A Reunion in Plotlands

Dawn Knox

© Copyright 2024 Dawn Knox

The right of Dawn Knox to be identified as the author of this work is asserted by her in accordance with the Copyright, Designs and Patents Act 1988

All rights reserved. No parts of this publication may be reproduced, stored in a retrieval system, or transmitted in any form or by any means, electronic, mechanical, photocopying, recording or otherwise without prior permission of the copyright owner.

A Record of this Publication is available from the British Library.

ISBN: 9798337692241

This edition is published by Affairs of the Heart

Cover © Fully Booked

Editing – Wendy Ogilvie Editorial Services

To Mum and Dad.
Thank you for believing in me.

Other books by Dawn Knox

The Great War – 100 Stories of 100 Words Honouring Those Who Lived and Died 100 Years Ago

Historical Romance: 18th and 19th Century

The Duchess of Sydney

The Finding of Eden

The Other Place

The Dolphin's Kiss

The Pearl of Aphrodite

The Wooden Tokens

Historical Romance: 20th Century

A Cottage in Plotlands

A Folly in Plotlands

A Canary Girl in Plotlands

A Reunion in Plotlands

Humorous Quirky Stories:

The Basilwade Chronicles

The Macaroon Chronicles

The Crispin Chronicles

The Post Box Topper Chronicles

Chapter One

October 1943

The knock on the front door was bold and unfamiliar. Evelyn jumped.

It wasn't Mr Leonard, the rent collector. He never came on Sunday afternoon, and anyway, the rent wasn't due for another week.

Neither was it Mrs Corfield from number six, come to 'borrow' a little sugar. Her rat-tat-tat would have been followed by another. And another. Until someone answered the door. She always knew when people were at home. Her patience when she was 'on the scrounge', as Mother described it, was legendary.

Evelyn's gaze flew to her mother, searching for instruction.

"Open it." Mother's voice was brittle. "And then get rid of them. The Sabbath is no time to disturb people."

Evelyn suppressed a smile. Mother probably assumed it was Father Brian – the only person she feared and respected. Getting rid of him was wishful thinking on Mother's part. No one turned the priest away.

Evelyn put down her knitting and left the warmth of the kitchen, closing the door behind her. She padded slowly along the cold linoleum to the front door, hoping whoever had knocked had gone.

She didn't want to be inhospitable and send them away. On the other hand, her heart sank at the thought of dealing with Mother's annoyance.

The man on the doorstep was a stranger. A naval officer. He'd obviously mistaken the number. The terraced houses in Barnes Street, indeed in this part of Stepney, East London, were similar and the autumn evening was closing in. So easy to mistake one house for another.

"Miss Evelyn Quinn?" His voice was cultured. Not that of an East Ender. It was deep and rich. Pleasant. Very pleasant indeed.

"Yes?" How did this dark-haired stranger know her name?

He held out his hand to shake hers. "Lieutenant Jacob Adam. Pleased to meet you."

"Err, likewise." Clearly, he hadn't made a mistake. But she didn't know him. She didn't really know any men of her own age, and if she did, she'd definitely have remembered this man. Against her better judgement, she didn't ask him his business nor send him away. Instead, she lingered. Intrigued.

He pulled a sock from his pocket and held it up. "Your handiwork, I believe?" He smiled over the top of the sock.

She realised she was holding her breath. His smile was slightly crooked and, for some reason, that made it so appealing. And those eyes. Soft, brown, gentle. And yet, eyes that reflected suffering.

"Miss Quinn?"

Evelyn jumped. She'd been staring at him. Her cheeks reddened.

"The sock," he said, wiggling it. "You knitted it... well, the pair of them, naturally. And you put a message inside one of them."

Oh yes! How stupid of her. Along with the girls at the telephone exchange where she worked, Evelyn had knitted dozens of socks for servicemen. And on one occasion – like the other girls – Evelyn had included her address. She'd also slipped in a short poem and message of encouragement.

Later, she'd regretted it. If anyone responded, Mother would find out and forbid Evelyn to reply. Corresponding with a strange man would have been considered sinful. Both Mother and Father Brian railed about the sins of the flesh. They shared the same view on many things – it was a wonder they didn't get on better.

"Evelyn! Who is it?" Mother's voice was sharp and critical. Her words flew like barbed arrows down the hall.

Evelyn jumped, and Lieutenant Adam's smile dropped.

"I wanted to thank you in person. For the socks. And the poem. I didn't get a chance to wear the socks, unfortunately. I met with a slight mishap." He looked down and she saw the cane propped against his leg.

"You were wounded?"

He nodded. "Otherwise, I'd still be in Italy."

"Oh, I'm so sorry you were hurt." What a foolish thing to say. Of course she'd be sorry he was hurt. Who in their right mind would be glad someone had been wounded? She wanted to groan with embarrassment.

"Evelyn!" Mother's voice was threatening and sharp. As keen as a blade.

"Coming, Mother," she shouted, then with a nervous glance over her shoulder, added, "I'm sorry, Lieutenant Adam..."

"I only wanted to thank you, Miss Quinn. You wouldn't believe how much of a difference your message made. My grandmother lives a short distance away in Wellclose Square. I'm staying with her for a few days, and when I saw your address, I thought I'd come and thank you in person."

Light penetrated the gloomy hall as the kitchen door opened and

Mother stomped down the hall towards her. "Who is this?"

Lieutenant Adam politely held out his hand and introduced himself.

Mother's eyes narrowed. She stepped back, away from his outstretched hand, and turned to Evelyn. "I asked you who this person was. You appear to know him."

"Please, madam, I meant no harm." Lieutenant Adam lowered his hand, his face aghast. "I merely came to pay my respects."

"Your respects? To my daughter? Why would my daughter be interested in your respects?"

Evelyn swallowed and held her breath. Mother was about to find out she'd included her name and address in the sock.

Lieutenant Adam, his voice full of reason and politeness, held up the sock and explained how he'd been given the pair just before he'd been wounded, on arriving in Sicily.

Mother folded her arms across her chest. A tight jaw and a pulse that throbbed in her temple were signs Evelyn knew well.

Lieutenant Adam, however, did not. And he'd obviously mistakenly believed Mother was listening to his explanation.

How could anyone know how unreasonable her mother was? Evelyn sensed disapproval swirling around her in chilling, bitter waves.

"I see. And how did you know my daughter had knitted the socks?"

Evelyn winced and drew in a sharp breath as Lieutenant Adam held out the note.

Mother snatched it and read. "Evelyn! You encouraged a strange man to contact you?" She grabbed her daughter's upper arm and pinched.

Lieutenant Adam's eyes moved back and forth between mother and daughter. From his expression, it appeared he'd worked out the state of affairs.

"I apologise for any upset I've caused, Mrs Quinn. I assure you, that was not my intention. I have nothing but respect for your daughter."

"You may have nothing for my daughter." Mother's voice was icy. She pulled Evelyn by the arm and slammed the door.

Chapter Two

Jacob limped away from Miss Quinn's house, each step twisting and tearing at the muscles in his back. Nevertheless, he increased his pace, wanting to get away from Barnes Street. He recognised he was punishing himself for the upset he'd caused, even though he knew his pain wouldn't make anything up to her. How could his visit have caused so much bother?

He'd only wanted to make contact. To thank someone who'd been thinking of all the nameless, faceless men who were doing their duty. Just a moment of human warmth.

Instead of pleasing her by showing his appreciation, he'd caused her trouble.

Her sweet poem had touched him. And even now, the memory of the morning he'd first read it aloud; a ray of sunshine to slice through the black cloud that engulfed him as he walked towards Cable Street.

Despite having been in the Mediterranean, there had been precious little sunshine in his life. His recollection of the time he'd spent on duty was coloured black. Or grey. And during his nightmares, red.

The war...

His mouth dry, he pushed away the memories of his last days in Sicily. Not those spent in a haze of morphine, but the days preceding that when they'd landed in Italy.

The explosion. As deafening as a steam engine. Noise and brightness that defied his senses. Agony that had mercifully lasted an instant until he'd woken in the hospital, his back peppered with shrapnel.

The medical staff had been outstanding, and they'd sent him back to England to convalesce. The doctor had said his determination had served him well, and now, although Jacob was in severe pain, he could walk – although it was more of a limp or hobble. He was supposed to use two sticks, but he'd wanted to try with only one. It would not beat him. He'd persevere until he could walk unaided. Day by day, as he pushed himself harder, it was already becoming easier. His muscles no longer going into severe spasm.

One day, it would be as if he'd never been wounded – to the outside world at any rate. Inside, he knew the scars would still be raw.

How young he'd been when he'd first left England to fight. He'd had no idea how appalling it would be. Now he found it hard to believe how sheltered he'd been as he'd grown up. Comfortable. Cocooned.

But the senseless death of his parents and younger brother had exceeded pain. Like being suspended in space. No sound. No feeling. No hope for the future. Nothing.

Although, he still had Gran. As far as he knew, anyway. Life was so precarious in the east end of London. But he'd soon find out because she only lived a few streets away from Evelyn Quinn.

He walked faster; jaw clenched, ignoring the pain, praying his gran would be safe.

Chapter Three

♥

Jacob turned into Wellclose Square, his eyes scanning the buildings for bomb damage. The area must have been quite a sight over a hundred years ago, with its grand Georgian houses. Many had been built for wealthy sea captains and Scandinavian timber merchants, although they had long since moved away, leaving dust and shadows.

Jacob slowly released the breath he'd been holding. No unexpected gaps in the terraced houses. No ruins. No heart-wrenching views of rooms with external walls torn away. No wallpaper strips still attached, flapping in the breeze and family belongings where their owners had left them.

A newspaper page blew towards him, cartwheeling along the litter-strewn gutter on the wind. Much of the square was now tired and dilapidated, but in Jacob's eyes, it was still a place of glamour. Of course, that had more to do with his grandmother than with the architecture. Gran owned one of the crumbling three-storey houses, where she'd lived for as long as he could remember.

He recalled wonderful parties with flamboyant, arty and bohemian guests. But not since the beginning of the war. His mother had tried to persuade Gran to move to Chelmsford in Essex, to be closer to her family. "We can find you a smaller, more manageable house, Mum.

You'll love the countryside around here..."

But Gran had always resisted. "Where would my cats go? And how could I put anyone up?"

Had she moved into the country, arguably, there wouldn't have been so many people who needed a bed. In this part of London, there were always many who were down on their luck. Poor wretches who'd slipped into debt and needed a room for a night or two, and a hot meal. And now, of course, with the war, so many who'd been bombed out and had lost everything.

No, Gran would never move from where she was most needed.

Jacob was one of those who'd be staying with her. It would only be for a while. He'd be moving to Hailcombe Cross, a village near Chelmsford, soon to work in a new radio research facility in the Marconi factory – an extension of the Admiralty Signal Establishment. He might not be able to walk far, but his hands were as nimble as ever.

Years before, he'd become interested in making crystal sets. He and his younger brother, David, had made the simple radio receivers that they'd put in their mother's china jug to act as a makeshift speaker.

Jacob had maintained a keen interest in radio technology ever since. And that knowledge was very useful. Across the country, wireless sets were tuned to eavesdrop on German messages, the operator faithfully recording each dot and dash of the Morse code being transmitted through the airwaves. Somehow, somewhere, those intercepted messages were decrypted and the information they contained was used to plan offensive and defensive operations.

Jacob didn't know where the messages went, how they go there nor who decrypted them – that was all top secret. Information was supplied on a need-to-know basis, and he didn't need to know.

Not that he'd be working on decryption. He'd now signed the Official Secrets Act and had been informed he'd be involved in top secret research, working on HF/DF – or High Frequency Direction Finding – more usually known as 'Huff-Duff'. The race was on to develop new ways to detect enemy attacks. Novel ways to win this war and find peace. Exactly what he would be doing regarding Huff-Duff, he had no idea. He'd have to wait until he started his new job to find out more.

Crossing over the road, he arrived at Gran's door. It had been glossy, dark blue once. Now it was scuffed and worn. For the second time in the last hour, he raised a knocker. There would be more of a welcome in this house than the last.

A woman cradling a baby in her arms opened the door and a cat shot past her legs out into the street. She smiled and let Jacob in. Another of Gran's guests. She didn't ask his name or his business. It wouldn't matter to Gran, and this young woman was hardly likely to turn anyone away.

This was typical of Gran's house. People came. They went. A few returned and then disappeared again. Occasionally, people appeared, having improved their lot, and they paid Gran for her kindness. She used the money to help those who were the worst off.

As Jacob stepped past the young woman and put his duffel bag down, Gran came out of the parlour, her face lighting up as she recognised him.

"Oh, Jake!" Such a world of love, longing and shared unspoken thoughts in those two sounds. She held her arms wide and, blinking back tears, he embraced her.

He felt her frail bird-like chest heaving beneath his arms.

"My dearest boy, you're early. Thank God," Gran whispered in his ear. "Let me look at you."

She held him at arm's length. No words were needed. Both of them still keenly felt the loss of their family. It had been so senseless.

Although, no more senseless than any other death during this terrible war. But when they met, the emotions they both held in check, rose to the surface and doubled their grief.

Thousands of people had been killed or displaced during the London Blitz. Bombs had rained down for days and the destruction had been heavy and widespread. But the explosion that had taken Jacob's parents and younger brother had been caused by one random bomb. The pilot had most likely been aiming for either Hoffman's, which made ball bearings or Marconi. Both strategically important factories for the Allies, and both based in Chelmsford.

Instead of hitting either of those targets, the bomb had struck the Adams' house. His parents and younger brother had all been taken. And even worse, Jacob knew that if it hadn't been for him, they'd have been in the bomb shelter. Once again, he felt his heart was being torn in two.

It had been Jacob's birthday.

He would never celebrate that day again.

Later, as he shared supper with his gran and her guests, his thoughts turned once again to Evelyn Quinn.

He'd had no expectations of the meeting. Obviously, she might have a sweetheart, or after having slipped the note into the sock, become a wife. He hadn't wanted anything from her. He'd wanted to see a friendly face. Someone who knew nothing about his background, his family, or his guilt.

He'd been so surprised when she'd opened the door. He hadn't expected anyone so exquisite. Not that she'd been dressed up. Far from it. Her dress and cardigan had been so nondescript, he had no recollection of them. But her face... That had taken his breath away and now remained imprinted in his mind.

Those green eyes, those full lips...

But even at that moment, he'd had no romantic intentions. It had been a surprise, that was all. He had to admit; the thought had crossed his mind – how wonderful if he'd been returning home to her. If she'd opened the door to him, held her arms wide and welcomed him back. Instead, he'd inadvertently caused friction between her and her mother.

He should have heeded the warning signs when she'd nervously looked over her shoulder after the mother had called out. But then, hindsight is a wonderful thing.

He'd try to make it up to Evelyn Quinn. Perhaps ask Gran to go round to Mrs Quinn and explain – woman to woman. He'd need to think about it over the next few days.

Chapter Four

After Mother slammed the door, Evelyn ran upstairs to her bedroom to watch the naval officer through her window. He'd limped across the road, and she'd gasped, her hand flying to her mouth as he stumbled when he stepped up onto the pavement. Pausing for an instant to steady himself, he'd turned the corner and was gone.

In the past, Evelyn had accepted Mother's words and obeyed her without question. She'd tuned in to her mother's expressions and gestures. A lowering of the brow. Pursing of the lips. Arms crossed and tapping of one toe. So many ways of showing Evelyn her conduct was unacceptable. So many ways of showing she'd found her daughter's behaviour wanting.

Evelyn often wondered if her elder brothers and sisters had satisfied Mother. Or, as the youngest, had she been singled out for constant disapproval?

Her brother, Gordon, had been born eighteen months before Evelyn, and they'd grown up together. Mother had always favoured him, and he'd often taken the blame to save his little sister. After a while, Evelyn had decided that since Mother doted on Gordon, she must prefer sons rather than worthless daughters. Indeed, she'd often described Evelyn as 'useless' – but she'd never applied that word to her beloved son, Gordon.

Her elder brothers and sisters had left home, and during the last twenty-three years, not one of them had returned. Did they know they had a younger sister? Did any of them care? No one had ever contacted her. Was that another sign Evelyn was worthless?

Mother's opinions – which Evelyn had been expected to adopt – had been a constant in her life. They'd never wavered, either black or white, but never acknowledging shades of grey. Evelyn hadn't shared those views but had never said so. Why bait Mother and earn more disapproval? Better to keep quiet and avoid a row.

But this treatment of the friendly naval officer was too much.

How could Mother have been so rude to a man who'd been wounded serving his country? Evelyn was appalled. He'd grimaced with pain. Had Mother not noticed? Had she not seen his walking stick and realised his disability? If she had, she'd disregarded it, appearing only to see him as a man. A stranger. A threat.

But a threat to whom? As Mother had barrelled forward, he'd stepped back, wincing with pain. Then she'd slammed the door. He couldn't have caused harm, even if he'd wanted to. Neither Evelyn nor Mother had been in danger.

Thoughts ricocheted around Evelyn's brain like bullets in a small room – Mother's aversion to men made no sense. It was blind hatred. And yet she adored Gordon. Did her ill-will only apply to the men who might be interested in Evelyn?

Before the war, she might have met someone her age at church – under the supervision of her mother who would have made it clear what she thought about the man concerned. But now, so many young men were away serving their country; Evelyn never met anyone, so it was hard to say what was on her mother's mind.

Surely Mother had considered the possibility her daughter would marry one day? Although that was unlikely to happen if Evelyn was never allowed to talk to a man – even one who'd simply come to thank her for an act of kindness. But it was one thing to be wary of strange men on a daughter's behalf, and quite another to treat an innocent man with such coldness.

Didn't Father Brian always tell them to be kind and to love one's neighbour? Mother had displayed none of that love.

Evelyn turned away from the window. The man would be almost at Cable Street by now, although, she suspected it would be a while before he forgot about the unpleasant encounter he'd had with Mother.

Evelyn sighed at the thought of going downstairs to apologise for the note in the socks. As she descended the stairs, she wondered what to say to minimise the inevitable period of Mother's silence and disapproval.

Evelyn expected to see her mother sitting in her armchair near the range with her eyes on her knitting. There'd be an air of martyrdom about her. She'd meet Evelyn's apology with haughty silence at first and then a few derisory snorts. But eventually, she'd accept her daughter's words with a regretful sigh and a shake of the head – even if it took several hours.

However, when Evelyn entered the kitchen, she was surprised to see her mother standing, waiting for her. This was not good news. Her arms were crossed. Her foot tapping and her face was white and pinched.

"To bring such shame upon this house, Evelyn…"

The words tumbled out before Evelyn had a chance to think. "But I didn't…"

She'd been about to say she hadn't done anything, then realised that she had, indeed, done something. She'd sent the note and poem. No one had forced her to do that. It had been her fault.

But the word 'fault' somehow lodged at the forefront of her mind. Where had there been any fault? What harm had she done in reaching out to someone who was serving his country?

And the young man certainly hadn't been to blame. He hadn't deserved to be treated with such discourtesy for merely wishing to show his gratitude.

Evelyn was torn. Mother was always right. Even if it appeared to Evelyn to be most unfair. But in this instance…?

"How many other notes have you passed to strange men?" Mother's upper lip twisted in contempt.

"What? No! I've never—"

"Well, Evelyn, it's a slippery slope you've embarked on." Mother's arms were crossed over her chest. She'd already decided on her daughter's guilt.

Evelyn stared at the woman she'd obeyed for twenty-three years, as if seeing her for the first time. Before, she'd quietly accepted that although she didn't always agree with her mother, there was no point in making life hard for herself. It was best to do as she was told. But now, she'd done nothing wrong and yet she'd been condemned.

How would life unfold from here? If Evelyn gave in now, she'd lose the right to speak to anyone of her choice – including men. Not that she knew any. But she wanted to retain the right to, at least, speak to anyone of her choice. It wasn't as if she'd ever consider going to a dance or the pictures with a man. Heaven forbid. But just to have a civilised conversation with anyone she chose. Surely that wasn't too much to ask?

Did Mother expect Evelyn to remain under her roof in Barnes Street for the rest of her days? It was as if a heavy door was swinging shut in Evelyn's face, and once it closed, there would be no access through it. Ever.

A REUNION IN PLOTLANDS 17

Evelyn had always felt her mother would be glad to see her go. But how was that ever going to happen? Not that Evelyn had any great desire to marry but it was supposed to be the next step in life. Even Father Brian agreed on that. How would she ever find a husband if she couldn't talk to a man?

But despite Mother being of accord with Father Brian on the issue of morality, she seemed to be at odds with much of what the priest taught. The memory of the utter ruthlessness that Mother had displayed towards the naval officer... That would have drawn a sharp rebuke from Father Brian, Evelyn was sure.

Why was her mother so spiteful? Had she always been like that, or was it the result of having been widowed just before Evelyn had been born? Would Gordon know? Probably not. He'd have been too young to understand.

Evelyn's thoughts, which until then had been a colourless, random selection of shapes, clicked into vibrant kaleidoscopic precision.

If she didn't make a stand at some point in her life, she'd always be obliged to do her mother's bidding – exactly how and when she wanted. Until one day, Evelyn might become just like her mother. Bitter and alone.

No, she must make a stand.

Think carefully. This will cost you dearly.

Evelyn swallowed, squeezed her fists together and pulled back her shoulders. She said slowly and deliberately, "I'm not on a slippery slope, Mother. I was merely showing courtesy, unlike you who displayed such rudeness to a serving officer."

If Evelyn had slapped her, Mother couldn't have been more shocked. She stepped backwards, only stopping when she felt the chair against her legs.

"What did you say?" Mother's voice rumbled deep and menacing like distant thunder.

If you have any sense, Evelyn, you'll stop now...

Evelyn was quivering inside, and she feared her lips would betray her by forming half-stuttered, muddled sounds. Yet when she spoke, her words were clipped and determined. "I said that I have done nothing wrong and that you were most rude."

Mother's eyes were huge and round, as was her mouth. Silence hung between them – the quiet moment that comes before a lightning strike. But before her mother could gather her thoughts, Evelyn pressed on. "That poor man had been wounded in the war, fighting for our freedom. And you sent him away so coldly."

The words Evelyn had expected finally erupted from her mother's mouth. "How dare you? Ungrateful girl! Don't you dare make it sound like I'm in the wrong. Go to your room." She pointed towards the kitchen door, and for a second, Evelyn hung her head, and was about to obey. But the strength that had flooded through her, remained.

"I... will... not." She pronounced each word slowly and with determination.

With lightning speed, Mother slapped her face.

Evelyn gasped in shock and raised her hand to her burning cheek. There was no going back now. She would not apologise for her words.

And that, she decided, would be the last time her mother would hit her.

Evelyn sat down in her chair. She didn't want to remain in the kitchen, but to have gone upstairs to her room would have been to admit defeat.

Mother did not move. "I said go to your bedroom." The voice was strong, but there was a hint of doubt.

Evelyn's cheek still throbbed, but she forced herself to place her knitting on her lap. She stared straight ahead as if her mother wasn't there. Then picking up her tea, she slowly sipped the cold liquid. She could barely swallow for the lump in her throat, but she was determined to act as if she didn't care.

Her mother stared at her, then sat down as well, but she did not resume her knitting. Evelyn could feel her eyes boring into her.

No, she would not go upstairs to her room. She would not give way.

Time passed slowly, and even the *tick-tock* of the clock appeared to slow down. Evelyn had taken a stand against going to her bedroom, but eventually, she'd have to go to bed. Had she made a stand for nothing?

When the sharp click of the door rang out, Evelyn jumped, and her mother appeared startled, too.

"Hello!" Gordon's cheery voice echoed down the hall.

Evelyn closed her eyes as relief washed over her. It was hard to see how this impasse could possibly be broken without apologising and losing all the ground she believed she'd won. But now her brother was here, perhaps she'd have the chance to slip upstairs without appearing to give way.

Chapter Five

"How are my favourite ladies this evening?" Gordon rubbed his hands together and blew on them. "It's a chilly one tonight. Nice and cosy in there, though..." He paused, the cheerful smile slipping. His eyes moved back and forth between his mother and younger sister.

He took the paper-wrapped loaf from under his arm and placed it on the table. "Everything all right then?" he asked slowly. The icy waves of hostility rippling from his mother had obviously reached him.

Mother curbed the sharp retort that Evelyn guessed was on her lips. This was her favourite son. He had no part in this quarrel.

Mother stood up. "I'll put the kettle on, shall I, son?"

Gordon warily stepped towards her and pecked her cheek. "That would be lovely, Mum."

As their mother turned away, Gordon shot Evelyn an enquiring look.

But how could she explain? All she could do was look helpless and shrug.

"You're looking thinner," Mother said. "Are you sure that wife of yours is feeding you?"

Gordon smiled, but once his smile had dropped, Evelyn noticed he was biting his bottom lip. Their mother would not accept that Gordon's wife, Sarah, looked after her beloved son as well as she had. Sarah was a lovely girl, only a year older than Evelyn. She and Gordon adored each other, and aware of Gordon's weak heart, she did everything in her power to help him. Mother's misgivings about her daughter-in-law were unfair.

That thought fuelled Evelyn's resolve. Why hadn't it occurred to her before that Mother was fallible? She was wrong about Sarah – both she and Gordon knew it. And she'd been unkind to treat Lieutenant Adam with such coldness. If she'd been wrong then, how many other times had she been misguided? An unmarried daughter was expected to do her mother's bidding, but surely, at some stage in her life, Evelyn must form opinions of her own? Was she brave enough for that time to be now?

As usual, Gordon laughed and made light of the criticism of his beloved wife. "Sarah fusses over me as much as you do, Mum. I must be the luckiest man in the world to have two women look after me with such care."

Mother sniffed and raised her eyes to the ceiling, but Gordon ignored her response.

Evelyn sighed. Even Gordon behaved unnaturally in front of Mother just to keep her happy. He'd faltered when he'd spoken, and Evelyn guessed he'd been about to say that Sarah fussed over him *more* than their mother but had changed it mid-sentence.

What choice did he have? The more he stood up for Sarah, the more Mother took against her, so it was easier to brush off any disparaging remarks with a joke and ignore them.

Their mother appeared not to have noticed. "You've taken on too much, son," she said lovingly. "You're too good, that's your trouble."

She placed a cup of tea in front of Gordon who was now seated in Evelyn's chair. Mother had waved the back of her hand at her to tell her to move to one of the hard, upright dining table chairs.

Gordon shot Evelyn an apologetic glance but they both knew it was simpler to do as they were told. "I'm fine thanks, Mum. Oh, by the way, did you finish darning my socks?"

"Yes, of course." Mother bobbed up. "I'll just fetch them."

Sarah's hands had been cut during a bomb explosion, and they were still bandaged. Mother had eagerly taken on any tasks, thinking she'd won back a small portion of her son's regard.

As soon as the kitchen door shut behind her, Gordon looked intently at Evelyn. "What's happened?"

He had enough to put up with while Sarah's hands were injured, so it was pointless pretending everything was well. If she protested nothing was wrong, he'd simply worry until he found out. And Mother would soon be back.

The words tumbled out between sobs. "Please, Gordon, can I come and live with you? I can't bear it any longer. I could help Sarah..."

Gordon's expression crumpled, but he shook his head. "I'm so sorry, Evie. We have Sarah's aunt and her family staying with us at the moment. They were bombed out last week. There's no room. And even if there was, where's the first place Mum would look? It'd only cause trouble for Sarah. I'm so sorry, love. But tell me what happened?"

Evelyn held her hand to her cheek. "Mother's impossible, that's what."

Gordon frowned. "Did she hit you?"

Evelyn nodded.

He frowned and shook his head in dismay. "We'll sort something out, Evie, don't you worry. Leave it to me."

The door handle rattled, and Mother stepped quickly into the room with socks laid over her arm.

"I unpicked the darning that'd been done before. It was quite shoddy, but I've redone it now. You won't have any complaint there, son." She held them up so he could see.

Gordon thanked his mother and sat for a while longer until he'd drunk his tea, telling them amusing stories about the customers in the bakery where he worked. He'd been keen to join up at the beginning of the war, but his weak heart had excluded him.

"It's far more important work making loaves for the home front than being a soldier," Mother had told him on many occasions.

He placed some money on the table next to the loaf he'd brought and winked at his mother. "That'll keep the wolf from the door. Well, I'd better get home." He paused for a second. "Is there any chance you could darn a hole in the sock I'm wearing now if I bring it back tomorrow, please, Mum? I can feel my toe poking out."

She assured him he could bring anything to her, and she'd look forward to seeing him the next day.

Gordon shot Evelyn a meaningful look, and she nodded imperceptibly to show she'd understood.

Gordon knocked early the next morning. Mother was still dressing, but Evelyn was ready to leave for work. She was surprised to see Gordon on the doorstep so early.

He held out a sock and for a second, Evelyn was dragged back to the previous day when the officer had called.

"I haven't got time to come in, but if you could give this to Mum, I'll pop by this evening." He peered past Evelyn along the hall and up the stairs. When he'd satisfied himself his mother wasn't there, he whispered. "I've thought about what you said, Evie. Are you still keen on leaving home?"

"Oh, yes! Can I come and stay with you after all?"

"No, love. 'Fraid not." Gordon still looked over Evelyn's shoulder. "I've got a plan, but I need to check a few things first. If everything works out, can you be ready to leave London on the last Sunday of the month?"

Evelyn could only stare at him. Leave London?

"Don't look so worried. I'm going to find out if our eldest sister, Ada, will look after you. She lives in Essex, so it'll mean handing in your notice. Don't tell anyone anything until I let you know if it'll be all right—"

"Evelyn! Is someone at the door?" Mother's voice boomed down the stairs.

"It's only me, Mum. I brought that sock I mentioned last night. Can't stop. I'll come back this evening if that's okay."

By the time Mother had made it down the stairs, Gordon was pulling away from the kerb in the bakery van. He tooted and waved cheerily.

Mother snatched the sock from Evelyn's hand.

"Won't you be late?" she said as she walked into the kitchen for her darning things.

Chapter Six

Her eldest sister. Ada.

Why hadn't Evelyn heard the name mentioned at home? Mother had never spoken of her.

Of course, Evelyn hadn't been interested in the elder brothers and sisters who'd never bothered to find out about her. She didn't even know with certainty how many there were in her family. There were no photographs of them in the house, no memorabilia. Mother never mentioned any of them except Gordon.

In the past, when the subject had come up, Gordon had given her the impression he didn't know much about their siblings either. Over the next few days, it was a surprise to discover he had the addresses of three sisters and one brother who regularly corresponded with him, although he'd lost track of two other brothers who he suspected had emigrated to Canada.

Ada. What would she be like? Would she favour their mother in either looks or temperament? If Gordon knew, he wasn't telling. All Evelyn could get him to reveal was that their elder sister lived alone in a place in Essex called Dunton Plotlands. Evelyn was certain Ada wouldn't welcome suddenly having to look after a much younger sister who she didn't even know.

Well, not to worry. Evelyn would pay her way and be polite and cheerful, and as soon as she could, she'd rent a room on her own. In the meantime, she wouldn't give Ada anything to complain about, although if she was anything like Mother...

As soon as Gordon had told her Ada would allow her to stay, he'd tried to find as much information as he could about Dunton. He was a friendly chap and popular with the bakery's customers, many of whom had been able to provide him with useful tips.

Several of the ladies who queued for bread knew of others who owned weekend cottages on the Plotlands of Dunton.

Years before the war, the area had been farmland, but hard times had forced many farmers to divide up their fields and sell the plots. A new railway link from London to Laindon Station had opened up the area. It had allowed many East Enders who wanted to escape the smoke and grime of London to buy a small parcel of land and build a holiday home.

Typically, families left London from Fenchurch Street Station on a Friday night, arrived at Laindon Station, then walked to Dunton and spent the weekend on their own piece of countryside. On Sunday evening, they crowded together on the London-bound platform in Laindon Station, to make the return journey.

For years, Dunton Plotlands had been a weekend rural idyll for city-weary East Enders. And it may have stayed that way, with the air of a holiday village, if the Luftwaffe hadn't inflicted such devastating damage on London.

Apparently, many of those lucky enough to own a cottage in Dunton had moved there permanently during the London Blitz or after they'd been bombed out. Others had fled there for some peace. Not that the area hadn't periodically been attacked by German bombers, but not to the extent that they'd targeted the London docks and factories. Occasionally, pilots had dropped their bombs on the way back from London to Germany, rather than having to carry them home.

However, as much as Gordon had found out about the Plotlands of Dunton, he didn't know much about Ada, nor why she'd chosen to live there.

Evelyn had been dreading handing in her notice at the telephone exchange. She'd started working there after leaving school and Rita Sinclair, the supervisor, had recently suggested she thought enough of Evelyn to promote her to trainee supervisor within the next few months. Girls were discouraged from moving from one exchange to another in London, but it was particularly frowned upon if a girl wanted to move out of the area. All that training would be lost.

Suppose Miss Sinclair refused to let her go? Could she do that? Evelyn didn't know but suspected she could. With the war on, people couldn't simply move from one job to another without permission.

But there was worse – Mother knew Miss Sinclair because they all went to the same church – St Patrick's. Suppose the supervisor had a quiet word with Mother? That would cause untold trouble for Evelyn. And for Gordon, too.

There had been a frosty atmosphere at home since the evening Mother had hit her, but that would be nothing to how things would be if Evelyn's escape plans were revealed.

In the end, it had been easier than Evelyn could have dreamt.

"Leave?" Miss Sinclair's eyes had narrowed; her expression was suspicious and disapproving – perhaps even puzzled, and she'd glanced down at Evelyn's stomach.

It was Evelyn's turn to be puzzled.

"Are you in the family way, Miss Quinn?" she asked bluntly.

Evelyn had recoiled. She'd been appalled. "Oh no! Nothing like that. I... It's that... well..." This was going worse than she'd expected.

"Tess!" Miss Sinclair shouted to one of the women, "Take over here for Evelyn for five minutes. I need a word with her."

Outside in the corridor, away from listening ears, Evelyn explained she was hoping to start a new life with her eldest sister in Essex, without mentioning anything about Mother or Gordon. It would have been disloyal to her family to have revealed more. She hoped Miss Sinclair wouldn't consider her one of the 'flighty' girls she so scorned, believing Evelyn was acting on a whim.

"I see." Miss Sinclair squeezed her lower lip between finger and thumb thoughtfully. "And this would be Ada or Margaret you'd be going to stay with?"

"Ada!" How did Miss Sinclair know?

The supervisor's eyes lit up. "I've been going to St Patrick's all my life, Evelyn. I've grown up with all your brothers and sisters. I keep my ears and eyes open and I know what's what. I suspect it'll be Gordon who's suggested this scheme?"

She smiled mischievously at Evelyn's amazement. "Not that I know much about your brother. He hasn't put in an appearance at Mass for some time. But he always was a kind lad. As for your mother..." Miss Sinclair nodded, her mouth set in a firm line. "Well, let's just say I understand your decision to leave. And, luckily for you, I may have a contact at the telephone exchange near Laindon. I'll put in a good word for you."

"Oh, thank you, Miss Sinclair." That had been a surprising and remarkable piece of luck.

"Don't celebrate too early, Evelyn. I won't lie to your mother. If she asks me where you are, I shall tell her."

"No, of course, Miss Sinclair. I expect Gordon will tell her anyway once I've left." For a second, she thought about adding it was unlikely

Mother would care once she'd gone. The idea of slipping away was to avoid the inevitable rows, not because Mother could stop her going. She'd probably consider it a blessing Evelyn was no longer there. And that would most likely be the first time Mother would consider anything to do with her daughter 'a blessing'.

On the Sunday morning Evelyn was due to leave home, Mother got ready for Mass as usual. When Evelyn told her she wouldn't be accompanying her, the news was met with a slight flare of the nostrils and eyeballs rolled to the ceiling, as if one could expect no less of a such a sinner as her wayward daughter.

The reaction tempered Evelyn's excitement. If only once, her mother hadn't been so dismissive – hadn't made her feel such a disappointment. Evelyn had tried her best, but it hadn't mattered what she'd done, Mother had never, and would never, approve of her.

According to Gordon, Evelyn had been the only Quinn child to pass her scholarship and gain a place at grammar school. She hadn't been allowed to go. Mother had said she couldn't afford to send Evelyn there and anyway, she considered an education a waste of time for a girl. Evelyn had doubted her mother would allow her to go, yet she'd prayed in St Patrick's – eyes squeezed tightly shut and hands locked together – that her dream would come true.

That was the last time Evelyn had prayed for a miracle. Mother told her she must find a job and start contributing to the running cost of their house. And if Evelyn didn't gain employment immediately, Mother would find her a job.

But Evelyn's success with her exam had opened up a place in the General Post Office where she'd trained as a telephonist. It was a good job for a woman and any other mother would have been proud of her daughter's achievement.

Despite various invitations, Evelyn hadn't frequented the dance halls and cinemas – she knew Mother wouldn't approve of that. And other than the error in judgement with the note in the socks, she'd done whatever she thought her mother had wanted. So, why did Evelyn always feel guilty? Wasn't sinning supposed to be fun? At least until you got caught and then had to pay. But for Evelyn, there was just guilt. Weighty and smothering.

Mother took her missal out of the sideboard and slammed it on the table. She noisily assembled everything she'd need to go to church, as if she thought the display would prick Evelyn's conscience and convince her to change her mind.

Finally, she left the house. Evelyn stared into the bottom of her mug, not allowing herself to breathe until the front door closed with a thud. Then, she ran upstairs, and looked out of the bedroom window to see her mother straight-backed, black hat pinned firmly on her head, handbag dangling from one arm and missal in her hand, turn the corner of the street.

Evelyn slid her suitcase and bags from beneath the bed and took them downstairs. She put on her coat, hat and gloves. As she opened the door, Gordon pulled up in his bakery van. He'd obviously been watching for his mother to leave.

He leapt out and took her bags, then loaded them inside. "Right, Evie, let's get cracking. We've got quite a drive ahead of us."

Chapter Seven

Evelyn had expected the guilt to fade the further she and Gordon drove from London, as if the miles could separate her from Mother and the problems of her life. But despite the increasing distance, the weight still bore down on her.

Yes, she was escaping from an unhappy household, but she'd drawn Gordon into the situation, and soon, she'd involve the sister she'd never met. It was as if she couldn't avoid spreading trouble.

"I'm sorry, Gordon."

He glanced sideways and caught sight of her wiping a tear from her cheek.

"Nothing to apologise for, Evie. Dry your eyes. None of this is of your making."

"But Mother will be angry with you—"

"Let me worry about that. She'll forgive me. Well, as far as she can, anyway. She's never forgiven me for marrying Sarah. But that's her loss. She's a complicated woman and often, there's no pleasing her. You must live your life as you want. That's what I decided to do. And for you, that must start now." He patted her hand reassuringly.

"But what about Ada? Suppose she doesn't like me?"

"Why wouldn't she?" Gordon's voice was calm and comforting.

Evelyn was silent. She really didn't know.

"Don't worry, Evie. I know Mother's always given you the impression you're in the wrong, but really, that's just her way. You're fine as you are. And by the way, I don't think Ada's anything like our mother."

"What makes you say that?"

"I don't know really. It's just a feeling. Ada left home when I was about three. I don't remember much about her going except for a huge argument. Everyone shouting, doors slamming and you in your cot, screaming. Then I don't remember Ada being there anymore. As time went on and no one mentioned her name, I forgot all about her. I suppose she reached the end of her tether and walked out. I don't need to tell you Mother isn't the easiest woman in the world to get on with. Perhaps if our dad hadn't died so young, things might've been different."

Gordon carried on driving in silence. They'd both talked about their father in the past, but Gordon barely remembered him, and Evelyn didn't recall him at all. Mother had refused to discuss him. Indeed, her lip always curled with scorn if anyone referred to him.

Evelyn stared out of the windscreen, watching rows of shops give way to tall town houses and small villas. Then detached houses set in large gardens and finally, hedgerows, behind which fields stretched to the distance. Church bells chimed, their peals rolling across the countryside, summoning their congregations.

Would Mother have discovered the letter yet? At first, Evelyn had decided to simply walk out and leave some money, but no word. However, she decided that would have been an ungrateful ending. After all, Mother had given her a roof for twenty-three years. In the end, Evelyn had kept her letter brief. She'd simply said goodbye and wished her mother well. She'd also included her previous week's wages.

"What do you know about our other brothers and sisters?" Evelyn asked.

"Not a great deal," Gordon admitted. "I met Harriet a few years ago. She lives with her husband in the north of London somewhere. I know she was in touch with several others, and she gave me their addresses. I write each Christmas, but now, I only hear from Ada, Harriet, Margaret and Bob. Ada's always the first to reply. She always asks after you."

Evelyn hadn't expected to hear that. But perhaps Gordon was exaggerating to make her feel better. She suddenly felt lighter, full of hope, as if she might, indeed, break free from the suffocating guilt.

When they'd set off, Gordon had handed Ada's letter to Evelyn. It contained instructions on how to find her cottage and Evelyn studied her sister's handwriting, trying to imagine what sort of person she was. Ada's writing was difficult to decipher. The words were nothing like their mother's neat, regimented, plain script. Mother's letters rigidly conformed to each other. But Ada's scrawl was loopy and, at times, sharp and jagged, making it hard to read. What did that signify?

Once they'd reached Dunton, Evelyn had read the instructions out, guiding Gordon down grassy avenues flanked on either side by the most varied collection of homes she'd ever seen. When she'd learnt Ada lived in the country, she'd imagined she owned something like one of the pretty thatched cottages in the villages they'd passed through on their way to Dunton. But in this place, most of the cottages were relatively new and each was different from its neighbour. Many were simple, single-storey buildings – some wooden, some brick, some pebble-dashed. Others looked as though extensions had been hastily added.

That had probably been the case, as East End people had poured out of London since the Blitz. Tiny cottages that had served as weekend homes were now permanently inhabited and had grown to accommodate the enormous influx of homeless people.

Before Evelyn realised it, Gordon had pulled up outside a cottage, and was peering at the name on the gate.

"Swallowmead," he read, and leaned over to check the letter in Evelyn's hands. She could say nothing. Her mouth was completely dry.

"Yes, this is the place," Gordon said. He patted her hand.

Evelyn followed his gaze to the front door where a tall, thin, grey-haired woman stood. She was half-turned, holding on to the jamb with both hands. Swaying slightly, as if blown by a strong breeze, Ada Quinn watched them from the doorway.

Gordon got out and hastened up the path towards their sister. Evelyn wondered if she was ill. She certainly didn't look well. Getting out of the van, Evelyn followed Gordon and as she drew closer, she could see Ada's pale face and enormous eyes, so similar to their mother's, and yet so different. Ada's eyes were softer and kinder. The lines radiating outwards had been drawn by sadness, not bitterness and resentment like Mother's stark creases. Deep emotion filled Ada's eyes.

Gordon gently steered their elder sister into the cottage and fussed over her as she sat down.

"Just feeling a little faint. Nothing to worry about." Ada's voice was weak and apologetic. "So sorry. I'll be fine in a moment. The kettle's on." Her eyes sought Evelyn and she appeared to hold her breath.

Her earlier nervousness forgotten, Evelyn offered to make tea and went into the kitchen. Everything was clean and tidy, but not with Mother's compulsive neatness.

Comfortable. Not obsessive.

She carried a tray of mugs back into the living room and set it on the table. Ada's colour had returned, and she smiled at Evelyn. "Welcome," she said. One simple word, and at that, Evelyn's stomach unknotted, and the anxiety that had gripped her since she'd slipped out of Mother's house drained away.

Evelyn sat quietly while conversation flowed easily between Gordon and Ada. Although he'd been very young when Ada had left, the brother and sister still shared many memories. Gordon's favourite knitted toy, the next-door neighbour's dog that barked so loudly it always made Gordon cry, the song she'd taught him which he demonstrated he still remembered…

Ada told them about their father, although her recollections of him were few.

"Every so often, he'd arrive home from the sea, brown-skinned and smelling of tobacco and rum. Then one morning, he'd be gone. It was quite a few years before I realised he was my father." Ada blushed. "And of course, each time he left, a new baby was born nine months later. Our poor mother. It was so hard for her."

Evelyn listened in amazement. She'd always thought of her mother as someone who was in control. But Ada had described her as a downtrodden wife who'd been deserted most of her married life. A sad, sorry, forgotten woman who'd raised so many children, they'd worn her out. It was hard to reconcile this woman with the one Evelyn knew.

But as Evelyn listened, there were undercurrents, too. Neither Ada nor Gordon spoke about the woman who'd given birth to them with affection. With respect, yes. But not with love. None of their fond memories involved Mother unless it was to relate how she'd stopped their fun.

There was pity for their mother and resignation, with both Gordon and Ada recognising their lives might well have been different had their mother been more loving.

But there was more. Occasionally, Ada's eyes filled with tears. When she spoke, her words concealed anguish, although Evelyn could see through the carefully arranged smile that was designed to hide it.

There was no hint as to its nature or cause, but her clipped and carefully phrased comments revealed she was trying to be scrupulously fair to Mother – perhaps for Evelyn's benefit. And yet, neither she nor Gordon wholeheartedly excused their mother for her lack of feeling and warmth.

During Evelyn's work as a telephonist, she'd occasionally overheard snippets of conversation between callers. Unintentionally, she'd tuned in to their emotions, picking up on the careful choice of words, the silences, the exclamations. Brief conversations between parted lovers. Heart breaking calls to inform someone of a death. The happy news of a birth. Often, Evelyn wondered if she was simply being fanciful and had put the incorrect interpretation on the call. After all, she couldn't see the callers' faces. She couldn't see their expressions. But it was as if the lack of love in her life had trained her mind to pick up on other people's emotions, like a wireless set tuned in to invisible radio signals.

She'd learnt expressions could be misleading. People could lie with their faces. Hadn't Mother often smiled when she was anything but happy? But Evelyn knew her mood from her voice.

Gordon stood up and put his cup and saucer back on the tray. "Well, all this talk of Mum is telling me I need to go back and face the music. No point putting it off."

Evelyn's mouth had been so dry, she'd drunk the tea quickly, although she'd continued to cradle the empty cup, reluctant to put it back on the saucer and interrupt the conversation. While they'd been drinking tea and talking, Gordon and Ada had chatted easily, and she'd been able to observe. Now, her brother was leaving to face Mother's wrath on her behalf and Evelyn would be left alone with the sister who was a stranger.

At Gordon's cue, she reluctantly put her cup and saucer back on the tray. There was such an air of finality about those three empty cups sitting side by side.

Or perhaps she ought to see them as a new beginning?

Chapter Eight

♥

On his drive back to London, Gordon had deliberately not considered the inevitable meeting with his mother. He couldn't guess what she'd say nor how she'd react.

Fury? Sadness? Regret?

He'd done the right thing. He knew that. And if this ruined his relationship with his mother – such that it was – well, so be it. He'd tiptoed around her for too long in case she took it out on Evelyn. Now, that wasn't possible, and he didn't intend to take any more nonsense. He'd be kind but firm.

His mother greeted him with arms crossed over her chest, her mouth set in a thin line. "So, she's gone, has she? Well, good riddance."

"Mum, I—"

His mother held up her hand to silence him. "You're a good man, Gordon. I know that. But I don't want to know where she is. She's gone. Let's not discuss her anymore. A cup of tea?"

"No thanks, Mum. I need to get home."

At that, her face fell, and he marvelled she could be so cold to one child yet favour another. He'd once thought it was because she preferred boys, but his brothers had left home as soon as they could and had never returned. If she'd shown them as much favour as she'd shown him, surely, they'd have kept in touch. No, she was simply a complicated woman who found it difficult to form a relationship.

He shivered, trying to shake off the coldness inside that he often experienced when he visited his mother. As she closed the front door, he stepped backwards towards the kerb, staring at the house, trying to imagine what life might have been like had their father not been a sailor, and had their family been a close one.

"Excuse me, please."

Gordon jumped. He turned, realising he was blocking the pavement, but the naval officer didn't move past when he stepped out of the way.

"I wonder if you know Miss Evelyn Quinn," the naval officer asked.

"I... Yes, she's my sister." Gordon's eyes narrowed. "Why d'you want to know?"

"I'm afraid I caused a rumpus when I knocked to thank her for the socks she'd knitted a short while ago."

Ah, the officer who'd set Evelyn's flight in motion. Poor bloke. On the journey into Essex, Evelyn had explained what had happened. Gordon couldn't imagine what he must think of their family. And more specifically, their mother.

"I'd appreciate it if you'd pass on my apologies for causing so much fuss when I called before. I'd knock but I suspect it might simply create more trouble. I thought of sending a letter but... I've passed several times hoping I might catch sight of your sister, but I knew the chances were slim."

"She's gone, I'm afraid," Gordon said, peering over his shoulder to make sure his mother hadn't heard voices and was peeking through the curtains.

"Gone?" The naval officer frowned.

"Gone. Left home."

The officer gasped. "Oh no! I hope it wasn't anything to do with my visit."

Gordon felt sorry for him. He seemed like a decent bloke. He lowered his voice. "Don't worry. Evelyn'll be much happier now she's left home. Trust me."

"Even so…" The lieutenant staggered slightly, and Gordon saw the cane in his hand. A serviceman. Probably wounded in action. And his mother had rudely told him to go away. Gordon sighed inwardly. Life was brief. It was best to grab every opportunity when it presented itself.

In a second, Gordon had made up his mind.

"Look, if you'd like to write to Evelyn and tell her what you've told me, I can give you her new address."

Jacob mused how strange it was that a woman as cold as Mrs Quinn could have two such engaging children. Gordon had offered him a lift in his van back to Gran's; he was warm and generous.

As for Evelyn, Jacob had only met her once, so he could hardly make an informed decision. But Gordon had spoken about his sister with such love and respect. Surely Jacob's instincts about the girl who'd been on his mind constantly were correct?

Gran had cautioned him to be careful of causing further problems when he'd described what had happened on the doorstep in Barnes Street.

"I'll go around and see Mrs Quinn if you like, Jake. But to be honest, I'd let it rest if I were you. A woman as opinionated as she sounds is hardly likely to change her mind just because I tell her to."

"No, Gran, I don't want you to tell her to do anything. But…"

"But what, love? A woman who treats a daughter like that will be set in her ways. A stranger turning up on her doorstep isn't likely to make a jot of difference. And anyway, what would be the point? If the girl does exactly as her mother says, then it doesn't matter how sweet you are on her, there's no future in it."

He'd assured her he wasn't sweet on Evelyn Quinn. But even to his ears, the denial had rung hollow.

Sweet. Oh, he was so sweet on her. Even saying her name was like sliding honey across his tongue.

So, now, the news that she'd left home both cheered and discouraged him. Family was all-important and Evelyn's had now been broken apart as a result of his visit, although her brother had convinced him it had ultimately been a good thing. But the best news was that when he consulted a map of Essex, he saw that Evelyn was living about fifteen miles from where he'd be lodging in Hailcombe Cross. That wasn't far.

He'd planned to buy a bicycle. The doctor had told him it would be good to build up his strength. Yes, he'd see how strong he was and if he didn't think he could make the round trip, he'd persevere until he could. Then he'd visit her and apologise. She'd probably have forgotten who he was by then.

No, there was no point trying to fool himself he merely wanted to say sorry. He wanted to see her again. To talk to her.

And after that, he dared not let his mind wonder.

Chapter Nine

Evelyn retrieved the letter from the mat and noted the handwriting belonged to Gordon. This was the third letter he'd sent during the few weeks since she'd been staying with Ada.

The first two letters had been hastily scribbled and contained news about Sarah and their son, Tommy. A fire had started during a bombing raid in a clothing factory a few streets away and had burnt to the ground. Their next-door neighbour was doing as he'd threatened to do at the beginning of the war and was moving to Devon with his family. Sarah's uncle had rescued an abandoned cat that had subsequently bitten him. Inconsequential news. But the letter contained nothing about Mother. If she'd been angry with Gordon, he hadn't thought to mention it.

Good. The last thing Evelyn wanted was to cause problems for her brother. The lack of information about Mother merely underlined Evelyn's suspicions. She simply hadn't cared her youngest daughter had gone. Not enough to enquire after her. Not enough to be angry with Gordon. It had hurt Evelyn, but it hadn't surprised her.

She urged herself not to spoil the present by dwelling on the past. Since she'd arrived in Plotlands, her life had been more agreeable than it had ever been with Mother. She'd settled into a routine in the cottage with Ada and her diffident cat, Titan, although from time to time, Evelyn wondered whether her sister might have preferred her privacy.

Ada was sometimes remote. Not keeping herself distant in the same way that Mother used to – as if she believed associating with Evelyn would taint her. No, Ada was sad. Filled with troubled thoughts. Frequently, long silences settled between them, but they weren't hostile like they'd been at Mother's. They were easy and friendly, and Evelyn didn't feel waves of chilling disapproval flowing from Ada.

Strangely, she felt the opposite, as if Ada accepted her unconditionally.

Fanciful? Probably.

Evelyn was so used to Mother's constant disapproval, she might be misinterpreting Ada's quiet reserve and reading more into it than was there.

She must remember that many years had passed since Ada had left Barnes Street. So much had happened to her that might have been the reason for her sadness.

As Mother had told Evelyn so often, "It's not all about you, Evelyn."

But if, from time to time, Evelyn wasn't sure what was on Ada's mind, thankfully, she knew she'd been fully accepted at work. With Miss Sinclair's recommendation, she'd found a job in the Laindon telephone exchange and the supervisor, Miss Miller, had expressed her satisfaction at her new recruit's work. Evelyn had even made a friend. Phyllis Potter was two years older than Evelyn. A timid woman who habitually bit her nails. She worried about everything.

Evelyn suspected there was something in Phyllis's past that caused her pessimism, although she'd never hinted at anything. But perhaps not all problems came from an unhappy family background. Perhaps some people were just born that way. And maybe others were affected by the people around them.

After all, Mother had made it clear Evelyn was unloved and unwanted. But now she was free of her mother, each morning when she awoke, she felt lighter as if a weight was gradually being lifted off her shoulders. Life now held promise. If it hadn't been for those occasions when she looked up unexpectedly and found Ada watching her with an unreadable expression, Evelyn would have been completely content.

Well, perhaps not completely content. She wasn't sure whether she'd ever be fully at peace with the world. How could she erase the idea that she must have done something wrong for her mother to dislike her? There would always be a piece of the jigsaw of her life that was missing. Perhaps the older she grew, the smaller that lost piece would become and the more the other pieces would grow into the gap until she didn't notice it at all.

If only she could read Ada's curious glances. Their intensity was unmistakable. Pain? Longing? Sometimes, she looked haunted. Perhaps Ada had also been scarred by their mother's cold-hearted behaviour.

How could one woman have caused her children so much misery?

"Is it from Gordon?" Ada was sitting at the breakfast table, pouring tea.

Evelyn nodded and turned the latest letter over in her hand. Would it be full of news about Sarah and their son, Tommy? Snippets of information he'd overheard in the bakery? Or this time, would there be something about Mother?

No, Evelyn decided. There'd be nothing about Mother.

"Are you going to open it, dear?" Ada asked. She sipped her tea and surveyed her sister over the top of the cup.

Evelyn slit open the envelope and handed the piece labelled 'Ada' to her sister then unfolded the other paper. She scanned it quickly and stopped as her eyes caught the word 'Mother'.

"Bad news?" Ada put down her letter and leaned forward.

"No, I don't think so. It's just puzzling. Gordon says that although at first, Mother insisted she didn't want him to tell her where I'd gone, she's now dropping hints she knows where I am. He says that since I left, she's had three lodgers. She asked the first one to leave after a few days, and the other two walked out after a week. She told Gordon to tell me it's time I went home."

Ada snorted in derision, and her eyes rolled to the ceiling. "Yes. That's typical Mother. She expects everyone to fall in with her plans. She's probably missing your wages. And of course, she loves people thinking she knows everything. So, if she didn't want Gordon to tell her, how d'you think she found out where you were?"

"Oh, I expect my supervisor, Miss Sinclair, told her."

"And are you concerned?"

Evelyn shook her head. "No, Mother can't make me go home. That is unless you want me to..."

"Oh no!" Ada placed trembling fingertips against her open mouth. Immediately, she curled her hand into a fist and dropped it to her lap. "Well, not unless that's what you want." Her voice was now casual, and her face once again composed.

Evelyn assured her she'd like to stay. Gordon's letter had been an unpleasant reminder, bringing Mother's oppressive shadow into Ada's home. However, Ada's response had raised Evelyn's spirits. Surely that reaction meant Ada would miss her if she went? Her sister had been kind and scrupulously polite – like a benevolent stranger. That was understandable, because, after all, they were strangers. They were tied by blood but had been separated by miles and years.

The clock chimed. It was time for Evelyn to leave for work.

"I put your lunch in your bag, dear," Ada said.

Warmth rippled through Evelyn, and she smiled her thanks. Mother had never made her lunch to take to work.

Chapter Ten

Ada waited as Ted Farrell, the schoolmaster, locked the school door. It had been a long and tiring day.

"I expect there'll be a few more children turning up tomorrow," Mr Farrell said, pulling on his gloves. He shook his head. "What a state some of those children were in. And so many of them."

During the last two weeks, thirteen new school-aged children had arrived in Dunton. Four families had come to stay with relatives in Plotlands after their homes in London had been destroyed.

"I don't know how you coped today, Miss Quinn. Thank goodness you were there. I shouldn't have been able to manage on my own."

Ada smiled. Three new children had arrived that morning and all had required delousing and washing. Ada, a member of the Women's Voluntary Service, had carried out those tasks and provided new clothes to replace their rags from the WVS stock.

The children had spoken of brothers and sisters who'd accompanied them to Dunton, and sooner or later, they would appear at school.

"Although I suspect from some of the children's comments today, the older ones may be rather resistant to the idea of lessons," Mr Farrell said, shaking his head. "We're going to have our work cut out..."

Some of the children who'd arrived from the East End had previously been allowed to run wild. Mr Farrell was a kind, but strict, schoolmaster and so far, he'd managed to tame all the children. His worried expression now suggested he was doubtful about the new intake.

Although, Ada mused, Mr Farrell perpetually looked troubled. And he had every right to do so. Life hadn't been kind to him. He'd barely recovered from his wounds after the last war when his wife had been taken ill. He'd nursed her until her death the previous year. Now, the worries about the school and its children had replaced those about his loss and loneliness. Or perhaps they hadn't. Perhaps they just mounted one on top of the other.

"That little black-haired boy who came today..." Mr Farrell said as he dropped the keys into his coat pocket.

There were several black-haired boys in the school, but she knew who he meant. "Michael?"

"Yes, that's the one." Mr Farrell sighed. "He was quite a handful. I'm so grateful to you for stepping in..." He tailed off.

Michael had knocked over a pile of books, causing a bang like an explosion; Mr Farrell had frozen. His time in the trenches during the Great War had taken its toll. Loud noises startled him, hurling him back to the violence of those mud-filled holes in the ground.

In similar situations, Ada always stepped in. She organised the children into clearing up whatever had been spilt or knocked over. She read to them or organised a game, giving Mr Farrell the chance to control his breathing and to bring himself back to the present.

Neither ever mentioned this, but his eyes told her he was grateful.

She sympathised. Indeed, she understood. The last war had caused untold misery.

"I don't know how you always remember their names," Mr Farrell said with a sad smile. "It quite puts me to shame."

Ada gave a modest wave of her hand, deflecting the compliment. The truth was that each child she helped was so precious; how could she not remember their names? She'd never had the large family she'd yearned for. And she never would now. Caring for other people's children was the closest she'd ever get.

At the beginning of the war, she'd taken in two evacuees, John and Sadie – a brother and sister. Her heart had nearly broken at their hollow-cheeked faces and stick-thin limbs. She'd deloused them, bathed them and exchanged their lice-ridden rags for the best clothes she could obtain. She'd had such hopes for them; teaching them manners and appreciation of the countryside. Willing them to allow her to love them.

Within weeks, their mother had appeared on the doorstep. The poor woman couldn't have been more than thirty, but the grey complexion and dark-smudged sunken eyes had added years to her.

Ada recognised that worn-out, resigned look from years ago when she'd lived in the East End. Her mother's haggard face had reflected much of that weariness. The continual births and a new mouth to feed every year until the woman could no longer bear children.

When Sadie and John had left with their mother, Ada had felt betrayed. She had more to give them than that downtrodden drab – more time, more food, more of everything except the love and attention of their own mother.

The woman was obviously exhausted. And yet, her hands rested on her children's shoulders as she resolutely trudged along Second Avenue, back to Laindon Station, showing what sort of mother she was.

She was certainly displaying more love than Ada's own mother had ever shown. As the eldest child, she'd seen how Mother behaved towards Ada's brothers and sisters. Gradually, Ada had taken over the childcare as her father periodically returned and months later, a new charge arrived. Ada had noted her mother's resentment towards those poor children who hadn't asked to be born.

At the end of the High Road, where they would go their separate ways, Mr Farrell paused. "And how are you getting on with your sister?"

Ada's face broke into a huge smile. "Everything is going swimmingly, Mr Farrell, perfectly swimmingly."

He thanked her again for the help and, with a wave, turned off to his home.

She walked in the opposite direction.

At the bottom of the hill leading up to her cottage, Ada stopped and rested her knees, her mind still whirring with images of the new children who'd arrived that day. Grimy faces with wide, frightened eyes that darted this way and that, taking in the schoolroom and its master.

Insolent, disrespectful replies to questions the children didn't want to answer. Ada had recognised it as bravado. The children's family had been trapped for hours in a bombed building, and Ada's heart ached for them. Especially the young boy who hadn't spoken a word since. She'd played with him by the sand tray that day, trying to gain his trust, but it would take more than a few hours to coax him to speak again. She'd try again tomorrow. And the next day.

Yes, it had been another heart-breaking day.

Now at the top of the rise, Ada stopped to get her breath back, and rest her knees again. Her fiftieth birthday loomed, but for years, she'd felt old. Since she'd left London and moved to Plotlands and recognised she'd left her past behind, she'd considered herself old – past it.

The doctor said it was the damp that caused her joints to swell and although they were worse when the weather was cold and wet, she'd noticed they were more painful when she was upset. It was as though the emptiness and ache in her heart set up pain throughout her body. Not that the no-nonsense doctor would agree with her, but experience told her otherwise.

She walked to her cottage and, once she'd let herself in, she put the kettle on the stove. Evelyn would be home in about half an hour. Ada got up, held back the curtain, and peered through the cross-taped windowpanes out to the road.

Yes, Evelyn would be coming soon. Warmth spread throughout Ada's chest, easing the pain in her heart and soothing her entire being.

Chapter Eleven

Jacob groaned with relief as he got off the bicycle. He'd been practising over the past few weeks, riding several miles from his billet in the tiny village of Hailcombe Cross to the Marconi research facility in Great Baddow where he worked. His muscles were strengthening – as the doctor had assured him they would – but his progress was pitifully slow.

Predictably, he'd pushed himself too hard at first, not heeding the doctor's warning. He'd barely been able to walk for several days. Sleeping had been a problem as his back had repeatedly gone into spasm. But with characteristic doggedness, he'd persevered and was encouraged by the outcome. It wouldn't be long before he'd trust himself to walk unaided. But not yet.

Once he'd acknowledged he had sufficient strength to cycle for two hours – an hour there and an hour home – he'd pored over his map and planned the fastest route. He'd spent so long studying the roads, he could have drawn the map freehand.

On his next day off, he set out from Hailcombe Cross and headed towards Dunton Plotlands with the address Gordon had given him securely in his pocket. Not that he needed the reminder. He'd also committed that to memory.

The journey had taken longer than he'd expected because, annoyingly, after all his preparation, he'd got lost. Once he'd left the familiar roads around Chelmsford, he'd travelled along several major roads. Road signs had been removed at the beginning of the war in case the Germans had invaded. However, using the direction of the sun and his map, he was certain he was going the right way until he turned off one of the major roads onto a grassy lane. His map hadn't shown all the tiny tracks, and the one he'd chosen had proved to be the wrong turning. It had cost him fifteen minutes while he'd found his way back to the main road. However, he'd committed the right turning to memory and was sure he wouldn't make the same mistake the next time.

The next time?

That was ridiculous. This would be the first and last time he'd need to do this journey. He merely wanted to find Evelyn Quinn and apologise.

No, you don't.

Well, all right. If he was being honest, he could have – and probably should have – written a letter of apology, but he wanted to see her face again, to hear her voice. He wanted to stare into those green eyes.

But he had no right to that, and he wouldn't blame her if she wouldn't listen to a word he said. Her brother, Gordon, had given him hope. He'd told Jacob that her departure from home had been for the best. He hadn't elaborated, simply implied she'd be happier living with their sister. Nevertheless, Jacob had inadvertently changed a relationship in a family.

Family.

That word brought faces crowding into his mind. His mother, her beautiful smile; gentle and patient. Father – mischievous and playful, yet despite all his light heartedness, regarding his sons with fierce pride.

And his younger brother, David, the one who would never grow up, still with the face of a young boy.

Jacob had been wheeling his bicycle along the country lane, lost in thought, and possibly looking like he didn't know where he was going. A woman with a basket of eggs over her arm called out to him, "Are you lost, ducks?"

Trying to orientate himself, he glanced right and left at the grassy avenue flanked on either side by a higgledy-piggledy collection of bungalows surrounded by vegetable gardens.

"I'm trying to find Second Avenue."

"Who yer looking for, ducks?"

"Miss Ada Quinn."

The woman smiled and pointed behind her. "Off to see Ada, eh? Well, you want to go down there. Take the turning on the right. Keep going and you'll see 'Swallowmead' on the gate. It's about five down on the left. Tell Ada I'll be over later with 'er eggs." She carried on walking in the opposite direction, whistling.

Jacob had thought he was close to the cottage, but there were no numbers on any of the strange buildings – just names. Nothing to measure his progress. However, according to the woman, it was nearby.

His chest tightened and his mouth went dry.

Perhaps it hadn't been a good idea after all.

He stopped, and plunging his hand into his pocket, he found the tiny fabric parcel. His fingers closed around it.

What would Evelyn think? A little gift that meant so much to him and yet would probably be meaningless to her.

Something to show her how sorry he was.

Something to bring her luck.

A round bead, the colour of her eyes. In fact, the concentric circles on it even looked like an eye. He'd wrapped it in a square of fabric that Mrs Shipley, his landlady, had given him and tied it with ribbon. Probably Evelyn would be more interested in the ribbon. It would be more use than a scrap of fabric and a glass bead – however precious it was to him.

Jacob winced. The ride had been rougher than he'd anticipated. His muscles felt as though they had no strength left in them. Once he'd found the house and made a fool of himself, he faced the return journey. He wasn't sure he'd be able to make it. Well, too bad. He'd simply have to keep turning those pedals until he got back to Mrs Shipley's.

It wasn't like he could spend the night under a hedge, although the thought of resting anywhere was remarkably tempting. He reached a turning on the right-hand side and carried on wheeling his bicycle out of the ruts.

Several people working in gardens greeted him as he counted down to Swallowmead. Finally, he arrived and leaned his bicycle against the hedge. He swallowed, trying to moisten his mouth. For a second, it occurred to him he might get on his bicycle, ride off and forget the whole thing.

He squeezed his eyes closed, trying to summon the courage to knock at the door. Running his fingers through his fringe, he paused, his hand on his head.

No, leave now...

"Hello."

Jacob looked up. A woman stood at the door of the house, a black and white cat in her arms.

Something about her resembled Evelyn, although she was much older. Yes, this must be the elder sister, Ada Quinn.

Well, she'd spotted him now. He could hardly ride off. He opened the gate and walked towards her, patting the bead in his pocket for luck.

The woman tilted her head. "Can I help you? Are you lost?"

"I'm looking for Miss Evelyn Quinn. I believe she lives here?"

The woman, who was almost certainly Ada Quinn, raised her eyebrows. "And you are?"

"Lieutenant Jacob Adam. I met Miss Quinn in London."

The woman's brows drew together, and Jacob braced himself. She would probably know what part he'd played in her sister leaving home. Perhaps it would have been wiser to write.

Of course, it would have been.

But he'd longed to see Evelyn and at least while he was there, he had a chance...

Then, to his relief, Ada Quinn smiled. Not a polite smile one might give a stranger. Her smile was one of welcome.

"Ah, the recipient of the socks. I'm so sorry, Lieutenant Adam, but I'm afraid my sister is still at work." Ada Quinn put down the cat and checked her watch. "She should be home soon. Possibly fifteen minutes..." She paused, then added, "would you care for a cup of tea until she returns?"

Jacob hadn't realised he'd been holding his breath. He slowly let it out now. So far, so good. He hadn't dared believe Evelyn's sister would be so welcoming. Of course, that didn't mean Evelyn herself would be pleased to see him. But taking tea with her sister was a good place to start.

The cottage was small, although everything was neat and tidy. Two armchairs sat in front of a wood fire, a sofa against the wall. Nearby was a dining table with four chairs. Jacob noticed as Ada led him towards the table that her movements were slightly stiff. Just like him. And later, once she'd made tea, she gripped the teapot carefully as she poured, the shadow of pain passing across her face.

"So, Lieutenant Adam, tell me how you came to be here. It's quite a coincidence, isn't it?" She looked at him with twinkling eyes.

"I ran into your brother Gordon in Barnes Street," he said, as if he'd accidentally encountered him somewhere rather than having been waiting outside Evelyn's house to see if she appeared.

"Gordon? My goodness. He certainly seems to meet a lot of people working in that bakery. I think he knows half the East End."

Jacob thought back to when Gordon had offered him a lift. 'Graham & Sons, Bakery' had been painted on the side. He smiled, nodded and said nothing, not wanting to lie to Ada, but not wanting to admit the truth either.

"So, what are you doing in Essex? You're a long way from the sea." Ada nodded at his uniform.

"I'm afraid my seagoing days are over." He glanced at the cane that he'd leaned against his chair. But now I'm based in Chelmsford." He wasn't allowed to talk about where he was working and what he was doing.

Again, Ada Quinn's brows drew together, and she surveyed him. "I imagine that would be at Marconi."

Jacob smiled. She was well informed about where a naval officer might work in Chelmsford.

"But say no more," she added quickly. "We all know careless talk costs lives." Her eyes were now sad.

The black and white cat crept out from beneath Miss Quinn's chair and, after sniffing Jacob's boot, he rubbed against his leg.

"Titan is a good judge of character," she said, affectionately shooing the cat away. "He dislikes most people, but he's obviously taken to you. Well, can I offer you more tea?" She pointed at the teapot, but before he could reply, the front door opened.

"Ada! I'm home. I couldn't get the pork chops—" Evelyn stared at the two people at the table. Her eyes quickly scanning back and forth.

"Oh, I'm sorry, Ada, I didn't realise you had company this afternoon—" She gasped as her eyes rested on Jacob, and recognition lit them.

"Lieutenant Adam?" She tilted her head to one side as her sister had done earlier.

Jacob stood as quickly as he could, fighting his stiff muscles. "Miss Quinn, I hope you'll forgive the intrusion, but I felt an apology was necessary. I had no idea my attempt to thank you at your mother's house would spark such an argument, much less result in you leaving home."

"H... how did you know?"

"I met your brother Gordon, and he told me. I hope you don't mind him giving me your address. Family is so important. And I felt wretched after I caused you trouble. That was the last thing I intended. I hope you will forgive me." The words tumbled out and his cheeks flushed.

Stop babbling.

Evelyn shook the hand he offered and smiled at him. As he held her gaze, it was as if they were completely alone, only their palms touching, but connected in every other way.

Had she felt it? Or was he being foolish?

She broke the spell as she let go of his hand, bringing him back to reality. "There's no need for an apology. In fact, I can't thank you enough, Lieutenant Adam." She smiled at him, and the breath caught in her throat.

A REUNION IN PLOTLANDS

Thankfully, Ada distracted Evelyn. "Sit, sit," she said, picking up the teapot again. "Let's enjoy a cup of tea together. Lieutenant Adam has ridden his bicycle all the way from Chelmsford, dear. Now, what do you think of that?"

"Chelmsford? That's miles and miles away." Evelyn's eyebrows raised in surprise.

Jacob shrugged modestly, as if it had been nothing, and explained his doctor had recommended exercise to help his muscles heal.

In fact, his muscles were screaming at him, and the thought of the return journey gnawed at his insides.

And yet, when he glanced at Evelyn, he admitted to himself he'd have cycled twice as far just to see her face and to know she'd forgiven him.

What was happening to him? After his parents died, he'd vowed never to get close to anyone again. The pain of loss was devastating, and he couldn't bear the thought of more grief. But it was unlikely he'd ever see Evelyn again. Why not enjoy this afternoon? What harm could that do? He'd had precious little pleasure for so long.

Ada chattered away and the conversation came easily. He learnt about Evelyn's work at the telephone exchange in Laindon, and although he couldn't explain exactly what he did at Marconi, he told them it was important war work. They probably wouldn't have understood that what he was doing involved new developments in rapid and accurate detection of enemy aircraft and ships and preventing attacks. But neither of them asked.

"I understand Marconi was instrumental in wireless technology," Ada said.

"Well, yes, that sort of thing," he said vaguely.

"All very technical, I'm sure, Lieutenant Adam. I don't suppose you'd know how to mend a wireless set, would you?" Ada asked. "I broke mine last week and I miss it so. But perhaps I'm taking liberties in asking."

"I'd certainly have a look at it for you. Sadly, I need to leave shortly but I could perhaps call again when I'll have more time." What luck! The sun was already low, and he knew he'd have to leave soon or risk getting lost in the dark. But the thought of never seeing Evelyn again kept him sitting there. He'd been trying to find the words to ask if he could call again. And now, he had a perfect excuse. Of course, when he returned, she might not be there. It had been Ada who'd asked him to mend the wireless, but at least it was better than walking out of the cottage forever.

At least there was a chance he'd see Evelyn again.

"Well, thank you for a delightful time, ladies. I'll write and let you know when I next have some leave, and I'll bring some tools." He smiled and rose, biting down hard on his lower lip as he turned away, willing his muscles to respond. His legs had stiffened while he'd been sitting, and pain stabbed his back. But he wouldn't falter.

And once on his bicycle, his muscles would surely loosen. Of course, he'd have to get on it first.

He clamped his jaws together. He'd have to rely on willpower.

Chapter Twelve

Evelyn watched as Lieutenant Adam wheeled his bicycle to the corner and waved. She sighed. He was obviously in great discomfort, but he'd been desperate to hide it. The impression of his teeth on his bottom lip as he got up from the table showed how much effort it had taken him to move.

"So, that's the pleasant lieutenant we have to thank for prising you out of our mother's house." Ada's smile was mischievous. "Such a handsome young man. So well spoken. And so obviously smitten with you, Evelyn."

"Nonsense." But Evelyn's heart was still thrashing in her chest. He'd said he would come again. Had he simply felt an obligation to please Ada when she'd mentioned her wireless set?

It hadn't appeared so. But he was such a well-mannered man he might not have wanted to refuse. Perhaps he wouldn't write, and they'd never see him again. No, surely, he wasn't that type of man.

Well, what did she know of young men anyway? Mother had made sure she knew nothing. This was the first time since she'd arrived in Plotlands that the subject of young men had come up and Ada obviously didn't share Mother's puritanical opinions. She'd taken every opportunity to praise her younger sister and to give Lieutenant Adam the impression she was the perfect woman. Evelyn's cheeks glowed at the memory. Mother had rarely referred to her daughter when speaking to others, much less praised her. But Ada had wholeheartedly expressed her approval.

As overwhelming as that was, Evelyn was worried. Back in London, life had been easy. She wasn't allowed to speak to men. So, there had been no reason to worry about how to behave with them. But Ada had opened a whole new world of possibilities.

Evelyn felt as though she was standing on the edge of a cliff, looking down at the sea swirling far beneath. Living with Mother, she wouldn't have been allowed anywhere near the cliff edge. But Ada had made it clear she must live her life as she wanted. To walk on the cliff edge if she desired.

To make her own mistakes.

To breathe.

However, that type of freedom brought hazards.

Was she brave enough to grasp every opportunity that was now open to her, knowing she'd inevitably make mistakes?

A letter arrived at Swallowmead several days later. Not the white envelopes that Gordon used. This was expensive cream-coloured stationery. Evelyn picked it up, assuming it was for Ada, but it was addressed to Miss E. Quinn.

She didn't recognise the elegant writing. Hope fluttered in her chest. Could it possibly be from Lieutenant Jacob Adam?

Please. Please.

She turned it over and over, reluctant to risk discovering it was from someone else.

"Are you going to open that?" Ada raised her eyebrows. She would also have noticed the envelope and handwriting, and deduced it wasn't from Gordon.

She passed Evelyn the letter opener. "You might as well get it over with, dear. He did say he'd call again and I for one, believe him. I don't think he'd have just said it without meaning it."

Evelyn blushed. They both knew who 'he' referred to. It was as though Ada had read her mind. She slipped the blade inside the envelope and sliced it open. After a moment's hesitation, she pulled out the letter and unfolded it. Her eyes flew to the name at the bottom. Jacob Adam in elegant script. It was him! Next, her eyes slid up to the message. He might simply have written to tell her he couldn't come to visit them.

But no. He wanted to come next Sunday. Evelyn couldn't help giving a tiny gasp of excitement.

"Good news?" Ada asked casually, her head down over the newspaper as if more interested in an article, but Evelyn could hear the smile in her voice.

"Lieutenant Adam would like to come and attempt to mend your wireless set on Sunday, if that's convenient."

"As far as I'm concerned, that's completely convenient. Is it convenient for you, dear?"

"Oh, yes!" The words tumbled out of Evelyn's mouth in a rush.

"Excellent." Ada pushed the newspaper away. "Then, we must plan Sunday lunch carefully." She tapped her mouth with a forefinger, her brows drawn together. "I fed Mr Turner's chickens while he visited his son a few months ago, and he said to let him know if I ever wanted one of them. Not that they're particularly large, but I'm sure there'll be enough for three people. Now, how can we make the meal really special? I know! Let's bake a cake. Between us and the neighbours, we can find enough coupons to gather the ingredients for a cake – and possibly even a few biscuits. I'll call in a few favours. When neighbours have had important events in the past, I've donated coupons to help them out. Now, I expect they'll be pleased to help me."

Evelyn looked at her sister in surprise. Ada appeared to be as excited as she was. Already planning a meal such as they'd never had before.

Ada placed the stationery box on the table. "Well, what are you waiting for, dear? Write back and tell him to come. You can post the letter on your way to work this morning and it'll catch the first post. And then we need to start tidying everything away. Oh, and cleaning. Everything must be clean and tidy."

Evelyn wrote back to say it would be most convenient if Lieutenant Jacob Adam would call on Sunday. She wondered how to finish the letter. Should she say she was awaiting the day impatiently, or did that sound too familiar? After all, she didn't really know him. Excitement bubbled up inside her at the thought of seeing him again.

Don't read too much into this.

He'd said he'd have a look at Ada's wireless. He was a gentleman. Of course, he would come. He was doing it to help Ada. But still, she couldn't forget his hand in hers and the way he'd looked at her, his eyes brightening as if he was drinking in every part of her.

Stop it! What nonsense. Eyes don't drink in anything. You're writing your own fairy tale. Stop it now or you risk making an utter fool of yourself on Sunday.

It was good advice and she'd do well to heed it. She would assume nothing. Yet as she walked along Second Avenue on her way to work with the letter in her hand, something thrilling quivered inside.

In the end, she'd finished the letter, Yours sincerely, Evelyn Quinn. Well, better to be too formal than not formal enough. And it was accurate. She was sincere. Sincerely eager to see him again. Sincerely impatient to hear his voice. Sincerely hoping he might feel the same about her.

And yet, 'Yours sincerely,' might also appear to be rather business-like. What would he read into it? Would he even notice? Well, it was too late now. She looked down at the letter in her hand. The thought of Lieutenant Adam receiving that same piece of paper filled her with warmth, keeping away the chill of the overnight frost.

The world glistened and sparkled as the lemony glow of the early sun reflected off the ice crystals that coated everything. The commonplace and ordinary had been made spectacular. And that didn't merely apply to the countryside – it described her life since she'd learnt Lieutenant Adam would be visiting on Sunday.

Not taking care where she was walking, she slid a few inches on a frozen puddle. Her heart raced as shock streaked through her body. She paused to recover; thankful she hadn't fallen. Hopefully Ada wouldn't slip when she made her way to school later. But by then, the watery sun would have melted some of the frost. Had that been a lesson? The beauty of the frost had so bewitched her, she hadn't been prepared for the treacherous ground beneath her feet.

No. She wouldn't be gloomy today. That sort of thinking came from having lived with Mother for so long. And yet being cautious still seemed prudent. Becoming keen on a man was fraught with danger.

Evelyn looked down at the letter again and the breath caught in her throat; her warning to be watchful was forgotten. How was she going to bear the wait for Sunday?

Evelyn had no intention of telling Phyllis about the lieutenant's forthcoming visit. She didn't want to admit she was so excited. And anyway, it would be inconsiderate to mention the dashing lieutenant when Phyllis was so desperate for news from both her brother and her fiancé who were both missing in Europe.

But mostly, it was because Phyllis would look for problems, and Evelyn didn't want to see them. She didn't want to consider the possibility that Lieutenant Adam might not come. They were at war. There was no certainty about anything. People could be moved to different parts of the country at a moment's notice. Others were picked off by bombs. One minute there, the next gone. Life was precarious at the best of times, but it had taken on such a brittle fragility that it hardly seemed worth making plans at all.

Stop it! She told herself, you're thinking like Phyllis now. Treat it like another day. Don't build it up in your mind. Forget about it.

Before she knew it, she'd told Phyllis. They'd hardly entered the telephone exchange before the words had tumbled out of her mouth.

"I wondered why you were looking so pleased this morning. So, tell me more about this man."

That was the point where Evelyn should have pretended Lieutenant Adam was no one in particular. An acquaintance who'd offered to fix – or at least to look at – Ada's radio. Perhaps a family friend. Or a distant relative.

Remain vague and pretend he doesn't matter. Phyllis will lose interest.

But of course, she didn't.

"You put a poem and your address in the socks you'd knitted, and he came to find you? Well, how exciting and romantic is that?" Phyllis clasped her hands together.

And strangely, she hadn't looked for problems.

Although if she had – as Evelyn was certain Phyllis would have – she hadn't mentioned them.

Surprisingly, she offered to lend Evelyn a dress she'd just made for herself. "It'll suit you perfectly and we're about the same height and size. I'll bring it in tomorrow and you can try it on."

Dress? Evelyn looked down at her shabby skirt, blouse and cardigan. Her cardigan was faded, and one elbow had been darned. It appeared to have grown and sagged with age, while her skirt was now slightly too tight.

She'd put on a little weight since she'd come to live with Ada. Not that she'd been eating much more than she had at Mother's. But everything tasted more delicious. Or perhaps she was just more content.

There was certainly greater choice in Plotlands. Many of the neighbours produced their own food and shared it with others when they had a glut. Ada's garden was overgrown. The neighbour who usually worked on it for her had hurt his back, and once he'd stopped helping, the weeds had taken over. Evelyn had begun to work on it but there was a lot for one person to manage. She was keen to give back to those who'd helped Ada. In the spring, she'd plant some vegetables.

The spring. The beginning of new life. Her skin tingled at the prospect of starting afresh.

She was comfortable with Ada, and for the first time she knew she was accepted for herself. And that set her free to think about who she actually wanted to be.

Such a strange thought. In the past, she'd been what her mother had wanted her to be. Or, more accurately, she hadn't been what her mother had wanted her to be. However hard she'd tried, that had always been an impossibility. She'd never been good enough.

"I'm sure the dress will fit you perfectly." Phyllis crossed her arms, tipped her head to one side and with brows drawn together, she scrutinised Evelyn. "But we need to consider your hair. I'll pop round on

Sunday morning and see if I can give you a more sophisticated look."

Evelyn wanted to laugh. Phyllis, usually so timid and full of foreboding, was intent on transforming her. On one hand, it was funny. On the other, it was disturbing to know her friend considered she needed to become someone new. Well, why not? It was merely another part of being the new Evelyn Quinn.

But where would it stop? Her skin tingled again as she realised there were so many possibilities. How could she not have seen them while she was living with Mother? It was as though she'd had an umbrella over her head, and when she looked up, all she saw was its underside. Now with no umbrella above her, she looked up at the sky with its clouds and the birds, and for the first time ever, felt that if she wanted to, she, too, could float amongst the clouds.

Chapter Thirteen

On Sunday morning, Phyllis arrived early to style Evelyn's hair. The dress she'd lent her fitted perfectly. It was navy blue with pale blue polka dots, a white collar, and cuffs around the short sleeves. She'd also brought a light blue cardigan that matched the polka dots.

When Phyllis had finished, Evelyn looked at herself in the mirror. She stared in silence.

"Don't you like it? I can do something else. If you like..." With eyes wide with dread, Phyllis hovered nervously behind her.

Evelyn swallowed the lump in her throat. "No, I really adore it. But it's so... different; I can't believe it's me."

Phyllis's shoulders sagged with relief. "Goodness me, I thought you hated it! Of course, it's you. And I'm glad you like it. You know what they say, during this dreadful war, 'beauty is a duty'."

When Phyllis finally left, the cottage was filled with the aroma of cinnamon and sugar. Ada lingered by the oven, reluctant to keep opening the door, but dreading the cake burning.

"I knew I should have done it yesterday. But at least it'll be fresh. And hopefully cooked properly. If I'd done it yesterday and burnt it, I wouldn't have had enough ingredients to make another, and I'd have worried about it all night. But even so. Perhaps I should have started earlier..." Ada nibbled her lower lip.

"I'm sure it'll be delicious." Evelyn had never seen Ada so agitated. Her cheeks were flushed, and hair had escaped from her bun.

"This is the first cake I've baked since I've been living here. There wasn't any point baking one for myself, and now, of course, with rationing..." She pushed a wisp of hair behind her ear and bent to risk another quick peep.

It had never occurred to Evelyn to wonder what life had been like for Ada when she'd first come to Swallowmead. She probably hadn't been much older than Evelyn was now. Before she'd thought it through, she'd asked, "Why did you choose to come to Plotlands? I understand why you might have wanted to leave Mother's, but you could have gone anywhere; why did you choose here?"

For a second, Evelyn wished she hadn't asked as she saw the haunted look pass across her sister's face. It was immediately replaced by a blank, impenetrable stare – the expression Ada assumed from time to time when she obviously didn't want to talk about something.

It hadn't happened often. The last time Evelyn had seen it was when one of the neighbours had mentioned two evacuees who apparently had briefly stayed with her elder sister at the beginning of the war.

Now, Ada's features gave nothing away. They were set, like a mask. Well, it was none of Evelyn's business and she would definitely not probe.

She changed the subject, drawing in several breaths, sampling the air, and said, "That cake smells delicious."

But to her surprise, Ada blinked several times, and once again, a shadow of pain darkened her face.

"I... I don't usually talk about it, but since you've asked, I'll tell you. I moved to Plotlands because I knew a family here. They've all gone now, unfortunately, but they were very dear to me when I first came."

"I'm so sorry, Ada. I didn't mean to pry." Evelyn was concerned at having started a conversation that was obviously loaded with disturbing memories. "You don't need to tell me. I can see it makes you sad."

Ada bowed her head. In a small voice, she said, "You deserve to know. We won't have time now. But one day I'll explain."

The timer for the cake went off and cut through the melancholic air.

Deserve to know? What did Ada mean? Well, Evelyn was not going to ask. She'd already upset her sister once.

Ada turned back to the oven and opened the door. The cake was lopsided and slightly darkened on one side, but the aroma was mouth-watering, and they both pronounced it a masterpiece. Lightening the mood, Ada joked she might have put too much carrot in the mixture.

"When I cut into it, let's hope it's not orange on the inside."

But at least the earlier awkwardness had been forgotten. Evelyn would not probe into Ada's past again. It was none of her business what had happened to her sister years ago.

"Well, I'd better go and tidy up," Ada said, pushing wisps of hair behind her ears.

Evelyn suppressed a smile. Her sister was almost as nervous about the visit as she was.

Almost – but not quite. Evelyn's stomach churned. Her chest had tightened, and her heart beat out an insistent protest at the constriction. Her muscles appeared to have lost their strength, and she fumbled with the teaspoons and cups. If she didn't pay attention, she'd break something. And if she couldn't get her body under control, she'd make a fool of herself in front of Lieutenant Adam.

He was coming to fulfil a promise to Ada to look at her wireless set.

Nothing more. And yet the shy glance towards her when he'd agreed to come had suggested he had wanted to see her again.

Oh, stop it! She told herself crossly. Expressions were too hard to read. Expressions could lie.

Mother had displayed her disapproval, disappointment or dismay of her daughter openly when they were alone. But if someone else was there, she masked it, making her face blank. Evelyn had found it easier to judge her mother's mood by listening rather than looking – a snort, a sniff, a tap of the foot, the way she said 'Evelyn', had all been more revealing that what she showed on her face.

No, Evelyn knew expressions could deceive.

She checked her watch. Not long until he arrived.

If he arrived.

Suppose he didn't come?

Her stomach sank.

Ada would be disappointed; she'd put so much effort into the Sunday dinner.

Evelyn looked down at her dress and patted her hair. Her stomach sank further. If he didn't come, she would be beyond disappointment.

Chapter Fourteen

Jacob dismounted the bicycle. After returning from his first visit to Plotlands, he'd been in agony and hadn't cycled for several days. He'd pushed himself too hard. But it had been worth it, and the proof was that he was now back in Dunton and had the perfect excuse to spend time with Evelyn.

He had various tools in the duffel bag that was slung over his shoulder, as well as a bottle of sherry and a chocolate bar, wrapped in a towel to stop them breaking. They'd cost him more than he could afford, but he hadn't wanted to turn up empty-handed.

Flowers had been his first choice, but what sort of state would a bouquet have been in after his bicycle ride? He bent his knees slightly, testing his thigh muscles. After his journey, they weren't too painful. That was encouraging.

He really should have brought an AVO meter so he could check the current, voltage and resistance of the wireless set, but although he could have borrowed one from his friend, it was heavy, and it would have added extra weight to his bag. And anyway, if more than a simple repair was necessary, he'd probably have a better idea of what he ought to bring the next time he called.

The next time...

Jacob wheeled his bicycle along the main road, then turned off onto the grassy track that led towards Second Avenue. He didn't need to check his wristwatch to know he was much too early, and he slowed his pace. Such had been his fear he might get lost again and waste precious time that he'd set off too soon.

Mrs Shipley, his landlady, had assumed he was going out on his own again for a day's bicycle ride as part of his exercise regime. She'd wanted to pack him sandwiches until he'd explained he was going to visit a friend. Although she hadn't asked for details, he'd seen the inquisitive expression on her face.

Dear Mrs Shipley – she had shown herself to be quite protective of him and had begun to fuss over him like a mother. Not like his own mother of course – no one could ever come close to her. But it was touching how caring the landlady had become.

Even walking as slowly as he could, Jacob arrived at the corner of Second Avenue, much too early. There was no point turning back to the main road where the going was easier; he might as well carry on and explore.

Dunton was nothing like the village in which he lived with its ancient thatched cottages and Norman church. The first time he'd visited the Plotlands, he'd been surprised at the strange collection of wooden sheds and shacks, as well as the modern cottages. But he hadn't taken much notice because he'd been eager to find Swallowmead – and Evelyn.

But now he had time to look about. Most of the dwellings were simple and well kept. Others had a ramshackle appearance – with rooms and lean-tos added on to enlarge them – probably to accommodate the people who'd escaped the bombing in London.

A group of chattering children hurried towards him, two carrying buckets of water that sloshed over the ground as they walked. They stared at him and one gravely saluted. Jacob returned his salute and smiled. The faint drone of conversation drifted out of several cottages and the clang of saucepans. Further off, someone hammered wood and closer by, the *buk-buk-buk* of chickens filled the air.

The aroma of burnt toast accompanied by a hint of what might have been coffee prompted Jacob to remember he'd been invited for dinner. He didn't feel hungry at all. His stomach was knotted with nerves and excitement.

He stopped to check his watch. One minute had passed.

How much longer would he need to wander?

He was still staring at his watch when a man came out of one of the front gardens, pushing a wheelbarrow. Just as Jacob was about to turn to go back to Evelyn's cottage, he heard the hum of aeroplanes. A jolt of fear shot through him, and he looked up, his eyes scanning the sky. The man also stopped and looked skywards.

Jacob had learnt a lot about the area and didn't think there were any large industrial targets in the vicinity. However, the mock airfield on a nearby farm had been laid out to draw enemy attention away from nearby Hornchurch aerodrome. Luftwaffe pilots had dropped explosive and incendiary bombs on the Dunton area, causing several deaths.

A cold sweat broke out on his brow, and he fought to control the waves of panic that rose inside. Of course, he'd endured air raids over Chelmsford, but he'd willed himself to disengage his fear. When the air raid siren had sounded, he'd forced himself to go as calmly as he could to the shelters at work or if he'd been home, he'd gone into Mrs Shipley's garden to her Anderson Shelter.

But here in open Plotlands, memories flooded back of that deserted, bombed-out village where there had been nowhere to shelter. He thrust his hand into his pocket and found the blue bead, still wrapped in its square of fabric and tied with a ribbon. Squeezing it tightly in his sweaty palm, his nails bit into his flesh.

"They're Spitfires, mate. Our lads. Hornchurch heroes." The man with the wheelbarrow picked up the handles and, nodding at Jacob, he carried on along the avenue muttering curses on the Germans.

Jacob could see them now. Five spitfires flying towards him. Probably on their way back to Hornchurch aerodrome.

As the man had said. 'Our lads.'

The hairs on the back of his neck stood up. Pride in his country and horror as he remembered the bomb that had killed three friends and wounded him. He released the blue bead and took hold of the handlebars of his bicycle. It was time to go.

Chapter Fifteen

The knock on the door had come as the clock chimed the hour.

"You open it, dear. I'll keep an eye on everything in the kitchen," Ada said. She nodded reassuringly.

Evelyn pulled off her apron and hung it on the back of the door. She patted her hair to ensure it was still in place and smoothed her dress. Had she made too much of an effort? Or perhaps she hadn't tried hard enough? Phyllis had suggested a little makeup, but Evelyn had been too nervous. Lieutenant Adam might think her fast. After all, she'd been the one to send her address to a stranger.

Don't be so conceited. He hasn't come to see you. He's come to fulfil his promise to Ada to look at her wireless.

The voice in her head had been her own, yet the words might well have been spoken by Mother. She sighed. The moment she gained a little self-confidence, the tiny voice eroded it. Would her mother's influence always pursue her?

She hurried to the door, anticipation fluttering in her chest. He was standing on the path, holding a bottle of sherry.

She could barely breathe.

That smile! His hair had been ruffled by the breeze and his cheeks were coloured after his bicycle ride, but the pain she'd noticed before in his eyes had been replaced by pleasure.

Do not read anything into anyone's expression. You cannot trust your judgement.

She realised she was staring. "Come in, come in," she said, words flying out of her mouth in an undignified volley. Too loud. Too enthusiastic. Too... well, just too much.

Flushing, she stepped back to allow him in. Ada appeared at the kitchen door and greeted him as she wiped her hands on a tea towel.

While he took off his coat, Evelyn cautioned herself again.

Stay calm.

He handed Ada the bottle of sherry and, turning to Evelyn, he shyly gave her the chocolate bar. Then, as they thanked him, he knelt and busied himself with the tools in his bag, as if hiding his embarrassment.

Finally, he stood. "Well, shall I look at the wireless now?"

Ada cleared a space on the sideboard, and he carefully laid out his tools on the towel he'd brought.

How thoughtful he was. A neighbour had mended Ada's dripping kitchen tap the previous week and had left the kitchen floor covered in mud. It was kind of him to have helped, but it had taken Evelyn a long time to clean up. He hadn't even appeared to have noticed the trail of dirty footprints he'd left behind.

But not Lieutenant Adam. He'd carefully considered in advance how to prevent causing damage or a mess.

He placed the wireless on the towel. Then turning it around, he started to unscrew the back. "If nothing's immediately apparent, I'll have to arrange another time to call if that'll be convenient. I may have to borrow a meter to test the components. But hopefully, I might be able to see something obvious now."

He was prepared to come back. Evelyn's heart soared. Not that she wanted Ada to be without her beloved wireless but the chance of seeing him one more time...

"I'm afraid it's broken because I dropped it," Ada said. "So clumsy of me. I was dusting, and as I put it back, it slipped. Only a few inches but after that, it wouldn't work."

He undid the last screw then removed the back of the unit to reveal cables, boxes and valves. Wires led from one part to the next, in what to Evelyn, was a meaningless jumble. Lieutenant Adam stared at it for a while, gently prodding wires to see if anything was loose. He touched each of the four valves in turn, pressing them home. The fourth moved slightly and appeared to be unseated. He pushed it into place with a grunt of satisfaction, then plugged the wireless into the mains. It crackled and as he turned the knob to tune it in, the faint strains of music came out of the speaker. Tuning into the BBC Home Service, orchestral music filled the room.

Ada clapped her hands in delight. Lieutenant Adam smiled in triumph, and Evelyn's stomach flipped over. How handsome he was. How clever too.

Like the valve being pushed into place, a weight pressed down inside her. He'd mended the wireless. Once they'd eaten, there would be no reason for him to return.

How she longed to see this man again. She couldn't take her eyes off his face, wanting to watch his various expressions and those gentle brown eyes. Wanting to commit it to memory.

Ada rushed back into the kitchen to start serving up, and Lieutenant Adam began to screw the back of the wireless into place.

"Well, that was fortunate; I thought it might be more complicated."

"Thank you so much, Lieutenant Adam, my sister loves music and we both like to hear the news. Not that there's much happening to cheer us at the moment, but it's best to know how the war's progressing." Had she really just said something so banal? She wanted to groan as Mother's voice mimicked her words and echoed through her mind.

He paused and swallowed. "I wonder if you'd do me the honour of using my first name, please. Lieutenant Adam is so formal, and I had hoped that we might..." He looked down at the screw. It was crooked. He undid it slightly, righted it and began to screw it in again.

"Yes? We might...?" She held her breath.

"That is," he said without looking up. "I had hoped we might become friends."

"Yes!" She said it so quickly, he jumped, and the screwdriver tip slid out of the screw head.

Evelyn flushed. *Fool!*

But when he looked up at her, his cheeks were pink, and he was smiling that delicious, lopsided smile that made her stomach flip over once again.

"Then that's settled; we're friends. And perhaps I may call you Evelyn?" His brown gaze rested softly on her face.

"Yes!" she said, once again, too eagerly, but this time, rather than being startled, he smiled delightedly, as if they were sharing a secret.

Ada came bustling in. "Well, dinner is ready. I'm sorry Lieutenant Adam, but I need to drag my sister away to help me serve up. I can be a little clumsy. She looked down ruefully at her hands.

"Then please, Miss Quinn, may I assist too?"

"Perhaps you could carve the chicken, Lieutenant. That would be a great help."

When Evelyn had first arrived at Ada's, she'd dreaded their first Sunday together. With Mother, the day been a silent affair. So, Evelyn had been surprised to find how enjoyable it was to spend the time with Ada. They cooked dinner during the morning. Then, while they ate, they either listened to the BBC on the wireless, or talked. They shared what had happened during the previous few days and discussed what the coming week would bring. It had been a time to learn about each other and for Evelyn to appreciate her new life with her sister.

Despite longing to see Jacob, Evelyn had wondered whether the meal would be as relaxed as usual. She needn't have worried. It had gone well and had been worth all the extra effort, expense and coupons. Jacob was good company and he and Ada were also now on first-name terms, too. Stand-offish Titan who didn't like strangers had been charmed by Jacob and sat by his feet.

After the meal, Ada suggested they have some of the sherry Jacob had bought.

"Please don't open it on my account. I've had more than enough wine and I need to keep a clear head for my ride home or I'll end up in the village pond," Jacob said.

Evelyn laughed, but she glanced repeatedly at the hands on the clock, willing them to slow down. The sun was still shining although it was low. Soon, he'd have to leave or risk cycling through dark lanes.

"Do you know, I haven't had a glass of sherry since the Christmas before war began," Ada said.

There was silence for a few moments, and Jacob bent over to stroke Titan, hiding his face.

The mention of Christmas. Was that what had caused the change in mood? Perhaps Jacob was remembering past years when he'd celebrated with his family.

"And this Christmas," Ada said decisively, "is going to be a good one, isn't it, dear?" She reached over and patted Evelyn's hand. "Because we can do exactly as we like."

They exchanged glances. Evelyn hadn't given much thought to Christmas, but now seeing the sparkle in Ada's eye she had a rush of optimism. This would be the first Christmas she would spend with someone she loved and with someone who loved her. Warmth filled her at that thought.

Someone she loved.

Yes, she loved Ada. Of course, she'd be expected to love her eldest sister; that was natural. But this wasn't a family obligation. This was unbidden and unexpected.

But poor Jacob. She guessed he was thinking about the family he'd lost, and how bleak his Christmas would be. From the little he'd said about his family and the tragedy that had struck them; Ada must have guessed, too.

"If you aren't working on Christmas Day, or have other plans, Jacob, then you're more than welcome to spend the day with us. If you can face the bicycle ride of course."

For a second Jacob stared at her, then he smiled and, after glancing at Evelyn with an expression she hadn't been able to read, he said he'd love to join them.

He'd sounded sincere. Even a little excited.

"Excellent. That's settled." Ada took the bottle off the table and put it in the sideboard. "That's for Christmas Day and you'll just have to risk wobbling all over the place on the way home."

Having almost ruined the jovial atmosphere by mentioning Christmas, Ada had succeeded in raising it to higher levels. And now, Evelyn had an extra reason to look forward to the day. She'd see Jacob again. Excitement bubbled up inside her.

After the meal, Jacob helped to carry all the dirty dishes into the kitchen, although Ada had forbidden him to help wash up.

"We don't have company often, so let's enjoy you while we can.

That can be done once you've gone."

Evelyn made tea and they gathered around the fire and ate the cake Ada had agonised over while it had been baking. It was delicious, although Evelyn realised she could have been eating cardboard and it would have tasted wonderful. Just being near Jacob made the world better, brighter, full of hope.

But when the clock chimed three, the time for him to leave had come. Evelyn felt as though something was squeezing her heart.

He had to go so soon?

At least he'd be back at Christmas.

"I expect you have a lot of Christmas parties and celebrations where you work," Ada said.

"I must admit, I hadn't really thought about it," he said. "But I believe so. There's always a lot of social events being held."

Ada nodded with understanding. "I've never really been interested in Christmas before. After all, it's not much fun on your own. The neighbours always ask me to join them but it's not the same. Now I've got Evelyn." She paused to smile. "Well, now it's different. And there's plenty going on around here. We have the Christmas dance in the hall in Laindon. That's always popular. I went a few times when I first came here but I haven't been since. The local shops and businesses club together and put it on for their employees. In fact, a mother of one of the schoolchildren didn't want her tickets and gave them to me. But really, it's not my sort of thing. Perhaps, if Jacob isn't too busy or working that evening, he could take my ticket?"

"Surely you'd like to go with Evelyn, Ada?" Jacob asked.

"I'm certainly not accompanying Evelyn and then spending the evening sitting in the corner. I'd only have to hear the music to want to be up on my feet. But my dancing days are over." She paused, presumably remembering that Jacob's dancing days might well be over, too. Her cheeks reddened, but to Evelyn surprise, Jacob smiled and said, "I would love to go if you're sure you don't need the ticket." Then turning to Evelyn, he said, "I beg your pardon, Evelyn, of course you may wish to go with someone else."

"No!" she said quickly. Too quickly. What was it about this man that caused such extreme reactions in her? "I'd love to go with you."

"Excellent." Ada beamed. "Then that's settled. I don't think I've ever looked forward to a Christmas as much as this."

Chapter Sixteen

"And?" Phyllis asked when she met Evelyn on Monday morning at the end of the High Road. "How did it go? Did he ask you out on a date?"

"No, of course not," Evelyn said. "He only came to mend Ada's wireless."

Phyllis arched her eyebrows. "Really? Well, that was a lot of effort you took to get dressed up just for the repair man."

"He's not a repair man. It's... well... all right. Yes, I do like him..." Evelyn blushed.

"I knew it! So, isn't he keen on you?"

"That's just it. I don't know. He's shy and he seems rather sad and... well, wounded. I don't just mean his back and legs. He's been hurt and I'm not sure he has room for complications in his life. But..." Evelyn smiled mischievously. "Ada gave him her ticket for the Christmas dance, so we'll be going there together."

Phyllis clapped her hands together. "How marvellous!" She paused for a moment and frowned. "But didn't you say he came over on a bicycle? The Christmas dance doesn't finish until midnight. He'll have to cycle back to Chelmsford after that. I wonder if the prospect of a long ride in the dark will put him off."

Trust Phyllis to have thought of a problem and a possible reason for Jacob to change his mind.

Unaware of Evelyn's dismay, Phyllis carried on. "Perhaps he could come on the bus? But it's still a long way. Oh well, never mind. I expect he'll find a way to get here." The doubtful note in her voice suggested she didn't think that at all.

Of course, it was too far to come for a dance. Evelyn's elation took a further beating as Phyllis told her about a friend who'd taken the bus to Chelmsford and had to walk for miles when the bus had broken down. No, Jacob wouldn't want the trouble of coming to Laindon for a dance when he'd probably have plenty of parties taking place where he lived. From what he'd said, Marconi had a lively social life. He'd have all sorts of invitations at Christmas. Why would he want to come to Laindon? If he wrote again, he'd probably say he regretted he couldn't make that day because he was on duty or make some other excuse.

They arrived at the telephone exchange and Evelyn was relieved there'd be no further opportunity to chat until their break. Having planted the idea Jacob wouldn't come to the dance, Evelyn's earlier excitement drained away. Of course, she'd see him on Christmas Day. But perhaps he wouldn't come then, either.

And if he didn't, there'd be no further excuse to see him unless he wrote to say he wanted to see her. And why should he? He'd said he hoped they could be friends, but that didn't mean anything. He'd sought her out to thank her for the socks, but he'd just been showing gratitude. She could have been anyone. He'd come to mend Ada's wireless. Again, Evelyn had been incidental. Ada had invited him to the dance, and he'd agreed to take Evelyn.

But at no time had he expressed a desire to be with her. True, they were on first name terms, and he'd said he'd wanted them to be friends. And he'd looked at her in such a way, she'd assumed he liked her. But she didn't trust her instincts.

The previous day, she'd offered to accompany him to the main road to show him the way, but he'd declined. He'd been most polite, but he'd said he knew the way and that he didn't want to put her out, nor Ada who was about to start the washing up.

She thought he'd looked at her as if he'd rather have accepted her offer. Another example of her reading what she wanted to see into people's expressions.

How long would she have to wait before Jacob wrote and told her he couldn't come?

She took over from the telephonist who'd been on the night shift, and as she was adjusting her headphones, a lamp on the lowest section of the panel in front of her lit up. She reached up to insert the plug into the jack. "Number please?" she asked in the voice she assumed at work – efficient, to give the person on the other end confidence their call would be dealt with competently, but at the same time, sunny and friendly. There was enough misery because of the war without people spreading more unpleasantness.

Evelyn repeated the number and as she plugged the jack into the correct socket, she added, "Putting you through, madam, please hold." After initiating the ringing signal, she waited until the recipient answered her call and then announced to the caller she was connected.

As she made a note in her logbook, she noticed Miss Miller, the supervisor, hovering behind, keeping an eye and ear on the telephonists. Evelyn dared not lose concentration. She desperately wanted to keep this job; Miss Miller had shown herself to be very hard to please. But even if she wasn't able to think about Jacob, she was aware of a gloomy feeling all morning.

When they stopped for a cup of tea, Phyllis started talking about the Christmas dance once again.

"Well, never mind if your Jacob can't go. You can sit with me at the dance. I shan't be dancing with anyone. It wouldn't be right, with Tim away..." Her jaw quivered.

Evelyn's spirits sank further. She hadn't realised Phyllis would be there, too. She then felt ashamed of herself. Poor Phyllis still clung to the belief that RAF pilot, Tim, was alive after having been shot down over France.

"I didn't really want to go at all, but my younger sister, Val, has a ticket and I need to keep an eye on her. She can be a little... well... a little wayward. She's a nurse and the independence has gone to her head. Our mum's at the end of her tether. Val's always out with different men. Honestly, she's such a Sunshine Suzy. Anyway, I got her a ticket and it turns out she's got her own, so I've got a spare. Oh, I've just had a marvellous idea. If your Jacob does decide to come, you could give him my spare ticket so he could bring a friend. If they both cycled, it would be easier and if they had a few drinks and one went into the ditch, the other could help him out." Still, Phyllis looked doubtful.

Always seeing the disadvantages. But at least, Phyllis had now offered Evelyn hope. She couldn't wait to write to Jacob to suggest it. He'd be more likely to come with a friend than he would on his own, where he only knew her.

Evelyn couldn't wait to start her letter. But first, she had to concentrate on the rest of her day connecting callers.

Jacob wrote back immediately and said his friend, Ronnie Howell, would love to come with him to the dance.

So that was settled. When Evelyn told Ada, she was thrilled Jacob was going with a friend. She appeared to be very fond of him and liked the idea of him becoming friends with Evelyn.

How different from their mother.

In fact, in every respect, Ada went out of her way to help Evelyn and to make her life happier. Perhaps she was trying to make up for her younger sister's earlier life. Although she hadn't been there, she'd have had a good idea of what Evelyn might have gone through.

Ada beamed broadly. "And I have some news for you. You'll never guess. Mr Farrell has given me his spare ticket so I can go to the dance, too. He said he might also drop in for a short time. He told me he hasn't been anywhere since his wife died, and he thinks it's time he started getting out a little. This is going to be such a marvellous Christmas."

After that, there was a scramble to look through their clothes to find something suitable to re-furbish for a dance. Ada brought a lilac crepe dress with matching embroidered bolero jacket into the living room and tried it on. It no longer fitted, hanging from her gaunt frame. She'd obviously lost weight since it had first been made.

When Evelyn asked her when she'd worn it before, Ada sighed and shook her head. "I never did wear it." Her voice was thin and wistful.

Then, more cheerfully, she added, "But the time has come to give it an airing. It's so beautiful, it deserves to be worn. And anyway, I don't have enough coupons for anything new."

Phyllis, who was an expert needlewoman and had come around to supervise, pinned the garments and promised to make a good job of the alterations.

"And what about you?" Phyllis asked Evelyn.

There was no question of buying anything new; Evelyn had used her clothing coupons on a winter coat and sensible shoes. Secretly, she was hoping Phyllis would lend her the polka dot dress again.

But it was Ada who saved the day. "I have a gown that I loved many years ago. It's much too young for me now. And possibly a little old-fashioned. But perhaps Phyllis can do something with it." She brought out a long silk dress with Grecian drapes to the left shoulder and waist. It was also lilac but with black lace trim. Phyllis and Evelyn stared at it in wonder.

"That's beautiful, Ada."

"I cut quite a dash when I was younger," Ada said, blushing with pleasure. "But now it's your turn, my dear." She patted Evelyn's shoulder. "Let's make you look like a goddess."

Chapter Seventeen

Jacob didn't have as much time as he'd have liked to get ready for the dance. Mr Isted, who was in charge of Section E, had wanted to talk to Jacob about the latest results of the tests on a new design for a quartz crystal oscillator, and Jacob had listened patiently. He was now late returning from his shift and hoped to make up the time, but he hadn't expected Mrs Shipley to have made him tea.

"You'll need something inside you to keep you going all evening," she'd said.

He'd eaten as fast as was polite. It had left him half as much time as he'd expected in which to get ready.

But needs must. He stared at himself in the mirror, exploring his face with his fingers to ensure he'd shaved properly, then rubbing a few drops of aftershave into his cheeks. People had described him as handsome. But what did Evelyn see?

Evelyn.

Yesterday, he'd been thinking about her, and he'd accidentally given himself a mild electric shock when he'd been testing an oscillator that had broken. He should have left it for the technician, but Jacob had thought he could save the man a bit of time if he diagnosed the problem first. He should have been concentrating, not thinking about

Evelyn, and he'd soon regretted not keeping his mind on the job. The mild shock had left him with a nasty, jangling feeling. But now, as he thought about meeting Evelyn later, a jolt went through him that was more intense than an ordinary electric shock, but every bit as disturbing. This shock, however, made his heart beat faster and left him feeling warm inside and full of longing.

Jacob would see her soon. He grinned at himself in the mirror.

Then he remembered his companion.

The last person he'd have invited to the Laindon Christmas Dance was Neville Harrington-Wade. He'd asked his friend Ronnie, who'd been looking forward to the evening. Ronnie was a quiet chap who longed to ask out one of the filter room plotter Wrens at Marconi, but he lacked the courage. He was so hesitant with girls, he made Jacob feel positively confident.

The chance to go to the Laindon dance had come at the right time. Gladys, the girl Ronnie loved from afar, had recently taken up with Neville Harrington-Wade and Ronnie needed something to take his mind off her. Perhaps he'd even meet another girl.

Neville was handsome, rich and from an aristocratic family. Not surprisingly, he was very popular with the girls who worked in the station. Less surprising was his popularity despite being married and being remarkably open about that fact. He was often out with one of the girls and currently, it was the turn of Wren, Gladys.

Three nights before the dance, Ronnie had been walking across the field to the hut in which he worked. In the total darkness of the blackout, he'd tripped, spraining his ankle and bruising a toe. Several of the men, including Neville, had heard his shouts and had carried him to the sickbay. Ronnie had asked one of them to let Jacob know he wouldn't be able to go to the dance and it had been Neville who'd taken it upon himself to relay the message.

He'd found Jacob in the canteen later and said he had Ronnie's ticket, adding he'd be happy to drive them both there and back in his car.

Jacob was annoyed Ronnie had handed over his ticket – to Neville of all people. But it was most likely he'd assumed if Neville only had one ticket, he couldn't take Gladys. Well, there was nothing Jacob could do about it, so against his better judgement, he'd agreed.

Jacob consoled himself it would be lovely to pick up Evelyn and Ada and take them in style to the hall in Laindon. He hadn't been looking forward to the cycle ride to and from Laindon, although it wouldn't have been so bad with Ronnie. He was quiet, but he had a dry sense of humour that Jacob appreciated, and together, the journey would have been pleasurable.

Neville had only just arrived at Marconi and Jacob didn't know him – other than by reputation. And what a reputation! But surely people exaggerated his outrageous behaviour? Well, it wasn't Jacob's business. So long as Neville behaved well in front of Evelyn and Ada, Jacob didn't mind what he did. After all, there was a war on, and lots of people were acting irresponsibly, drinking to excess and having love affairs.

Ronnie had told him Neville had drunk too much in the Duke's Head in town a few months before and, egged on by his friends to build a tower and climb to the top, he'd broken a table and three chairs. Jacob didn't know if this was true. Ronnie disliked the man because Gladys found him desirable, so he was hardly impartial. He'd grudgingly added that Neville had paid the landlord handsomely for the damages, although this hadn't earned any approval – Ronnie had simply complained about the seemingly endless supply of black-market goods the insufferable man always had. Silk stockings, French perfume and chocolate, amongst other highly prized commodities, he used to lure girls like Gladys to his arms.

But all those stories were told through the lens of Ronnie's despair at losing the girl he'd never had. In Laindon, Neville wouldn't know anyone except Jacob. Surely, he'd moderate his behaviour. Anyway, it was a relief to know they'd be travelling in Neville's Rolls Royce Phantom.

Yes, a real Phantom.

Ronnie had told him the Harrington-Wades had several of them. Despite the rationing, Neville always had enough petrol. Presumably, he had a black-market supplier for that, too. Jacob supposed he had enough money and connections to buy whatever he wanted.

Well, who was Jacob to cast stones? After all, he'd bought the bar of chocolate he'd given to Evelyn at their Sunday dinner at great expense from a colleague – and he hadn't asked any questions as he'd handed over his money. He wasn't proud of it, but his qualms had been salved when he'd seen the delight on her face. And that had encouraged him to buy another bar...

And he hadn't allowed himself to dwell on it, but the journey to Laindon and back on a bicycle in the pitch black would have been difficult – even with Ronnie. Jacob would have walked, if necessary, but he wasn't sure he was fit enough to get there and then to dance.

Dance?

That was the part he wasn't looking forward to. He hadn't danced since before his accident. It would probably be painful. Not that he cared. It would be worth it to hold Evelyn in his arms. For the first time, he might be able to talk to her on her own. Of course, they wouldn't actually be alone, but he hoped to be able to snatch a few moments of conversation with her. The dance floor wasn't private, but it would allow him to have her to himself.

Jacob fumbled with the buttons of his jacket. Then he patted his pocket. The chocolate bar and the wrapped blue bead were there.

Would he finally build up the courage to give her the bead? Somehow, he doubted it. After all, although it meant the world to him, it couldn't possibly mean anything to her. He'd have to explain its significance and he wasn't sure a Christmas dance was the place to do that.

Why was he so desperate to give her the bead? He'd puzzled over that many times.

Well, the answer was obvious. It was because he wanted to give her something special. Something that would bring her luck.

No, he told himself. He actually wanted to give her everything.

That thought had shaken him. In a nerve-jangling, electric shock sort of way. Thoughts like that were most unwise. They'd open him up to all sorts of risk. Perhaps she wouldn't feel the same way about him and would reject him. But what if she did return his... feelings? He'd faltered over the word 'feelings', deciding against 'love'. He hadn't known Evelyn long enough to love her, but he didn't think it would be long before he fell heavily. Suppose he did fall in love with her and, against all odds, she fell for him, too. Would the war keep them apart? Suppose the Navy suddenly decided to station him elsewhere?

At the thought of more separation and loneliness, his stomach twisted.

The prospect of happiness was so remote as to be almost impossible. Was it worth taking a chance? He'd take the bead with him. One day the conditions might all be favourable... And in the meantime, it would be his lucky charm and perhaps it might keep him safe.

Chapter Eighteen

Jacob was hurriedly tying up his laces as Neville pulled up outside Mrs Shipley's house and tooted his horn. Mrs Shipley shuddered at the noise and put down her knitting.

"I really wish you hadn't asked that dreadful chap to go with you, Lieutenant Adam. Martha at the Women's Institute was his landlady for a time until she got rid of him. He might have all the airs and graces of a lord, and he might speak as though his mouth's crammed full of plums, but he is no gentleman." She lowered her voice. "He entertained women in his room. Well, until Martha threw him out, of course. And what's more, she told me he has rather unsavoury contacts on the black market."

Mrs Shipley shuddered again as a horn blared. Jacob opened the front door, pulling on his coat.

"Well, have a good time," Mrs Shipley shouted after him as he slipped past the blackout curtain. "And don't let Lord Muck drag you into any trouble."

As soon as Jacob was in the car, Neville pulled away – wheels spinning and gravel flying in all directions. He swerved, straightened the wheel, then accelerated towards the corner. As he braked sharply, Jacob was thrown forward.

"Sorry, old man. I always like to arrive early. If we're going to detour to pick up your girl, we need to hurry. I want first pick of the rest of the ladies. Have you met any of your girl's friends? Are they pretty?"

Jacob was speechless. It appeared Ronnie had been correct. Before he'd had a chance to think, he'd said, "She's not my girl. She's a friend. And yes, she is pretty. Well, actually she's beautiful."

"Just a friend you say? Now, what did Howell say her name was? Ellen? Elizabeth?"

"No, Evelyn."

"And she's not spoken for?"

Jacob was appalled. "She's probably not your type..." But he'd already piqued Neville's interest.

"Well, you sound rather puritanical, Adam. But a word to the wise; I don't stick to 'types'. Variety's the spice of life, you know. It's what makes this war bearable. My wife, Margaret's, working in Bletchley. We hardly ever see each other. She's not living the life of a nun. And I'm certainly not going to live like a monk. When the war's over, we'll get together again and see what's what. But in the meantime, I'm going to grab all the fun I can. *Carpe diem* and all that."

Jacob knew husbands and wives weren't always faithful. At first, it had shocked him having seen his parents as role models. He'd had no doubt they'd been faithful, and they were now Jacob's gold standard. Once he'd joined up, he'd heard of many affairs, but most people were discreet.

Neville, however, was blatant. No pretence at obeying the rules. Jacob's chest tightened in dread. Suppose Evelyn preferred Neville? He was dashing and suave, and would undoubtedly be able to dance all night with style. There'd be no need for him to rest periodically, as Jacob knew he'd have to do.

Neville was amusing, engaging and would impress any woman.

Jacob couldn't compare. He was quiet, dull and had limited mobility. Neville had travelled throughout Europe and even to the Far East before war had broken out. Jacob had spent his time with his family or studying. He didn't have exciting tales to tell. He knew nothing of life – or he hadn't before he'd joined up and sailed to Italy.

Jacob pointed out the turning they should take, but Neville had been travelling too fast and had to brake sharply. The car fishtailed before it shot down the country lane.

"Once we come off the main road further ahead, the roads are unmade – mostly grass but they're very uneven," Jacob said, gripping his seat and hoping the warning would stop him speeding. The meal he'd hastily eaten curdled and churned in his stomach with the erratic movement of the car, and the thought of introducing Evelyn to this madman.

"Roger, old boy. I'll take them a bit slower. Don't want to prang the old Phantom, do we?" He patted the steering wheel.

Jacob put his hand in his pocket and gripped the bead again. How ironic it would be to have survived that bomb blast and then to be killed on the road in Neville's car on the way to a dance.

Why had Jacob never realised how boring his life had been before the war? Neville, always ready to fill silence with an amusing anecdote, was telling him about a girl he'd met in Singapore before the war. There didn't appear to be a country in the world Neville hadn't visited.

How had Jacob never looked beyond the horizons of his family life and seen the potential of the world? Perhaps because his parents had been so happy and his childhood with David had been so idyllic there had been no reason to look elsewhere. Maybe it was only people whose lives were sad or unfulfilled who searched for more.

Neville dispassionately told him about an incident that had happened to him at boarding school when he was seven. Jacob had been horrified that such a young boy had been sent to Scotland, away from his family and had been picked on by school bullies. If Jacob had been in that situation, perhaps he too would've searched for happiness wherever it could be found. Well, now he'd look for more. He'd be bolder. In fact, that night, he'd hold Evelyn in his arms, dance until his back and legs seized up, but most of all, he'd tell her how he felt. Determination coursed through him.

But please don't let Evelyn prefer Neville.

It was one thing making up your mind to change – to become more mature, to take on the world. But until he had time to put that into practice, as far as anyone else was concerned, he was still Jacob – reliable, steady, quiet – the underdog. To Jacob's dismay, when they pulled up outside Swallowmead, Neville got out of the car and followed him up the path to the front door.

The light was already out inside the cottage when Evelyn opened the door. She was merely a shadow against blackness, but Jacob's nostrils were filled with her floral scent. He introduced Neville, who thoughtfully produced a torch. He politely greeted Evelyn and Ada and then held out his arm towards Evelyn.

"Your carriage awaits, madam," he said gallantly.

She turned her head towards Jacob, but in the darkness, he couldn't see her expression. He hesitated, then, she took Neville's arm, and he illuminated the way down the path for her.

Had she wanted to take Jacob's arm? Well, if she had, he hadn't barged in and been bold as he'd promised himself he would. He'd merely stood by and let Neville lead Evelyn away.

Jacob extended his arm to Ada, who closed the door and held on to him. He felt her body stiffen as she stepped down onto the path, then he assisted her to the car.

How he admired Ada, never complaining, although he recognised she was often in pain. She'd patted his arm, and he wasn't sure if it was in consolation at Neville having claimed Evelyn, or encouragement to do better. Perhaps she was just grateful to have an arm to lean on.

Once they'd set off, Neville filled the car with charming and amusing chatter. Evelyn laughed and joined in, but Ada was quiet. So was Jacob. Had his grand idea of becoming braver failed before he'd started putting it into practice?

It definitely appeared to be so because once they'd arrived at the hall and Evelyn had taken off her coat, Jacob had simply stared. She was stunning. Understated, yet elegant. Like a Grecian statue with soft folds at her shoulder and waist. She was so beautiful he couldn't speak. Neville, however, had no such problem. His eyes lit up when he'd seen Evelyn in the light, and Jacob suspected all thoughts of Ronnie's Wren, Gladys, had been eclipsed.

For a second, Jacob wondered whether there was a bus back to Chelmsford. What would be the point of staying? If Neville had set his sights on Evelyn, he'd be unlikely to give up. But surely, she'd see through his fecklessness? She wouldn't be won over by smooth talk and the promise of silk stockings, would she? Jacob realised he didn't know.

That wasn't a side of her he'd seen, but he had to acknowledge he barely knew her. Yet she hadn't appeared to be one of those girls who was impressed by presents. He'd brought her a bar of chocolate and now wondered if he shouldn't have tried harder to get stockings, too. The man from whom he'd bought the chocolate had offered to get him some, but Jacob had turned them down, deciding they were too

A REUNION IN PLOTLANDS

personal. He felt sick again.

His life had become uncertain. At work, he measured range, angle, wavelength. They were exact values. His measurements were correct, or they were incorrect. There were no blurry areas. But tonight, there were no absolutes.

It was as though he was walking on ground made of thin ice. He might slip over or indeed, plunge straight through. Nothing was certain.

"Your friend is rather dashing. I expect he sweeps many young women off their feet." Ada was standing next to him, regarding him with dismay. Her eyebrows were raised in a questioning gaze. Almost a challenge. Was she telling him she hoped he'd fight for Evelyn?

If you fought for something, and you won, you couldn't walk away from the prize. You were committed. Well, that was exactly what he wanted wasn't it? Hadn't he decided to be bolder, braver, more resolute? If he didn't start now, there'd be no point at all.

He would risk all to win Evelyn. Resolution coursed through him. Tonight would be the night. But if only his opponent wasn't Neville Harrington-Wade, the man who skated on thin ice and always won the girl.

Neville found a table and sat next to Evelyn. She, however, had looked at Jacob, her lips parted slightly as if about to say something.

He must do something, but what?

"Shall we dance, Evelyn?" Neville said, holding out his hand in such a way that took her agreement for granted.

Jacob felt nauseous. What was the matter with him? Why was he always several steps behind? Once Neville got on the dance floor, he wouldn't let Evelyn go. Ada stared at him; her face frozen in... what? Dismay at his spinelessness?

Undoubtedly. Well, what could he do now? He'd delayed and Neville had swooped in.

Evelyn looked at him again, her expression questioning.

However, while Jacob was wondering if he had the right to leap in and claim Evelyn first, two young women approached the table, and to his relief, they saved the day.

Evelyn thanked Neville and, ignoring his hand, she leapt to her feet and explained her friend had arrived. She greeted a small, dowdy, worried, looking woman whom she introduced as Phyllis, her workmate.

Behind her was a younger woman. They were obviously related because their features were similar. But where Phyllis's features were sharp, gaunt, and worry-lined, the girl behind was glamorous – full red lips, large eyes and glossy, blonde hair.

She had nothing of Evelyn's elegance, Jacob thought. This girl's beauty was painted on. Phyllis introduced her younger sister, Val, and Jacob found two chairs so they could join their table. Neville kissed Val's hand and, after pulling his empty chair next to hers, he went to get drinks for everyone.

"It seems a shame to waste good dancing time, my dear," Ada said to Evelyn. "Why don't you and Jacob dance while Neville's bringing drinks? I'm sure he'll find another partner." She looked at Val who was checking her face in her compact mirror.

"I'll go and help Neville bring the drinks," Val said, closing her compact with a snap.

Phyllis's eyes rolled to the ceiling, but Jacob didn't wait to hear what she was about to say.

He'd had a reprieve he wasn't going to lose the advantage. He stood as quickly as he could and held out his arm to Evelyn.

"Would you care to dance?" He held his breath. She might still want to wait for Neville.

"Yes, yes!" She stood abruptly, almost knocking her chair over and took his arm, making her way to the dance floor with what seem to be speed and eagerness.

She wanted to dance with him. Jacob tingled with pleasure. Finally, he would hold her in his arms. Now he hoped he might regain some of the grace he'd once had. If only he'd thought to practice dancing. Would his back and legs work properly?

He would jolly well force them to cooperate. And once Evelyn was in his arms, he would not give way to Neville.

Chapter Nineteen

♥

Evelyn had wondered if Jacob intended to ask her to dance. She'd been surprised he'd brought Neville until he'd explained the friend he'd intended to bring had sprained his ankle. With a sickening feeling in the pit of her stomach, she'd then wondered if he was trying to pair her up with Neville. She'd determined to be polite, but she didn't want anything to do with the obnoxious man. The thought of his wolf-like stare set her teeth on edge.

And then, surprisingly, Phyllis had saved her. Or rather her sister, Val. Evelyn felt sorry for Phyllis who had enough worries of her own with Tim missing without having to babysit her sister.

And then Jacob had asked Evelyn to dance and the dreams she'd had of being in his arms were about to be fulfilled.

"I'm afraid I'm rather rusty at dancing," he said as he led her to the edge of the throng. His eyes implored her like a young boy seeking approval.

"I learnt how to dance at school and haven't done much since, so I've never been anything other than rusty," Evelyn admitted, not adding she only wanted to feel his arms around her and his body close.

"Then, together, we'll be perfect." Relief crossed his face, and he shyly took her hand.

His touch was like a spark on tinder. The world suddenly sprang to life. She knew nothing had changed except her perception, and yet the tiny twinkling lights that illuminated the hall sparkled like jewels and the pine branches that decorated the walls filled the air with the scent of Christmas. The colours of the baubles and ribbons that adorned the branches and large tree were brighter than they'd been when she'd entered the hall, and even the music was livelier, more urgent. Nothing in her life had ever been as exciting as this evening. When she'd dressed earlier, she'd known it was going to be a night of firsts...

For a start, she'd never worn silk before. Now her body was encased in its sleek folds. Not only the gown but also a pair of silk stockings Ada had somehow procured for her. It was the first pair Evelyn had ever owned. Earlier that evening, she'd shivered with pleasure as she'd slid them up her legs. But it was the dress moving against her body, that had surprised her. It slipped softly over her contours as she moved. A strange and sensual feeling. Nothing like the cotton or wool she was used to against her skin. And now, through the silk, she felt the touch of Jacob's hand on the small of her back. The pressure of each finger. Warm and intimate. And his other hand holding hers. Palm to palm.

Jacob's breath brushed her cheek, short and ragged, as if he was struggling to breathe. Was he as nervous as she? Her nostrils sang with the warm, spicy smell that clung to his skin. This far exceeded the dreams she'd had of this moment during the nights leading up to the dance. Nothing had prepared her imagination for this. She never realised how responsive her entire being could be to someone's touch. Her whole body throbbed with longing for him.

She turned her head slightly to look into his face. So gentle. There was no embarrassment as they gazed into each other's eyes. Could he see the longing inside her? She couldn't read his thoughts, but the pain she'd often noticed in their brown depths had gone.

Or was that wishful thinking?

He broke eye contact and placed his mouth near her ear. "Evelyn, I realise I haven't known you for long... or at least I haven't spent much time with you... but I feel as though I've known you for much longer..." He paused and swallowed.

She held her breath. This could go one of two ways. She dared not consider the unthinkable...

"So, I was wondering whether you'd be my girl?" He closed his eyes as if waiting for a blow.

"Yes! Yes!" The words flew from her lips. Too quickly. Too loudly. His eyes opened in surprise at her over-eagerness. She'd always been diffident and aloof before. What was it about this man that aroused such passion in her?

His face lit up and she returned his smile. They were so engrossed in the moment, neither realised they'd stopped dancing until someone nudged Jacob. "This is a dance, mate. If you want to stand and stare at yer girl, go and do it somewheres else."

They both started to move to the music again, and Jacob placed his cheek against hers. He whispered in her ear, "You are the most beautiful girl here, Evelyn, and I'm the luckiest man."

After a few numbers, she felt Jacob begin to tense. Slight lines had appeared on his forehead, and she guessed his muscles were hurting. She said she was thirsty and suggested they rest for a while. He'd smiled his thanks, although he'd been apologetic.

But Evelyn hadn't cared where they were or what they were doing, so long as he was with her.

She was officially Jacob's girl.

How happy she was.

He held Evelyn's hand as he led her back to the table. Ada smiled with satisfaction when she saw them and nodded her approval.

Even better, that ghastly man, Neville, wasn't there. When Jacob had first introduced him, Evelyn had been fooled by his cut-glass accent and seemingly impeccable manners. He'd taken her arm like a gentleman, but his other hand had stroked hers in an over-friendly way. And it had wandered down her back to her bottom as he'd helped her into the rear of his car. He definitely wasn't a man she wanted to spend time with.

Phyllis's sister, Val, however, was very keen to be with him and they were now on the dance floor.

Before Jacob had returned with drinks, a tall, grey-haired gentleman approached the table. Ada introduced him as Ted Farrell, the schoolteacher, with whom she worked. He sat next to Ada and Evelyn felt sad for Phyllis. Her eyes roved over the dancers as she watched her sister in the arms of Neville Harrington-Wade. How perfectly awful for Phyllis not being able to control her sister and now, as Mr Farrell joined their party, she was on her own. The deeper furrow than usual between her brows told Evelyn she was thinking of Tim.

But to Evelyn's relief, Mr Farrell and Phyllis were acquaintances, having both lived in Laindon for years, and he drew her into the conversation with Ada. That left Jacob and Evelyn to themselves. When he'd rested, he suggested they go back to the dance floor. Evelyn eagerly agreed and thrilled at the touch of his fingers against her back, and his other hand in hers as they danced to a slow version of 'Let There Be Love'.

When his lips feather-kissed her temple, she looked up, unsure whether it had been an accident. But his smile told her he'd done it on purpose. She didn't think she could be any happier. Of course, she longed to feel his lips on hers, but that would not happen in a public place like this. Still, he'd shown her how he felt.

Ada had danced once with Mr Farrell, and although he'd left early, she was in a good mood. And as for Evelyn, she'd never felt so light and free. She fizzed inside, like the sparkling wine Jacob had brought them.

She was Jacob's girl.

At eleven o'clock, Phyllis realised her sister and Neville had disappeared. She hadn't seen them for almost an hour and they were nowhere in the hall. Jacob hurried outside to where Neville had parked his car, but it had gone.

Chapter Twenty

Evelyn was in no hurry to get home. Above the Essex countryside, a silver quarter moon hung in the sky and the stars spangled in the darkness. In the frosty air, their breath blended into one cloud and wreathed their heads as they talked and laughed.

Neville hadn't reappeared by midnight when the dance had finished, and neither had Val. Phyllis had been furious. "What am I going to tell Mum?" she'd wailed over and over. "She'll go mad. Just wait till I get my hands on that floozy! She'll wish she'd never been born."

Neville's disappearance had caused more problems.

"Well, there's only one sensible option," Ada had said. "Jacob can't walk back to Chelmsford, so he must stay with us. Evelyn, you can sleep in my room with me, and Jacob can have your bed."

He'd protested he didn't want to impose, but he hadn't objected too strongly. There might be a bus. Then again, there might not. The only sure way to get home would be to walk back to Hailcombe Cross, and that would take hours.

One of their neighbours had offered to drop Ada home along with the others he'd crammed into his delivery van. But there'd been no room for Evelyn and Jacob.

"Two fine, strong young'uns like you can walk it in no time," the neighbour had said with a wink.

Hand in hand, Evelyn and Jacob had set off home.

Finally, a chance to be alone. To talk. To share their lives and get to know each other.

Evelyn explained what her life had been like before Jacob had called on that Sunday afternoon. "Mother often criticised people behind their backs. No one could live up to her standards, but I'd never seen her as nasty to anyone as she was to you. I'd always kept quiet before when she found fault with people. If I ever questioned her, she'd shout and then once she'd calmed down, she'd completely ignore me until she tired of it, then life went back to normal. But that day she was rude to you, I realised I couldn't take any more."

He squeezed her hand. "I was so worried I'd caused a row between you and your mother. It didn't occur to me things were so difficult for you. Foolish, I know, to assume everyone was as happy as my family…" He trailed off.

"There's no need to talk about it, if you don't want to." She certainly didn't want to cause him pain.

He sighed. "I haven't spoken to anyone about my parents and brother since… since they died." He was silent for several seconds before drawing a deep breath. "But I think I'd like to tell you."

Haltingly, he described how happy his life had been with his parents and younger brother, and how tragic and mindless their deaths were. He told her of the nagging guilt that he'd been the unwitting cause of their death.

It had been his birthday and he'd arranged to take leave so he could spend the day with them.

"I'd done something foolish and there was an argument. Stupidly, I walked out. When the air raid siren went off, I'd already left and for some reason, my parents and David didn't take shelter… There was a

A REUNION IN PLOTLANDS 111

direct hit on our house." His voice caught as he spoke, and when he paused, she knew he was fighting back tears. He'd been deeply scarred, and that pierced her heart.

He'd only given her a basic outline, but his well-chosen words had shown her how important family was to him. His parents had offered him unconditional love. The perfect family. Then they'd been torn from him.

How ironic she'd torn herself from a home life that had lacked the slightest warmth or compassion.

She stopped, and he turned to look at her questioningly. The tears in his eyes glistened in the moonlight, and she placed her hand against his cheek. How she longed to take his pain away.

He placed his hand over hers and pressed her palm to his cheek, swallowed, and then smiled. "That's enough of the past. It's gone and there's nothing we can do to change it. This is the first time I've been able to consider the future. Until now, I didn't want to know. I just stumbled from one day to the next, hoping the war would end yet refusing to consider what I'd do then. It didn't really matter." He shrugged and sadly shook his head. "I didn't care. But now..." He swallowed again. "But now I have you. And life's worth living. You mean everything to me, Evelyn. I know we haven't known each other long, but there's something about you that makes me feel I've always known you. I expect lots of people feel like that during the war. Time becomes compressed when you don't know how much more of it you have. But somehow, I think this is different."

He placed his hand against her cheek. "Do you believe each person has a soulmate? I'd never thought about it before, but it feels like you're mine."

A shadow of fear passed across his face. "Please tell me I haven't frightened you away, Evelyn. Please tell me you feel the same." Anguish filled his voice.

She pulled off her glove and placed her forefinger over his lips. "I feel exactly the same. Like I've been waiting for you forever."

He closed his eyes, and his body relaxed. Evelyn left her finger on his lips and traced their outline. She'd never touched anyone's mouth before. There was a hint of roughness on the skin above his mouth. Yet his lips were smooth. He closed his eyes and groaned her name.

Gently, he held her hand and after turning it palm up, he kissed each fingertip in turn, then leaned towards her and placed his lips against hers.

Nothing had prepared Evelyn for the sensations that cascaded through her body. Instantly, her heart hammered, while dizzy, swoopy feelings filled her head. She tingled, thrummed and melted inside.

Jacob broke away and an exclamation of delight escaped from his mouth. He wrapped his arms tightly around her and held her close, pressing his cheek to hers.

"I'm so glad you're my girl, Evelyn. You've awakened something in me I had no idea was there. I just want to put my arms around you and hold you tight, and never let go." Then, after another long kiss, he took her hand. "Come on. Let's get back to Ada. She'll be worried we've got lost in the dark."

Evelyn knew Ada would be anxious if they were too long, but she also suspected her sister would be very glad they'd spent time together.

"Just one more kiss?" she murmured. She was sure Ada would understand.

Evelyn stared at the ceiling. It was too dark to make out anything, but her eyes simply didn't want to close.

Sleep? Impossible.

She relived the evening, the music still playing in her head. *Let There Be Love.* She still fancied she could feel Jacob's arms around her, his hands caressing her face as he kissed her. And his lips... She shut her eyes and breathed in deeply; remembering his scent, the taste of him and the wave of euphoria that had swept through her when their lips had touched. She burnt with desire for more.

And now he was only yards away in her bed... She was tempted to creep to his room on a pretext of asking if he needed anything. But she wouldn't. The floorboards creaked in Ada's bedroom and there was no chance she'd get to the door without waking her. And even if she could, she didn't trust herself.

She longed to touch him, to wrap her arms around his neck and fill her nostrils with his scent. She groaned inwardly as warmth spread throughout her body, filling her with a need she'd never felt before. Should she take a risk and try to get to his room without waking Ada?

No. Best not. She didn't know how Ada would react. It was one thing actively encouraging Evelyn to get to know Jacob and quite another to approve of her younger sister throwing herself at a man.

And then, of course, there was Jacob. What would he think if she went to him in the middle of the night? So far, he'd behaved impeccably, and she suspected he wasn't the sort of man who'd approve of a loose woman.

On the other hand, he'd taken her by surprise that evening with his passion. He'd trembled as he'd held her to him on the way home, and his breath had been ragged with emotion and desire. Yet, he'd still suggested they return to Ada rather than risk worrying her.

No, she wouldn't go to him.

She wondered if he was lying awake thinking of her.

Chapter Twenty-One

♥

Jacob stared at the ceiling. There'd be no sleep for him that night. He was surrounded by the intoxicating floral perfume that always accompanied Evelyn. He breathed in, appreciating its subtle notes, hoping familiarity wouldn't rob him of its intensity.

Evelyn had lain in this bed where he now lay yearning for her.

She was tantalisingly close, and his arms ached to hold her. But she might as well be miles away. Well, at least he'd see her first thing in the morning. He silently blessed Neville for deserting him and forcing this unscheduled overnight stay on him. He'd have to rush in the morning to get back to Baddow on time for his shift, but it would be worth it.

He remembered the feel of Evelyn's lips on his earlier when they'd held each other and shared their first kiss. But the exhilaration of being alone with her was accompanied by a memory as jagged as cut glass. Why hadn't he been completely honest with her?

It had been their first kiss.

She'd told him it had been her first kiss.

But it hadn't been his. Someone had stolen that from him during a drunken haze. Or perhaps they hadn't? He'd never know.

Jacob hadn't intended to keep anything from her, but the end of the evening had taken him by surprise. If he'd had time to plan, he'd have told Evelyn everything before he'd taken her in his arms and kissed her. At least she'd have had a chance to decide whether he was worth knowing.

He'd have told her of his stupid and degrading attempts to show his fellow officers he was a man. The unfortunate argument with his parents and the tragedy that had occurred straight after. He'd even have explained his guilt when he'd survived the bomb that had killed his comrades in Italy. There'd have been a chance she'd have been repelled by him and then he'd have walked away. But at least his conscience would have been clear.

However, that frosty, star-spangled setting had not been a time for confessions. It had been a time for romance, not for revealing unpleasant memories.

Then when will you tell her? Ada will be there tomorrow. Will you explain to her, too?

Definitely not. He'd rather not have told anyone. But Evelyn deserved to know so she could make up her mind up about him.

Would she lose respect for him? What would she think about his foolishness? He couldn't comprehend how he could have been so naive, so why would she?

He needed to find the right words to explain. In the past, the images of being taunted mercilessly had played over and over in his mind without the need for words. Many of his navy colleagues had been older, and they'd picked on him for his boyish face and lack of worldly experience. They'd called him 'Mummy's Boy' and worse – attracting bullies who'd made his life miserable.

The message had been to grow up, and in an attempt to rid himself of his tormentors, he'd tried to throw off his youth. It was only later he realised he'd played right into their hands. How they must've laughed at him when he'd got drunk. How they'd enjoyed his first trip ashore with the men. He only had hazy recollections of the drink, the women and the gaming table.

The morning after one particular evening, when he'd sobered up, he'd discovered his empty wallet – a large sum was missing. Apparently, he'd gambled the lot and of course, he'd lost. They'd played him, and like the young fool he was – trying so hard to prove he wasn't, – he'd been their plaything.

The following morning, when he'd discovered his empty wallet, he'd vowed he'd never be manipulated again. He wouldn't allow anyone to take what dignity he had left, nor any more money – however much taunting it resulted in. There was nothing wrong with being young and naive. He discovered it was certainly better than feeling old, jaded and abused.

A lesson learnt.

But to his shame, he realised it wasn't a lesson he'd learnt in private.

On his next visit home, he'd had to explain to his parents how he'd gambled away large amounts of money. If only his mother hadn't probed. He hadn't wanted to lie to her. He'd wanted to forget it and move on, but she'd pressed him and predictably, his parents had been horrified at his gambling losses.

Although he hadn't admitted about the girls, he suspected they knew. And their disappointed expressions had prompted him to defensiveness and anger as he relived his humiliation.

He'd acted like a child and the argument had escalated. Just after he'd walked out, the air raid siren had sounded. He'd ignored it, desperate to get away from the house. He'd never know why his parents and David had not taken shelter.

He'd survived. They'd died.

It was part of the torment, wondering why they hadn't heeded the siren. He'd imagined his mother making tea, and the three of them sitting around the kitchen table, comforting themselves as they calmed down after the row. If he hadn't upset them, they'd probably have been safe in the Anderson Shelter at the end of the garden, and still alive.

What would Evelyn think? Her family life had been so troubled. His had been so wonderful, and yet his actions had resulted in its destruction.

He would tell her. Perhaps not tomorrow if he didn't have a chance to talk to her alone. But he wanted to build his future around her and he'd have to be scrupulously honest first. There was no future in a life of lies or omissions of the truth.

Chapter Twenty-Two

"I'll make the tea," Evelyn said as soon as Ada opened her eyes the next morning.

"Don't rush on my account, dear. I'm going to have another snooze. Last night was so tiring." Ada turned over and pulled the covers up.

Undoubtedly, she was tired but there was a smile in her voice. Was Ada allowing her to have a few moments alone with Jacob?

Evelyn pulled on her dressing gown, wishing it was less shabby. She combed her hair and prodded the dark shadows under her eyes with dismay. Well, there was nothing to be done about them. She'd hardly slept at all, so it wasn't surprising her eyes were sunken.

Hurry up.

If she delayed any longer, she'd have no time alone with Jacob.

She crept out of the bedroom; grateful she hadn't attempted to make the same trip a few hours before. The floorboards creaked alarmingly. They were louder than she'd remembered, but then she'd never thought to creep around the cottage before.

As soon as she opened the door, Jacob appeared. Silently, they hurried towards each other and embraced. He slid his fingers into her hair and kissed her hungrily, his passion igniting hers.

"I couldn't sleep for thinking of you," he whispered as he broke away, butterfly-kissing her neck.

"Nor I, you." She threw her head back, allowing him to carry on down her neck to the top of her chest.

His lips gliding over her skin filled her with dizzying delight.

The bed creaked in Ada's room and Evelyn reluctantly pulled away.

"Tea," she croaked. "I need to make tea."

Never had she wanted a cup of tea less. She longed for Jacob to carry on exploring her body.

"Tea," he said with that lopsided smile that further heated the furnace that raged inside her.

In the kitchen, he stood behind her, arms wrapped around her, nuzzling her neck while she added tea leaves to the pot with shaking hands.

"I'm not sure I'm going to be able to make this tea without scalding both you and me," she whispered, turning away from the kettle and allowing him to hold her tightly.

The last time Jacob had left Swallowmead with his bicycle, he'd been afraid his muscles had seized up and he wouldn't be able to mount it. He'd been so convinced he might fall off or make a fool of himself, he'd refused Evelyn's offer to accompany him to the bus stop on the main road.

When he left this time, he was grateful she suggested she walk with him. Despite dancing the previous evening, he didn't feel stiff at all. In fact, this was the best he'd felt since he'd been wounded. Perhaps the raging torrent of emotions that Evelyn had unleashed had pushed the pain out of its way.

The sky was grey and threatened rain as they walked, hand in hand, along the grassy avenues towards the main road. Their pace slowed the closer they drew to the point where they'd part. He hoped he wouldn't miss the bus or there's be a long wait. But perhaps it might be worth it if she'd wait with him. He'd be in trouble at work, but that was a small price to pay for this extra time with Evelyn.

Now. Tell her now about your foolishness and how it impacted on your family. You're alone. This is the perfect time.

"Will you be able to stay with us Christmas night?" Evelyn asked.

"I'd love to but I'll have to see. We've got some important work coming up and we've been warned we won't get much time off over Christmas."

"Oh." Her voice was small and lost.

"I want to, of course," he added quickly.

She'd smiled at him and nodded. "I understand. We've all got to do whatever we can to win this dreadful war."

His heart constricted as he saw the disappointment in her eyes. Now wasn't the time to tell her how he'd let his family down with his gambling and other stupidity. No. He'd tell her on another occasion. It was best if they spent the last few minutes together speaking of something pleasant.

"If I can come, I'll leave as early as I can on Christmas Morning. I'll ride like the wind…"

She smiled up at him and he felt so light with happiness, he wondered if he might float home.

Jacob made it back to work with minutes to spare. At lunch time, he was queuing in the canteen when Neville sauntered towards him, and smiling at the Wren behind Jacob, he persuaded her to let him in before her, to have a word with 'his friend'. The Wren giggled as Neville blew her a kiss.

"Awfully sorry about deserting you, old chap." Neville said to Jacob. "I got carried away. You know how it is when you meet a pretty girl..."

Jacob kept his face neutral and nodded. Well, if it hadn't been for Neville's thoughtlessness, he wouldn't have had the opportunity to spend extra time with Evelyn.

Neville's eyebrows drew together as he looked at Jacob, presumably searching for a sign of anger. But seeing none, he carried on, "That young nurse was quite a whirlwind."

"So, you've finished with Gladys, then?" Ronnie asked. Hope alight in his eyes. He was ahead of Jacob in the queue.

"Who?" Neville asked.

"Gladys Taylor. The Wren you've been seeing."

Neville frowned and looked up at the ceiling for inspiration. "Oh, you mean Ginny. The blonde with the long legs."

"Her name's Gladys," Ronnie said through clenched teeth.

"Yes, but her initials are GT. Gin and tonic. Hence Ginny."

Ronnie took the plate of stew the canteen women offered him and turned his back on Neville.

"By the by, old chap, your Evelyn was ravishing," Neville said with a low whistle.

"She's taken," Jacob said quickly.

"Shame. I wouldn't have minded a crack at her."

"You don't mind having a crack at anyone," Ronnie muttered.

"What's that, old boy?" Neville asked.

"Just saying I don't know where you get your energy," Ronnie said.

Neville tapped his nose and looked knowingly. "Mum's the word, chaps, but I have a little assistance." He reached into his pocket and pulled out a cylindrical container that he revealed to Jacob and Ronnie. He thrust it quickly back into his pocket. "I can stay awake for several nights in a row. Very useful. I've got a doctor friend…"

"Typical!" Ronnie muttered. He turned and limped away to find a table.

Neville tipped his head on one side and looked at Jacob. "I say, old chap. Why don't you take these by way of apology? I can easily get some more."

Jacob shook his head.

"Go on, old chap. They're perfectly safe. I live on them. And you might need them if you're going to see anything of your girl. I've heard whispers. We're about to start testing some new parts for the magnetrons. We'll be working all hours for the next few weeks."

Jacob allowed Neville to drop the container into his pocket. He didn't have to use them, but if it meant he could spend more time with Evelyn, why not? They didn't seem to have adversely affected Neville. Quite the opposite, in fact.

Chapter Twenty-Three

Jacob woke as his head jerked forward.

He groaned.

The columns of figures he was comparing softened, blurred and then melted into each other.

Wavelength, input, efficiency. Even the letters in the column headings were merging. He shook his head trying to banish sleep.

Sleep.

He couldn't remember the last time he'd slept.

The night of the dance when he'd stayed at Evelyn's house, he'd lain awake all night. His mind and body buzzing with excitement and exhilaration.

Since then, several people at work had gone down with 'flu and everyone had struggled to cover their duties. Several newly produced magnetrons had been tested and found to be faulty.

It was a disaster.

With his elbows on the table, Jacob's head sank into his hands.

Involuntarily, his eyelids slid shut and he jerked them open again.

This was serious. While most people would assume guns and bombs were the most vital equipment in winning a war, others who were in the know, would consider the cavity magnetron might be just as important.

Perhaps even more so.

An insignificant-looking item, not a great deal larger than Jacob's hand. However, the cavity magnetron had revolutionised the Allies' ability to detect the enemy by generating large amounts of power at microwave frequencies. That meant it had been possible to develop effective airborne, as well as ground-based radar. How different might things have turned out had this technology been available at the beginning of the war?

Jacob squeezed his eyes tightly together, then opened them wide, forcing them to remain open. He reminded himself of all those merchant ships and men who'd gone down, prey to the marauding wolf packs of German U-boats. Now the Allies had the means, they could hunt down the predators and significantly reduce the Allied merchant ship losses.

Focus.

Only the occasional cough or scrape of a chair punctuated the insistent hum of the machines and the intermittent bleeps. Across the smoke-filled room, Ronnie was drinking a cup of tea. It was obvious from his face he was struggling to remain awake, too. Not far from him, the gap-toothed Wren, Mary Reeves, who was always smiling, worked at an oscilloscope, green light reflecting on her face. Now she was intent on tracking the radio nets up and down the dial.

Beyond her, Neville sat at his desk smoking a cigarette. He was watching another Wren. No sign of tiredness on his face. Just that lazy predatory gaze beneath lowered lids. He yawned, but not with exhaustion – more like boredom.

How did he manage to remain so alert?

Then Jacob remembered. He patted his pocket and the small cylindrical container rattled.

Should he try a pill? He looked back at the columns of figures. Had the thermocouple they'd been using to carry out the tests been faulty? Were the magnetrons actually all right?

Concentrate.

Once again, the figures swam.

Yes, he would take one of Neville's pills. He could hardly perform any worse than he already was. Surreptitiously, he took one out of the canister and slipped it into his mouth. He had a large gulp of tea to wash it down in case he changed his mind.

Jacob gripped the handlebars of his bicycle and pedalled hard. Hairs stood up on the back of his neck and his skin felt as though it had been stretched so tight it was too small for his body. In his chest, his heart thudded so fast, his breath couldn't catch up.

Excitement at the thought of seeing Evelyn? Well, yes, of course he was excited, but this wasn't normal. He wasn't experiencing the warm feelings that were tinged with possibilities. This was jittery, jarring and raw. Everything was more intense. He could have been cycling across the craters of the moon, and through the icy blasts of the Arctic.

Why was everything larger than life?

It might be more pertinent to ask why he was posing that question, since he already knew the answer.

Jacob had remained awake and alert all week. No, not simply alert – it had been more than that – he'd been hyper-aware. Filled with unnatural energy, he'd been able to work hard and had managed with very little sleep.

In fact, he didn't remember having slept at all, but he must have done. No one could have kept up that pace without some sleep.

Could they?

There had been little choice. Lives depended on their work.

He guessed that Ronnie, too, had accepted pills from Neville because he also appeared to be suffering from the same symptoms. Like Jacob, he'd acquired unusual confidence. Or perhaps it was recklessness. For Ronnie, there'd been a bonus. He'd asked Gladys out and although she hadn't accepted, she hadn't refused either.

Jacob suspected she was waiting to see if she received a better offer. Finally, she said she'd go out with Ronnie if he'd get Jacob to go as well because her friend, Mary Reeves, the smiling Wren, was interested in him.

Jacob had refused and Ronnie had been uncharacteristically belligerent. More evidence that placid Ronnie had been taking Neville's pills?

However, Jacob wouldn't be pushed into anything by a colleague ever again. He would not let Evelyn down. That was why he was currently peddling towards Dunton as fast as he could.

He'd written to give her the disappointing news he wouldn't be able to see the New Year in with her because he'd have to return to be on duty, so now he wanted as much time with her as he could manage.

Well, at least they'd had Christmas together and she'd loved the ring he'd made for her. He'd been very proud of it. And without Ada seeing, he'd slipped Evelyn some stockings.

"In return for the socks you knitted me," he'd whispered, and although she'd blushed at the sight of them, she'd smiled shyly.

He'd even managed to buy a bar of rare lavender soap at great expense for Ada. They'd opened the sherry he'd taken on a previous visit and the three of them had toasted absent friends and family.

His thoughts had predictably turned to his parents and David. How he wished they could have met Evelyn. They'd have loved her.

There hadn't been an opportunity to tell Evelyn all the things he thought she should know about him. Christmas wasn't a time for such revelations. Even supposing he'd been alone with her.

New Year's Eve wouldn't be the right moment either. And it wasn't as though he'd be able to spend more than an hour or two with her before returning to Chelmsford. But next year, at the first opportunity, he'd take Evelyn out on her own. They'd go for a meal somewhere. Perhaps he'd even take her to London. Neville had spoken of the 400 Club in Leicester Square. Apparently, you could dance there until the early hours. He'd tell her then. If she decided to finish with him, well, at least he'd have Christmas to look back on.

His bicycle jolted down a rut and he bit his tongue. Why hadn't he seen how uneven the ground was? He stopped and blinked to clear his vision. The furrows in the road were moving like waves on the sea and his head told him he was leaning sideways, but he knew he was upright. What was happening?

You know exactly what's happening…

Those pills? Yes, he knew they were affecting him but what choice did he have? He couldn't have missed seeing Evelyn because he was too tired. That was unthinkable, although he wondered how he was going to string words together coherently.

He guided the bicycle to a flatter part of the road and started pedalling. His legs pumped with energy he hadn't known he'd possessed. Not long now until he saw her again. If only he didn't feel so sick.

Chapter Twenty-Four

As Evelyn waited on the corner of Second Avenue for Jacob, she looked down at the ring he'd given her.

"It's not gold," he'd pointed out.

But it was more precious than gold because he'd made it for her. It was fashioned out of metal that he'd cut and smoothed at work.

The bezel held a brown electrical resistor with colourful bands around it. Apparently, they were all parts that he'd had at work, and he'd said they reminded him how grateful he'd been to have the excuse of mending Ada's wireless set, so he could see her again.

"One day, I'll buy you an expensive ring, made by a jeweller."

Evelyn had assured him nothing could be more precious to her than his gift.

She'd made him another pair of socks and some gloves for the cold rides over to Dunton, and his face had lit up when he'd opened her gift.

She'd even slipped a poem she'd written into one of the socks and he'd said he'd treasure it with the other one she'd sent him.

He'd bought her stockings and had made a joke about them being a fair exchange for the first pair of socks that had brought them together.

But she'd felt his eyes on her burning bright, and she'd wondered if, like her, he was wondering what it would be like if she was wearing just the stockings for him. She'd blushed deeply at the thought.

Christmas Day had been marvellous, and Jacob had been able to stay until early on Boxing Day before he'd had to cycle back to Chelmsford.

She'd been bitterly disappointed when she'd received his letter explaining he wouldn't be able to stay overnight again. But it was nearly the new year and surely, the advancements that Jacob and his colleagues were working on would help to end the war sooner.

How many more years could the hostilities continue?

Excitement fizzed inside as she saw him turn the corner, but as he approached, her eagerness was replaced by concern.

There was something wrong.

He was pedalling fast, and perhaps that explained why he appeared so unsteady. He braked hard as he approached, and she saw the film of sweat on his face.

He'd been cycling furiously; was that why he was so wobbly?

His skin had a grey tinge, and his eyes were sunken and red-rimmed. Although he looked at her, he blinked repeatedly, as if trying to focus.

She was imagining it, surely?

He'd simply ridden fast, so they'd have maximum time together.

But as he dismounted, he staggered. Nothing surprising in that with the wounds he'd suffered in Italy.

What alarmed her was the blank look on his face, as if he didn't know where he was, nor that he was overbalancing.

Evelyn caught his arm and steadied him.

"I'm so pleased to see you." The words tripped over themselves in

Jacob's haste to speak and he clung to her too tightly.

Something was very wrong.

Evelyn led Jacob into the cottage and, after taking off his coat, she suggested he lay down on the sofa to rest while she tended to dinner. Reluctantly, he agreed and within seconds, his eyes were closed and his breath was deep and even.

That wasn't what she'd planned when Ada had announced earlier, she was going to visit the neighbour next door for a few hours. She'd known Ada was allowing her time alone with Jacob, but now that time would be spent with him catching up on his sleep.

But it couldn't be helped. He'd explained he couldn't remember the last time he'd slept and once he was on the sofa, he'd gone from bright agitation to faded exhaustion like a torch with a dying battery.

But at least she could see him. Other than check the rabbit stew, there had been nothing to do in the kitchen because Ada had prepared everything before she'd gone out. Evelyn crept back into the living room and knelt next to Jacob.

The grey colouration was fading from his cheeks, but he still looked remarkably pale. His eyes moved beneath his eyelids, flickering from side to side as if, even in sleep, he was working.

Evelyn leaned forward and smoothed the fringe off his forehead and, after trailing her fingers down his head and neck, she allowed it to rest on his shoulder. Jacob's face softened slightly, and his lips moved in the merest hint of a smile. She had to stop herself from touching his cheek, tracing the outline of his lips and pressing hers to his. But that would waken him and he needed to sleep.

Evelyn turned to sit on the floor, her legs curled beneath her and after placing her arm on the edge of the sofa seat, she laid her cheek on it. Her other hand still on Jacob's shoulder rose and fell gently with each breath. Thankfully now, the rhythm had calmed from when he'd first arrived.

She tilted her head so she could study his face. His lashes trembled against his cheeks as his eyes periodically moved from side to side beneath his closed lids, but that rapid movement had also begun to subside. What a luxury to be able to take in his face, to be able to study each feature and to imprint it on her memory.

Chapter Twenty-Five

Loud voices drilled into Jacob's consciousness.

Mrs Shipley? No, definitely not. She'd never shouted like that.

There were two people arguing.

It was too much effort to open his eyes. Perhaps he wouldn't bother. The shouting would surely stop.

Voices again, closer this time. And something near his face moved. He opened his eyes in alarm, blinking to clear the blurriness. A floral scent told him Evelyn was close and he felt her gasp of surprise hot on his cheek.

Evelyn. Her face was next to his.

That thought cleared his head and as his vision sharpened, he remembered where he was and how he'd come to be sleeping on the sofa. But why was everything happening in slow motion?

Evelyn turned slightly, looking towards the front door. He could still see enough of her face to register the colour drain from her cheeks and the alarm in her eyes.

Following her gaze, he saw Ada, her hands, with fingers splayed, framing the silent 'O' of her mouth. She looked towards him still lying on the sofa and with Evelyn curled up next to him on the floor. Ada's eyes were wild as if witnessing an accident happening in slow motion, and she threw her arms sideways as if barring entrance to the person behind her. But she was too late. The woman barged past, knocking Ada to one side.

He'd seen that disagreeable face before.

It was the formidable Mrs Quinn – Evelyn's mother.

She stood, hands planted on hips, nodding with self-righteous satisfaction.

"Well, what a pretty picture this is!"

Evelyn leapt to her feet.

If a bucket of iced water had been tipped over Jacob's head, it couldn't have brought his consciousness into sharp focus faster nor more completely. He leapt to his feet and staggered, trying to balance.

"Mrs Quinn, I..."

She held up her hand and cut him off. "I suggest you leave now before you cause more harm."

"I..." He looked at Evelyn, unsure how best to proceed. She stood, swaying slightly. Had Mrs Quinn thought they'd been behaving inappropriately?

Surely not. So why did Evelyn appear to be so horrified?

And Ada, who was usually calm and dignified, was silent, statue-still.

Mrs Quinn crossed her arms over her chest. "I said go." She spoke slowly and deliberately to Jacob in a voice dripping disdain. "Now."

Jacob looked at Evelyn, but she still stared at her mother. He wanted to explain to Mrs Quinn. She'd obviously misunderstood. They might have been alone together, but he'd been asleep. Nothing had happened.

"Get out!" Mrs Quinn screamed; her features twisted in spitefulness.

The charged atmosphere told him something momentous was taking place, and if he interfered, he'd make things worse.

He picked up his coat, shoes and bag and walked to the kitchen door.

"I'll wait in here," he said, "until you're finished." He looked at Evelyn for confirmation that he wasn't making things worse, but she still stared at her mother as if she hadn't heard him.

He went into the kitchen and closed the door. In the living room, Mrs Quinn screamed abuse at Evelyn, and guilt pricked him. What might it have looked like with him lying on the sofa, making himself at home as if he lived there? When he'd woken, Evelyn's face was next to his. Had she been lying on the sofa with him? Surely he'd have known. Oh, why hadn't he been more alert?

He knew Evelyn's relationship with her mother had previously been troubled and that undoubtedly was part of the problem now, but his presence had triggered her mother's initial reaction. Mrs Quinn was still calling Evelyn unspeakable things, although she was now defending herself, denying the accusations. He wanted to go back into the living room and protect her.

What should he do? His presence in the house could only make things worse for Evelyn. Perhaps he should leave?

Leave?

How could he desert her? But in truth there was nothing he could do to repair the damage. If she managed to persuade her mother their time together had been innocent – which seemed unlikely – then as soon as Mrs Quinn saw him again, he might simply remind her of what she thought she'd seen. The best thing would be to go now. But he didn't want to slip away without explaining to Evelyn. He said he'd stay. Or had he? Perhaps he'd just thought it. It was hard to remember.

Ada's voice was now raised. But not in anger. She was pleading with her mother.

This wasn't how families were supposed to behave. He placed his hands over his ears. It was a childish gesture, but he couldn't bear to listen to the argument anymore. He'd slip out and ride round and round until he was certain Mrs Quinn had gone. Then he'd go back and see if he could do anything to comfort Evelyn and Ada.

Or would Mrs Quinn stay? What would he do then?

He'd worry about that later. Now, he couldn't bear to hear Mrs Quinn's merciless rant while Ada begged her to stop. Voices raised. Harsh. Hateful. Reminding him of another argument. Another day. His birthday. And then the regrets that he'd never know his parents' forgiveness.

He crept out, mounted his bicycle and pedalled rapidly down the grassy avenue.

Chapter Twenty-Six

Mother mimicked Evelyn's voice. "It's not what you think!" She snorted in derision. "Really? Well, perhaps you'd care to explain exactly what it was then? A man and a woman alone in a room, both lying on the sofa."

As Evelyn denied she'd been on the sofa with Jacob, Mother held up her hand. "Don't lie to me, girl. I saw your lewd behaviour with my own eyes. I came to take you back with me. To give you a second chance. I still can't believe you ignored your own mother at Christmas, but now I know why."

Evelyn felt sick. All the confidence she'd built up over the previous few weeks had dissipated the instant she'd seen Mother. All the pleasure in her new life had drained away, leaving her with the dread, doubt and – above all – guilt she'd carried throughout her life before she'd come to Ada's.

Was there no escape from the inexplicable shame she'd borne for as long as she could remember? She'd thought she'd made herself anew. But Mother had shown her all her new attitudes and beliefs were illusions. Insubstantial. Meaningless.

Mother turned to Ada; her lip curled in distaste. "And as for you... Well, I'm not surprised. No, not surprised at all."

Ada put her arm around Evelyn's shoulders and squared up to her mother. "Don't try to pretend you came to ask Evelyn back out of duty. You only want her to go home with you because she pays the rent reliably."

"And why do *you* want her to stay?" Mother sneered.

To Evelyn's surprise, Ada was silent. She'd drawn in a deep breath but hadn't let it out, and her arm around Evelyn's shoulders was rigid.

Mother appeared not to have noticed the change in Ada. "It's better Evelyn comes back with me. I can keep her on the straight and narrow. But you..." Mother's face was contorted with contempt, and she jabbed her finger at Ada. "You never did have any morals. You take after your father."

Evelyn felt Ada tremble.

Mother stepped forward and jutted her face towards Ada, her voice low and menacing. "Your father had the morals of an alley cat. He passed them on to you. And now, like mother, like daughter."

Ada's hand flew to her throat, and she went white. Was she going to faint? Evelyn put her arm around Ada's waist to support her.

"You... You promised..." Ada's words came as if she was tearing each one from deep inside. Her eyes filled with tears.

"Well, I think it's about time," Mother said, a nasty twist to her mouth. "After all, I would've thought by now you'd have made everything clear. Doesn't your conscience burn with shame, Ada?"

Their words made no sense to Evelyn. A quarrel from the past, perhaps? The reason, or perhaps one of the reasons Ada had left home so long ago?

Ada held one hand out. Fingers splayed anxiously towards their mother. "Please. I'm begging you. Don't..."

The raw emotion in her voice sliced through Evelyn. She wanted to draw Ada away out of this bubble of confusion and hatred. She recognised Mother's expression. It was the one she assumed when she knew she had the upper hand.

"It's time you paid for your past sins, Ada. You know sins will always find you out."

Evelyn gripped Ada's waist tighter. She appeared to be shrinking into herself. As if she was ageing rapidly and losing her strength.

Evelyn opened her mouth to scream at her mother to stop, but no sound came out. Her mouth was completely dry.

This was between her mother and Ada, and it would continue until one of them ended it. She was merely a bystander, watching a bomb drop from the sky in agonisingly slow motion.

With narrow eyes and a curled lip, Mother turned to Evelyn. "So, Ada hasn't thought to inform you of the truth. Well, allow me, my girl. If you're under the impression, Ada is your elder sister, think again. She is your mother."

Evelyn gasped. What nonsense was this? Her mother wanted to disown her? Well, that didn't come as a surprise. Evelyn expected Ada to say something, to stop Mother's vindictive words, but she stood, frozen. Her head hanging.

Black waves of shock washed over Evelyn. It was as though she'd been knocked from her feet by a strong wave, tumbled over and over and dragged down into the depths.

"The shame!" Mother said, spitting the words out, looking both Ada and Evelyn up and down. "Well, I wash my hands of you. You're both nothing to me."

A sound like air escaping from a tyre came from Ada and she sagged even more. Evelyn had been holding Ada up. Now, she felt herself in need of support, clinging on to stop sinking into the depths of the murky water that appeared to swirl around her, dragging her down.

Scenes from the past flashed through her mind. Angry words.

Scornful, hateful looks. Her mother's disapproval. Sneers, pinched arms, and coldness. But since she'd been with Ada, her life had been filled with light, love, acceptance, and a home.

But her mother? Ada was her mother?

Could it be possible?

No, of course not...

Then why hadn't Ada denied it?

With one final sneer, Mother turned and then, glancing over her shoulder, she said, "You are both dead to me."

As she walked out of the bungalow, Ada began to tremble violently, and Evelyn led her to a chair. She helped her sit and then knelt in front of her, laying her head on Ada's lap. Together, the two women cried.

Chapter Twenty-Seven

Jacob had ridden slowly away from Swallowmead, his ears filled with the echoes of raised voices and angry accusations, and his head throbbing with painful memories of a different family argument.

His mother's disappointment. His father's outraged condemnation. His own resentful denials and objections.

As he pedalled harder, Mrs Quinn's hateful tones blended into his mother's anger and her show of sorrow and regret at her eldest son's stupidity.

How right his comrades had been when they'd accused him of being a Mummy's Boy. When they'd laughed at his inexperience. He *had* been young and, compared to most of them, he'd known nothing. He hadn't been prepared for life in the Navy. He certainly hadn't been prepared for war.

On that fateful evening of his birthday – the last time he'd seen his parents and brother – righteous indignation had bubbled up in him, too. Why hadn't his parents prepared him for life?

But later, after they'd gone, he'd understood a parent couldn't possibly warn a child about everything. Instead, they'd gifted him a safe, healthy and balanced upbringing, and once he'd gone into the world, it had been up to him to deal with the rest.

The fact that he hadn't dealt with it sensibly had been his fault. The war had thrown many different people together who, under normal circumstances, might never have met.

His life now, although he was still in the Navy, was kinder, gentler. The people he worked with were mostly thinkers. Those he had associated with on board the ship had been men who preferred action and adventure.

A deep rut jolted Jacob out of his reverie. He looked around for something he recognised. There was nothing. He'd ridden with no thought to direction, merely turning left or right as the bumps and dips in the grass had dictated he should. He was lost.

Well, eventually, he'd arrive at something he recognised. He cycled faster. If Mrs Quinn had gone, he wanted to be there for Evelyn.

At the memory of the encounter, once again, his head filled with screams and angry shouts. He wanted to slap his hands over his ears to keep the sound out but knew it was pointless. His brain was perversely amplifying the memories and muddling them until they merged like a cacophony of radio signals, all blaring at once.

He stopped and shook his head as if to banish the sounds reverberating in his memory. He must think clearly, or he'd still be cycling when it got dark.

Having checked the direction of the sun, he judged he needed to turn left to get back to Swallowmead. But he was now in a country lane. Little more than a narrow, rutted track between two fields.

Still, the shouts rang out inside his head. His mother. Evelyn's mother. Screams and denials. Until he realised the shrill sounds that penetrated those imagined voices were the shrieks of whistles. An air raid warning. Had he wandered close to the mock airfield which had been set up to lure German bombers away from the RAF station at Hornchurch?

He wobbled and quickly righted himself. What good would he be to anyone if he broke his neck? He needed to be sensible. He dared not be late for duty in a few hours. Was there time to go back to see if Mrs Quinn had gone? If only he knew where he was in relation to Swallowmead.

There was only one thing to do. He'd promised himself he wouldn't, but this was an emergency. He'd take another pill. It would make him sick, he knew, but it would lend him the energy to find Evelyn and then to make it back to Great Baddow.

He fished in his pocket. The cylindrical container wasn't there. He gasped in dismay and, for the first time, allowed himself to acknowledge how much he needed those tiny tablets.

Jacob forced himself to breathe in slowly, hold, and breathe out. He wouldn't panic. A plan. He needed a plan.

Energy was draining out of him. He must get back to Baddow for his shift. And perhaps Neville would have some more pills. Or Ronnie...

Evelyn? A tiny voice asked.

He'd write to her and find out what happened. There was nothing he could do now. If he returned, he might make things worse. And if he didn't start pedalling now, he might not have the strength to get back to Hailcombe Cross.

Overhead, two aeroplanes swooped out of the sky with a deafening roar. Jacob braked hard and pulled up sharply. Probably two of 'Our lads' from Hornchurch.

Or perhaps a German plane fooled into believing he'd found the aerodrome at Hornchurch and an RAF fighter seeing him off.

A REUNION IN PLOTLANDS

A shiver went through Jacob as he realised the two planes were identical and both had swastikas on their tail fins.

Messerschmitts.

One plane skimmed over the field next to Jacob. It was so low he could see the pilot in the cockpit. The second plane was several seconds behind the first and swerved away from his original course to fly straight towards Jacob – the pilot obviously lining Jacob up in his gunsights.

The rapid *crack, crack, crack* followed by the thud of bullets into the ground threw earth and grass up into the air, spraying Jacob. He hurled himself from the bicycle and dived into the ditch at the side of the road with his hands over his head.

Chapter Twenty-Eight

Evelyn sat up in bed, dry-eyed. Her tears had long since stopped. Jacob had silently left and not returned. How she longed to have his reassuring arms around her.

A short distance away in her bedroom, Ada repeatedly blew her nose. The floorboards in her bedroom creaked at regular intervals as she paced back and forth.

It was just a short walk to Ada's bedroom, but Evelyn could not move.

Betrayal. Overwhelming betrayal by the unpleasant woman who, for so long, she believed had been her mother. Well, that was in character.

But Ada... the woman she'd admired and loved like a sister had lied by omission.

Ada had been too distraught to speak after the woman Evelyn had once thought of as 'Mother' had left. Neither could Ada look Evelyn in the eyes. Although they'd cried together, they might as well have been in different rooms. Or on different sides of the planet. Ada had

A REUNION IN PLOTLANDS

shut herself off and, once again, Evelyn felt alone and rejected.

Eventually, Ada had gone to her room. Evelyn had remained in the darkened living room for some time hoping Ada would come out and talk to her. To explain.

Eventually, Evelyn had gone to bed.

Questions pressed in on her. There was so much she wanted to know.

Who was her father? And how would she live her life from this day on? Would she be different? Undoubtedly so. Thoughts slipped in and out of her mind as the hours progressed. Betrayal and desertion. Evelyn felt as though the ground beneath her had crumbled to nothing and she was falling. Spinning. Tumbling over and over. There must be a bottom to this void through which she plummeted. Everything must have a solid surface which provided support. Soon, she'd find something stable to hold on to. But not yet. Just the feeling she'd lost everything that tethered her to life. Nothing was certain. Everything was shifting.

With no points of reference, how could she ever trust anything again?

Why hadn't Ada told her?

Well, perhaps Evelyn could understand that. It would have been difficult to initiate such a conversation.

Had Ada ever intended to tell her? Evelyn could have lived a full life and never known who her true mother was. Wasn't it her right to know who her parents were?

Every time Evelyn moved a piece of information into place, all the other things she'd always believed changed position. Everything was a blur. A lie.

Who was she? Surely all the things she'd done and thought, couldn't just have evaporated? Didn't they count for something?

Evelyn lay awake all night with thoughts ricocheting around her mind. She was tempted to stay in bed when the watery light of dawn seeped into her bedroom.

She could hear Ada in the kitchen and guessed that she, too, wouldn't have slept. She had half-hoped Ada would come to her during the night. Why hadn't she? A spark of defiance and anger grew inside Evelyn, and she got up, put on her dressing gown and padded barefoot into the kitchen.

There was no point wondering. She'd go and find out.

Ada looked up at her as she entered. Her eyes were sunken and smudged with purple shadows. Her face white and drawn. Neither spoke. Not the usual greeting that heralded another cheerful day.

Mother had destroyed everything. Ada sighed and placing two cups and saucers on the table, she gestured for Evelyn to sit down.

"Please allow me to tell you the truth." Her voice was flat. Her expression one of defeat. "You deserve that, Evelyn. You've deserved it from the start, but I was too cowardly to tell you. I thought I'd lose your respect. It was selfish of me. But I was so enjoying having you with me at long last."

It took a while before Ada could compose herself. She shook so violently, the cups and saucers chinked together as she prepared tea. Evelyn was afraid she'd scald herself on the boiling water and took over. Ada watched her silently with tear-filled eyes, for once ignoring Titan who rubbed himself against her legs as if he knew she needed comfort. In her lap were several framed photographs, all face down.

When Evelyn had put a cup of tea in front of her, Ada placed the photographs face up on the table and slowly slid them across the tablecloth towards Evelyn.

"Your father. Walter Gaynesford."

Evelyn's eyes flew from one image to the next, drinking in the details hungrily. A young man. Tall, slim and blond-haired. A soldier from the last war, with pride and confidence shining in his eyes, posing in a photographic studio. At the top of each picture, in neat script, was written: *To my dearest Ada, with love from your own Walter.*

"They were taken in northern France." Ada lovingly stroked the frame of one of the photographs. "This was the last..."

Her eyes filled with tears and Evelyn placed her hand over Ada's on top of the frame. Two women. Flesh and blood. Linked to a sepia photograph of a man who'd long since gone. Evelyn swallowed repeatedly, fighting back the tears.

Eventually, Ada managed to speak. She closed her eyes as if looking into the past. "I met Walter at school." She smiled. "We were childhood sweethearts. Of course, no one took us seriously when we were children, but we both knew we belonged together. There was no one else for me, and Walter felt the same. We'd been made for each other."

Tears squeezed out from between her closed eyelids and after wiping her cheeks, she began again. "When we were of age, I told Mother that Walter had proposed. She was horrified. At first, she said we were too young and insisted we wait a few years. It was true we were young, but I later realised that hadn't been her primary concern. She'd merely tried to delay the day I left home. I was too useful to her. At first, I agreed to wait until we were older. I knew she was exhausted and needed my help. My father didn't come home often but when he did, he drank his money away. Our lives were a struggle until some of the older ones went out to work."

Ada paused and opened her eyes. "And then war was declared. Fairly early on, only single men were conscripted. If Walter and I had married as we'd longed to do, it might have bought us a bit more time together. But... but..."

Evelyn waited until Ada could continue.

"Walter was sent to northern France. He was reported missing at first. His mother and I wrote repeatedly to his regiment for news. But his body was never found. After a year, he was presumed to have died in an ambush. Shortly after we'd heard he was missing, I realised I was expecting you." She buried her face in her hands and sobbed.

Evelyn felt as though her heart was being ripped to shreds. How Mother must have made Ada's life miserable once she'd known. She rose and put her arm around Ada's shoulders.

"I thought you'd despise me," Ada whispered. "I brought shame on you."

It was hard to push words past the lump in her throat, but Evelyn eventually managed to croak, "I'm so proud you're my mother."

Ada sagged with relief. "I don't deserve it, but you'll never know how relieved I am to hear that." She swallowed several times, unable to continue. Finally, she patted the hand Evelyn had placed on her shoulder. "I promised you the whole story. But I expect you've guessed the rest."

"Yes, there's no need to explain more. I can see it's painful." Evelyn was desperate to know everything but was reluctant to push Ada too far.

"No, I want you to know." Ada paused and after clearing her throat, she continued, "I was desperately afraid of Mother's reaction, and yet thrilled that a tiny part of Walter remained with me. She was furious, as I'm sure you'll have guessed. It was Dad's idea for Mother to pass you off as her child. He was on one of his rare stays at home and he wasn't angry. Just matter-of-fact. Remote. But then I'd seen him so few times in my life, we were almost strangers. At first, mother refused to go along with his plan, saying I should be honest and accept my punishment, but Dad convinced her she'd also be judged. After Mother still refused, he told Father Brian who spoke to mother and managed to convince her..."

Father Brian? Ah, so that was why Mother had such a strained relationship with the priest of St Patrick's. So many things were now beginning to make sense.

Ada continued, "So, we passed you off as Mother's. I stayed home as I grew larger, and Mother put a cushion inside her clothes when she went out. When you were born you were just another Quinn child, and nobody questioned it. I never saw Dad again. I sometimes wonder if he died or if he simply chose not to return."

As if he knew the next part of the explanation might be difficult for Ada, Titan jumped on to her lap and rubbed his face against her. She held him tightly and took a deep breath. "I suppose you're wondering why I left you with Mother?"

Evelyn nodded. More than anything, she wanted to know that.

Ada sighed. A long, heartfelt sigh. Almost a moan. "I was very weak physically after you were born and by the time I'd regained some strength, Mother had taken over. Nothing I did was right, regardless of the fact that I'd looked after all my brothers and sisters. We argued constantly about how to look after you. Of course, I ignored her, but life was one long battle. At first, she hinted that when you were old enough to understand she'd tell you the truth about me. That was enough to make me back down, but it was so hard when you cried, and she wouldn't allow me to pick you up and comfort you as I yearned to do. In the end, she threatened to tell you about me when you were old enough to understand – unless I left home. I was so ashamed. I couldn't bear to think of you hating me. Better you believed I was your sister than know such shame. Then, after one awful row, I could take no more. I left for France."

France! Evelyn had no idea Ada had been to France.

"Walter's mother and I still held out the hope he was alive. After all, they had no proof of what happened to him. I decided to go to France and find out. Perhaps if I'd told Mrs Gaynesford about you, she might have looked after you and your life might have been happier, but again, I was too ashamed. So, I went to France to find Walter. A mad notion. But I reasoned that if I'd found him, we'd have married, and you would have come to live with us. I volunteered as a nurse and remained after the war was over." Ada picked up the photograph and tears filled her eyes. "But in the end, I had to accept Walter had gone. After that, I couldn't bear the thought of coming back and seeing you accept your grandmother as your mother. Cowardly? Yes..." Ada clenched her jaw, her eyes fierce. "And I was so ashamed. I was so distraught, I lost interest in life."

She stroked Titan's head; her face one of shame and defeat. "I ran out of money and I'm not proud of how I earned my living after the war was over. I met an artist in Paris and became his model for a while. I tried to forget about the past. But with nothing to look forward to, I saw how empty my life was. Thoughts of you filled my head and, in the end, I saved enough to come back to England. The first time I saw you, my heart melted, but you cried when I tried to pick you up. You didn't recognise me, although now I wonder if mother wasn't gripping your arm so tightly you were crying because of that."

Instinctively, Evelyn ran her fingers over her arm above her elbow in the place where mother had often pinched her. The bruises had faded while she'd been with Ada, but not the memory of the pain nor the tenderness afterwards. Her skin tingled with feelings of longing, regret and love. One woman's bitterness at her husband and situation had damaged the lives of those around her. Ada, Evelyn and how many of their brothers and sisters? An utter tragedy for the entire Quinn family.

"I moved to Dunton to be near Walter's mother. But she died shortly after, and her children moved away. And that's why I came to this cottage. After they'd gone, there wasn't any point moving anywhere else, so I stayed."

Evelyn stood behind Ada and wrapped her arms around her. "Thank you for telling me." She placed her cheek against Ada's. They remained silent for some time.

Evelyn wondered what life might have been like if Ada hadn't been forced to leave.

She couldn't guess at Ada's thoughts.

Chapter Twenty-Nine

Evelyn decided to go for a walk. Ada had gone to lie down after she'd answered all Evelyn's questions. She hadn't slept the previous night. Although Evelyn was tired, she knew her sleep wouldn't come until she'd had a chance to think everything through. A walk might clear her head.

It had been a lot to take in, but if only she'd known before. What a difference it would have made to her life. Far from being ashamed as Ada had feared, Evelyn was fiercely proud to be Ada's daughter.

Of course, as far as society went, she was tainted, but what a relief to know Mother hadn't given birth to her. It hadn't been a tale of shame, as Mother had claimed the previous day. But a tragic love story. And if there had been a villain, it had been Mother, not Ada.

Evelyn rearranged her scarf to keep out the chilling wind that hurled icy daggers down her neck and gnawed at her fingers. She'd forgotten her gloves. But there'd been too much to think about and there was still so much to process. Evelyn's life was being rewritten from a different point of view. Having learnt so much about Ada's past, it was difficult to superimpose that on top of her own life and merge the two together.

And as if she didn't have enough to occupy her mind, like a shadow lurking behind her, Evelyn was aware of another matter that was casting gloom over her life. Jacob had gone. And he hadn't returned.

Her shock had been so great at Mother's arrival, her mind had frozen. She hadn't even noticed when he'd slipped out. When she finally remembered, she imagined he'd have gone for a walk until things had quietened down, but later, she'd seen his bag and bicycle had gone. Had he pedalled up and down the road waiting until it was safe to go back into Swallowmead? She was certain there'd have been no doubt Mother was still there from the raised voices – one voice in particular. Such vitriol had poured from Mother's lips. A lifetime of bitterness – both real and imagined.

Even when the air raid whistles had blown, no one had left the cottage for the bomb shelter at the end of the garden. Where had Jacob been when the alert had sounded? Had he found shelter? Perhaps by that time, he'd almost been back in Great Baddow? He'd have been aware of his next shift and wouldn't have wanted to be late.

When Evelyn got back to Swallowmead, she'd write to him and apologise for her mother's outrageous accusations. It wasn't as though she'd caught them doing anything – Jacob had been asleep. But the sight of Mother had reawakened the old, ingrained feeling of having sinned that Evelyn had borne all her life – whether she'd done something wrong or not.

They hadn't done anything wrong.

But a niggling doubt wriggled inside like a maggot.

Wasn't it a sin to imagine doing wrong? While she'd watched Jacob asleep, she'd wondered what it would be like to lie next to him, to hold him in her arms, to feel his body and his naked skin against hers.

Perhaps wearing only the silk stockings he'd given her. That had been enough to bring a guilty flush to her cheeks and a warm glow deep inside.

But her mother hadn't been able to read those thoughts. By acting as though she was guilty, it had merely confirmed Mother's shameful suspicions of Evelyn.

Jacob would write as soon as he could. Perhaps he'd even cycle back to see her...

But the spectre that still haunted the shadows of her life lowered her mood further. Had he been so appalled by Mother's outrageous accusations he was reconsidering his relationship with Evelyn? He had a rosy-coloured notion about families. And hers had, in no way, reached the high standards he admired and expected. When he'd talked about his mother, father and brother, everything had sounded perfect. How could he possibly take in Evelyn's mother's nastiness? No, not her mother, her *grandmother*, she reminded herself. Perhaps that was it, Evelyn thought. Needles of fear piercing her skin. He would now know she was illegitimate. Would that have made a difference? Surely not. She stopped abruptly, icy fingers gripping her heart.

Jacob wouldn't hold that against her. He was a kind, gentle man. And yet if he compared their upbringing and families, hers would be lacking. Having met Mother before in London, he'd known what she was like, and he'd still come to find Evelyn, but she'd left Mother far behind. *Grandmother,* Evelyn corrected herself. But it was no good. The word 'grandmother' didn't come to her mind for that woman. She was Mother, with a capital M. And always would be.

The front door to Ada's cottage would now always be locked in case Mother returned. She would not be allowed in. But Jacob didn't know that. And realistically, if she suddenly appeared on the doorstep, it would cause a scene. Ada would have to let her in. So, if Mother could reappear when she wanted, perhaps Jacob was having second thoughts about being with Evelyn? If, indeed, he wanted to be with her at all.

During the next few days, the atmosphere remained subdued in Swallowmead. Evelyn and Ada were both aware of their newly revealed relationship and were wary of each other. The easy camaraderie they'd once shared had gone.

Evelyn took care to show Ada she understood, but the shame was deeply ingrained in Ada, and she appeared to be unable to forgive herself. She'd spent so many years hiding her secret and suppressing the memory that now it had been so cruelly exposed, she couldn't face her past and the implications. Her arthritis flared up and she was in more pain than usual, although she appeared to embrace it, almost as if it was punishment.

Early one morning, Evelyn awoke – the events of the past few days swirling like a whirlpool in her mind. It was 2:13am. Once again, she knew she'd lie awake until it was time to get up for work, puzzling about how they could get over the chaos Mother had stirred up.

It occurred to Evelyn, the best way of dealing with the problem might be to simply ignore it. Mother had made it clear she didn't want to see them again, so although it was possible, it was unlikely she'd return. No one else in Dunton needed to know. Mother might tell as many people as she liked in Stepney, but Evelyn was certain she wouldn't. It would merely show her up as a liar with a fallen daughter.

No, she'd wanted to lash out at Evelyn and Ada to pay them back for all the pain she believed she'd suffered.

But Mother was no longer part of their lives. Now, between Ada and Evelyn, they must be able to sort out the problem. If neither she nor Ada acknowledged their true relationship, then why should it matter? Evelyn didn't want to address Ada as 'Mother'. The word carried too many unpleasant memories and feelings. She and Ada were the same people they'd been before the fateful visit. Indeed, nothing had changed other than Evelyn's awareness. Could things return to some sort of normality if Evelyn didn't think of Ada as her mother at all? Suppose Evelyn still treated her like a sister and used her first name? Would they ever achieve the carefree relationship they'd once had?

In the morning, she'd talk it over with Ada and see what she thought.

Having arrived at a possible solution, Evelyn eventually drifted off to sleep. She awoke late and realised Ada was still asleep. Presumably, she, too, had slept badly. If Evelyn hurried, she wouldn't be late for work. However, now, there wasn't the time to discuss something as important as their relationship – that would have to wait until they were less rushed.

As they hastily made breakfast, Evelyn heard the rattle of the letterbox. At last. Jacob had written. She rushed to the door to find Titan nosing one single letter on the mat. It was addressed to Ada – in Gordon's handwriting.

Evelyn had been so certain it would be from Jacob; tears pricked her eyes. True, she hadn't sent him a letter. She'd written one but hadn't dared to post it. She'd been desperate to hear how he'd taken Mother's visit and the life-changing revelation.

The whole thing had been so undignified and degrading.

Illegitimate. Such a stigma in some people's eyes.

Was that how Jacob saw it? If only he'd write and give a clue as to his thoughts…

Suppose he didn't write? Dare she travel to Hailcombe Cross and knock at his landlady's door unannounced? At the beginning of the week, the thought would have been inconceivable. But now...

At the breakfast table, Ada gently squeezed her hand as she handed over the letter. Was it that obvious how desperate Evelyn was to hear from Jacob? It appeared so because empathy glowed from Ada's eyes.

The letter consisted of one sheet of paper. That was unusual because Gordon usually wrote at length about his family and life in the war-struck capital.

Ada continued to stare at the words long after she'd finished reading them. Evelyn paused, a spoon of porridge halfway to her lips as she took in Ada's horrified expression.

"What is it? Has something bad happened to Gordon?" Evelyn asked.

Ada nibbled her bottom lip and passed the letter to Evelyn, who scanned it quickly.

"Dying?" She looked up sharply at Ada. "Mother's dying? How can that be? She was in fine form last week."

"I know. If this letter had come from her, I wouldn't believe it. But it's from Gordon and he says he's spoken to the doctor and Father Brian. Apparently, she had a strange turn when she got home after her..." Ada paused, her eyes narrowed, and her voice grew bitter. "After her visit."

"But she wants to see us? She wants to see *me*?" Evelyn's voice rose with incredulity.

Ada returned Evelyn's surprised expression. "Perhaps she wants to make peace?"

"What shall we do?" Evelyn asked. "I'd got used to the idea I'd never see her again. And now this..."

Ada nibbled her lip again. "Well, I'll go for both of us. I'd understand if you didn't want to see her hateful face again."

Ada was right, and yet the doctor and Father Brian had said she was dying. Evelyn could hardly refuse the woman her last wish.

She'd never forgive herself if she denied the woman she'd called 'Mother' this one final request. Not for Mother's sake but because she wanted to do what was right. She wanted to be her own person.

Chapter Thirty

Dazzling light penetrated Jacob's eyelids. He risked opening them a little and winced at the glare. It was so much effort, his eyes immediately closed. Why was he so tired? Perhaps he ought to sleep again. When he woke later it might be darker. More comfortable.

"Lieutenant?"

He recognised the voice but couldn't quite place it. A kind voice. But not Gran's. She'd have called him Jake. Perhaps he was dreaming. Yes, that was it.

"Lieutenant? Are you awake?"

The voice sounded real.

Jacob opened his eyes again and blinked repeatedly, trying to make sense of the brilliant blurry colours and shapes that filled his vision.

Gradually, his eyes focused and he saw Mrs Shipley's face, her hands clasped together, pressed against her chin, as if in prayer.

"Ah, there you are, Lieutenant. I can't tell you what a shock you gave me."

He frowned. Shock? What had happened? Pain shot through his head as he tried to sit up, and he fell back against the pillows.

He looked about. This wasn't his room in Hailcombe Cross.

This wasn't his bed in Mrs Shipley's house.

Intensely bright lights. The sharp smell of antiseptic. A clipboard at the end of his bed and a nurse outside in the corridor.

Hospital.

Oh yes, he knew all about being in hospital.

Was he dreaming he was back in the Royal Naval Hospital in Gosport recuperating after his return from Italy?

Or perhaps he really was still in Gosport. That would mean the life he thought he'd lived after he'd been discharged had been a dream.

"I was getting quite worried about you," Mrs Shipley said.

Jacob gasped. If Mrs Shipley was there, then he wasn't still in the naval hospital. She belonged in Chelmsford in a life that had come after he'd left Gosport. What a relief.

"Shall I call the doctor?" Mrs Shipley's brows drew together with concern. "Are you in pain?"

"No... no, thank you, Mrs Shipley. I'm just trying to remember what happened. Where am I? Why am I here?"

Her face relaxed. "Well, you're in Broomfield Hospital. You were found on a quiet country lane outside Laindon. My goodness, you had such a lucky escape. Some young boys out collecting bullets found you and who knows how long you might have lain there if they hadn't? It snowed that night. The temperature dropped to well below freezing. The state you were in, you wouldn't have made it 'til morning."

"Boys?" He didn't remember seeing any boys. Not that he remembered much at all. Velvety blackness filled his mind, and scenes appeared and disappeared before he had a chance to pin them down and inspect them.

"Yes, just some youngsters. Apparently, they heard planes and gunfire and, after the all-clear siren, they rushed over, looking for souvenirs. You know what little boys are like. Apparently, you gave them quite a turn because they thought you were dead. But when they fetched the constable, he discovered you were unconscious."

"Was I near the decoy airfield?" He shrank back into his pillow as an image exploded into his mind – sharp and vivid. A plane was heading towards him, inside the cockpit, the blurry face of a man leaning forward, his attention on Jacob and bullets bursting from the guns.

"Decoy airfield? Ooh, I wouldn't know about anything like that," Mrs Shipley said. "They don't give that sort of information out willy nilly, but it sounds likely. Now, are you sure you're all right?"

"Yes, yes, thank you, Mrs Shipley. I just remembered something, that's all."

She leaned closer to him and wagged her finger in mock indignation. "You gave me quite a turn, Lieutenant. The doctor told me he'd expected you to have recovered much faster. It seemed you'd knocked yourself out and were suffering from exposure, but after you came round, you were unexpectedly poorly. Fever and chills. Delirium."

"How long have I been here?" He recalled images of nurses and doctors flickering in his mind, but he'd assumed he was back in Gosport. All the time he'd been in Chelmsford.

"A week—"

"A *week*?" Jacob tried to sit up again. One whole week had passed, and he hadn't known?

"It's all right, you're not to worry. The doctor spoke to one of your senior officers at work and explained what had happened. You're not expected back for a while. The doctor asked me if you'd been well before the accident, and I told him about the outbreak of 'flu at work. He thought that might account for your symptoms, but he wasn't completely convinced. Still, you seem perkier now." Her bright smile was reassuring.

One whole week had gone? Could it really have been 'flu? It was possible. Likely, even. So many of his colleagues had succumbed to it. And yet, in that black nothingness of his mind was the lurking suspicion his strange symptoms had been the result of the pills he'd been taking.

But Neville took them and appeared to thrive.

Yes, the most likely explanation was that he'd had 'flu. And that was the most comforting thought. Because if it had been the pills, then much of his stay in hospital had been avoidable. He'd been taking up a bed that could have gone to someone who really deserved it.

After Mrs Shipley had gone and the doctor had examined him, Jacob tried to rest and sort out his memories. The doctor had told him he'd be kept under observation for the next few days, but Jacob was determined to leave as soon as possible.

What if his symptoms really were the result of having taken those tablets? He must leave hospital as soon as he could walk out and vacate his bed for someone who really needed it, and anyway, he had to get back to work.

He'd made up his mind. If necessary, he'd discharge himself the next day.

That night, he tried to sort out his thoughts. He still hadn't been able to remember exactly what had happened before the German pilot had shot at him. The doctor had told him not to worry. It wasn't unexpected.

But Jacob was horrified. Fragments of thoughts darted into his mind and then vanished before he had a chance to examine them. He needed to remember exactly what had happened because, somehow, he knew it was of the utmost importance. Something had led up to that event he felt was significant.

The next morning, he got up and although his head had spun, he hadn't fallen. A short walk around his bed had been painful as his muscles had not been exercised for a week, but in the past, they'd certainly caused him more discomfort.

He could manage.

Jacob sat on the bed and after a short rest, he got up again and walked to the window. It was only a few steps, but it would get him used to using his legs again. He was fortunate to be in a tiny side room – a precaution in case he'd been suffering from 'flu or another infectious disease.

Jacob looked out of the window and braced himself. A strong wind was driving the rain against the windowpane. It didn't matter what the weather was like. He must leave.

First, he would dress and then he'd sign whatever was necessary to discharge himself.

He turned back to the cupboard by the side of his bed for his clothes, as a crash reverberated along the corridor. A man began to yell at the top of his voice and after another clatter, nurses ran past Jacob's door, their footsteps hurrying in the direction of the commotion. The man yelled again and then a stern woman's voice rang out.

Jacob sank onto the bed, his head between his hands.

Voices.

He'd been searching for visions in his mind, but now, voices came to him. Loud female voices, or more accurately, one voice, harsh and strident. He closed his eyes and tried to hear the words, but nothing other than angry sounds came to him.

A woman's face, angular and twisted with rage. She hurled words at him. He replied politely, but she continued to shout. Then there were two other voices, also raised, but not full of hatred. They were tinged with anguish, and he wanted to help, but before he could do anything, they'd faded to be replaced by his mother's voice. She was furious, and so was his father. Their words, rapid and staccato, grew louder and rhythmic until they became the *rat-tat-tat* of German machine gun fire.

Rage filled his head. Not his own rage. Rather, people were furious with him. The cacophony filled his head. He pressed his hands against his temples, squeezing the sides of his skull as if to push everything out.

Perhaps he was going mad.

Chapter Thirty-One

Evelyn and Ada walked along the Stepney street where they'd both once lived, their arms linked. The earlier awkwardness between them had gone while they dealt with this latest crisis. They both paused outside, looking up at the house that had once been their home.

Evelyn's stomach twisted. Fear? Dread? Perhaps both.

"It's not too late if you don't want to go in," Ada whispered.

Evelyn shook her head and took a deep breath.

Gordon opened the door and greeted them sadly. His usual cheery smile replaced by a look of relief.

"Is she...?" Ada asked.

"She's still with us. The doctor says it could be any time now, though."

He led them upstairs into their mother's bedroom where Father Brian sat next to the bed, his rosary in his hands. His face lit up when he saw them, and he rose to allow Ada to sit next to her mother.

"Mrs Quinn, you have visitors," he said in his loud 'pulpit' voice. "Ada and Evelyn. Remember, you were asking for Evelyn?"

Mother's eyes fluttered open, and she blinked as she peered at the faces in the gloom around her bed.

Evelyn held her breath as her mother's gaze passed over her. Did she know her? Was she too far gone? But Mother's eyes stopped as they reached Ada's face and recognition lit her eyes. Her fingers worked at the counterpane as she opened and closed her mouth. Ada beckoned to Evelyn to stand by her.

"Evelyn's here. Did you want to speak to her?" Ada asked gently.

Mother's eyes filled with tears, but still, no sound came from her mouth. Finally, her eyelids slid shut and a single tear dribbled down her cheek.

Evelyn gripped Ada's hand as they watched, barely able to breathe, but Mother's chest still rose and fell, rose and fell.

"Perhaps give her a chance to rest," said Father Brian.

Chapter Thirty-Two

The BBC's *Music While You Work* blared from the loudspeakers in the canteen, playing a rousing marching band tune that set Jacob's teeth on edge. His hands were clenched into fists, his nails biting into his palms. He'd finally found Neville and asked if he had any more pills.

"You must be overdoing it, old chap." Neville was speaking to him but at the same time, glancing over his shoulder at the Wren in front of Jacob in the queue.

"Not at all," Jacob said, forcing himself to sound casual. "I've simply left them at home." He didn't add he hadn't left them at *his* home. They must have dropped out at Evelyn's and he fervently hoped she hadn't found them. Would she know what they were? Would she think less of him?

Neville wasn't listening. "Best not to leave them lying around, old man. But luckily for you, I have a few I can spare. Unluckily for you, it's going to cost you. It's getting harder to get hold of them on the..." He glanced about and lowered his voice. "Black market. And I need something for myself, you know. Going out with one of the Wrens tonight. And I'll be grateful for a boost in energy. If you know what I mean..." He winked.

Jacob knew what he meant but didn't care. He needed something to lift him out of the overwhelming despair that sucked at him like quicksand. Once he felt better, he'd be able to function again. He just needed a little help. His accident and stay in hospital had taken its toll. On reflection, it might have been wiser to have stayed in hospital for a day or two longer. It was taking so long to get back to normal. But this would be the last pill. And hopefully soon things would quieten down at work.

They'd made real progress, and the manufacture of the magnetron was once again up to speed. Their research had shown the modifications they'd made to their new radar systems were proving successful and had increased their detection abilities. The 'flu epidemic had run its course and people had returned to work. Yes, things would be better from now on. He just needed a little assistance until he felt better.

Later, Neville found Jacob at his bench and surreptitiously slipped a small bag into his hand.

"You owe me a guinea, old chap," Neville whispered, slapping Jacob's shoulder benevolently. Once Jacob had paid, he wandered away whistling and, after a word with one of the Wrens, he carried on back to his seat while her eyes followed him adoringly.

A guinea? The size and weight of the bag told him that huge sum of money hadn't bought many tablets. Another reason for Jacob to stop taking them – if indeed he needed one. Since he'd been using them, he'd lost his appetite and felt nauseous when he forced himself to eat. When he stood up quickly, his head and vision swam, and without warning, his heart thrashed disturbingly in his chest.

And if that wasn't bad enough, there were yawning gaps in his memory.

That morning as he'd been about to put on his coat to leave for work, Mrs Shipley had called out that his breakfast was ready. When he'd gone into the kitchen, she'd placed a plate of toast on his place at the table. He'd assume she'd made a mistake, but a tiny doubt niggled at him. Mrs Shipley was careful with food. She wouldn't have fed him twice. On the other hand, he might have forgotten he hadn't had breakfast; after all, he couldn't remember getting up, washing, shaving or dressing. But he obviously had.

He'd walked through the last few days as if wandering through fog. When he couldn't remember what should have happened, his mind filled in the blanks. How much was reality, and how much had his mind fabricated?

The previous day, he'd asked Mrs Shipley if he'd left Evelyn's letter downstairs. He couldn't find it. She wouldn't have touched it if she'd come across it in his room but if he'd forgotten to take it upstairs, she might have put it somewhere for safekeeping. Mrs Shipley said she hadn't seen it and added that he hadn't received a letter addressed in Miss Quinn's handwriting since before New Year.

He'd been sure she was wrong. But the landlady was adamant. Indeed, she was quite affronted he didn't appear to believe her, puffing herself up indignantly. Eventually, he'd been forced to accept it was true. He'd wanted to hear from Evelyn so badly; had he imagined the letter? If that was true, what else had his mind made up? And more importantly, why hadn't she written?

He turned his back on everyone in the room and tipped the tablets into his palm. Three. A whole guinea for three tablets? He tapped two back into the bag and put the other in his mouth, then swilled it down with a mouthful of tea.

It didn't matter how many were in the bag. He only needed one, and that would be the last. He had three days leave due to him at the end of the week and once he'd had a chance to sleep, he'd ask if he could stay with Evelyn for a few nights.

He wouldn't need pills then.

Evelyn.

The echoes of voices came to him as if they were floating the length of a long corridor. Shouts and accusations. Mrs Quinn sneering, and Ada pleading. Evelyn's sobs. How was she now? Why hadn't she replied to his letters to let him know?

Which letters?

Well, the ones he'd written to her.

He had, hadn't he?

He'd certainly composed them in his head even if he couldn't remember actually writing them... But he must have done. It would be unforgivable if he hadn't contacted her since that horrible afternoon. Good gracious, that was weeks ago... Two? Three? No, surely not that long. But he'd been in hospital for a week... When had it been?

Of course, he'd written.

His heart punched out a rhythm against his ribs and he had the desire to run. He longed to feel the release as his arms and legs pumped until their muscles gave out.

Calm down.

His teeth were chattering.

Too much energy. Yet, at the same time, he felt drained.

Jacob looked at the data he'd been given to analyse, and the figures melted into a black splodge.

Evelyn.

With steely determination, he willed the letters to unscramble. He'd finish his work and before he left his bench, he'd write to Evelyn. He had a stamp so he could post the letter on the way home.

By the time Jacob had finished his shift, he could barely keep his eyes open nor hold his head up, nevertheless, he wrote the letter he'd promised he'd write to Evelyn. It wasn't as long as he'd intended, and he wasn't sure it made sense, but it would let her know he was thinking of her. He folded it sealed it in an envelope, then stuck the stamp in the corner.

Sleep; he needed to sleep. And yet, his heart was racing, and he felt as though he wanted to leap out of his body and run, like a terrified animal trying to escape its cage.

How could he simultaneously feel exhausted and energised? Another wave of nausea hit him and as he stood abruptly, he swayed, grabbing the edge of his desk for support.

Home. Go home. Try to sleep. Allow the effects of the tablet to wear off. Then he'd never take another. If he was too exhausted to work, he'd have to go to the sickbay. Not that he wanted to. He might have to own up to taking the tablets. How could he explain where they'd come from? He certainly couldn't tell them about Neville... Oh well, he'd worry about that once he felt better.

Jacob put his coat on, and weariness swept through him as he anticipated the cycle ride home. He clenched his fists, telling himself he could do it. And if he didn't have the strength, he'd just have to push the bike home. Perhaps the cold night air would wake him up.

As he left the room, he remembered he hadn't tidied his bench, but it would have to wait until he returned.

Chapter Thirty-Three

Neville Harrington-Wade looked up as the door swung shut. He yawned as he put his slide rule back in its case. He'd return to his room, grab a few hours' sleep, and then later, he had a date with that delectable nurse, Val Potter. What a firecracker she was.

Fancy Lieutenant Adam not tidying his desk before he finished his shift. Tut-tut, he'd be in trouble. Untidiness was frowned upon. Tidy desk, tidy mind, and all that.

It suddenly occurred to Neville that Adam might have left the small bag of tablets he'd given him earlier on show. That might take some explaining. Screwing up a piece of paper into a ball, he strolled towards the wastepaper basket, taking a long route via Adam's desk.

No small bag on the desk, thankfully. However, there was a stamped letter.

Interesting. To whom was Adam writing?

He picked it up. Miss Evelyn Quinn. He scanned further down the address. Dunton.

Ah, yes! That pretty girl he'd driven to the dance in that dreadful backwater town. The one where he'd met the delicious Val.

Neville picked the letter up and slipped it in his pocket. He glanced around. One of the Wrens, Mary Reeves, was looking at him, her brows drawn together. Neville tapped his pocket. "Going to post it for Adam." He smiled at the girl. "He's obviously forgotten about it. Never mind. I won't let his girl think he's forgotten him." Neville patted his pocket again and the girl glanced back at her oscilloscope screen.

Neville knew she was sweet on Adam. She wouldn't want to know about a letter to his girlfriend and most likely wouldn't mention it to him.

Perhaps on his way to see Val, Neville might just drive past the lovely Evelyn's cottage and stop to see her. Adam had said they weren't serious, so no harm in asking her out for a drink. For a second, he wondered whether it was worth the trouble as he remembered the dark, unmade roads. Then Evelyn's face appeared in his mind, and he remembered her body draped in that silky, Grecian robe. Oh yes, he'd like to see more of the lovely Evelyn.

Well, why not? It would be a diversion.

He committed the address to memory and after shredding the letter, he put the pieces back in his pocket. He'd dispose of them later.

Chapter Thirty-Four

Ada, Evelyn and Gordon sat in the parlour in front of the range. Upstairs in her bedroom, Mother still clung to life, despite the doctor's prediction she wouldn't last long. Her breathing was rapid and shallow. From time to time, her eyes roved around the room, searching, searching, while her lips moved as if they wanted to form words that never came.

Several days had passed. Ada and Evelyn took it in turns to sit with the dying woman and on several occasions, she'd woken, and had breathed the word 'Evelyn'. Her eyes had then scanned the room, although it wasn't clear whether she could see anything. Evelyn had whispered that she was there.

The first time, she'd extended her hand to place it over the dying woman's, then quickly drew it back. Even under the circumstances, Evelyn doubted her touch would be appreciated. Each time, she'd sat forward and spoken gently, asking what Mother wanted and moistening her dried lips. But although her eyes had locked onto Evelyn's face and her mouth tried to form words, only stale breath emerged.

"Father Brian says her soul is troubled." Gordon stared gloomily into the fire in the range. "I'm not surprised. She must have a lot on her conscience." He paused. "Although to be honest, I'm not sure she's got one. She always assumed she was right. But it might be different when you're staring death in the face. I wonder if she wants to apologise for the way she..." he paused again and with a shrug, added, "you know."

Ada had told Gordon about their mother's visit and what she'd revealed, as soon as they'd arrived at the house. She'd discussed it with Evelyn on the train on their way to London.

"Better he hears if from us," Ada had said. "Although he may already know."

Gordon hadn't known that rather than being his sister, Evelyn was his niece. He'd been shocked. "Well, that certainly makes sense of the arguments and constant shouting before you left all those years ago, Ada."

Evelyn had wondered if Gordon's attitude towards her would change, but thankfully, after the initial surprise had worn off, he'd been the same loving person he'd always been.

"There's obviously something on Mother's mind. I wonder if that's what's keeping her alive," Ada said.

There was no way of knowing whether that was true and, if so, what she was thinking.

Eventually, Evelyn offered to remain at the house while Ada went back home. She'd had a letter from Mr Farrell, who'd informed her more East London children had arrived at the school. Although he hadn't asked her to return, Evelyn knew Ada wanted to help Mr Farrell with his new charges. Gordon offered to continue dropping in to see Evelyn every day, and at the end of the week, if mother was still with them, then Ada would return, too.

Evelyn was the obvious choice to remain. Mother still woke periodically asking for her, although those occasions were less frequent as the days passed.

If only she'd say what she wanted. During Father Brian's last visit, she'd woken, muttering Evelyn's name. It appeared she hadn't known he was there because her gaze had meandered across the room, but when she'd focused on the priest, her thin lips had clamped together, and she'd closed her eyes.

Later, outside the room, he'd sympathetically patted Evelyn's shoulder. "Her soul is in torment, my child. Do not judge her too harshly; she has endured much."

Evelyn had wanted to shake the priest's hand from her shoulder. He'd been kind to her but his attitude towards Ada had been less charitable and he'd barely spoken to her. Evelyn had heard him preach on many occasions in the past about the dangers of women being tempted into sin and falling from grace. Evelyn assumed he now classed Ada amongst those poor wretches. What was the matter with the man? Years ago, he'd advised Mother to pretend she'd given birth to Evelyn. Had he forgotten? Or did he feel now it was out in the open he needed to take a stand and to ensure everyone was aware he disapproved?

If only he'd leave them alone. He hadn't been able to get Mother to say what she wanted.

Of course, it was possible she wanted to rant at Evelyn again. That would be distressing. But the anger in her eyes had burnt away to leave sorrow. Suppose she wanted to say something kind?

Please let that be so.

Just one kind word. That would make all the difference to Evelyn. It would have shown that despite her puritanical views on Evelyn's arrival in the world, she hadn't considered the girl she'd passed off as her daughter, worthless. Perhaps she wanted to apologise. That would have been hard for Mother, Evelyn knew but she had obviously realised this would be her last opportunity.

Why didn't she speak?

And why did it matter so much to Evelyn?

Was it possible that on her deathbed, Mother was accepting Evelyn after years of rejection?

Why her worth should be decided by this woman, Evelyn didn't know. She knew she shouldn't care about her opinion. But she was pinning her hopes on something that might mitigate those years without love. Something that would give her back her self-esteem. Mother's last blessing.

Just one kind word.

Please.

But still, Mother tossed and turned in her bed, keeping her secrets.

Chapter Thirty-Five

On Ada's return home, the first thing she did was to check the post. There was nothing from Jacob. A heavy weight pressed down on her. Had she been wrong about him? Was he really so judgemental as to be bothered by Evelyn's illegitimacy? She'd believed his love had been more resilient than that.

Perhaps she was doing him an injustice. Perhaps he was ill – or worse. There'd been an air raid on the day Mother had visited. Would they have heard if he was ill or wounded?

Well, there was only one way to find out. And now was the perfect time to do so – while Evelyn was in London.

If Ada discovered Jacob no longer loved Evelyn, she would not tell her. She didn't think her daughter would appreciate interference. But if there was a possibility that Ada could mend Jacob and Evelyn's relationship, then she must take a chance. Of course, it was possible there was nothing to mend. But someone had to find out why he hadn't contacted Evelyn.

The following morning, Ada dressed up warmly. Snow had been forecast for the next few days. She hadn't told Mr Farrell she'd arrived home from London, so he wouldn't be expecting her. When she finally went back to the school, she'd have to work twice as hard, but

Evelyn needed her, and she was determined not to let her daughter down.

Ada had never been to Chelmsford, and when the bus driver let her off at a crossroads, she felt panic rise in her chest. He hadn't been very friendly and had vaguely waved his hand towards the right when she'd asked for directions to Hailcombe Cross. He'd driven off before she realised she should have asked how far it was. Not that it mattered. She had no choice but to walk however many miles it was from where he'd left her.

Woods on either side of the road prevented her from spotting anything that indicated a village was nearby. No church steeple or smoke rising from a tall chimney. There were no signposts either. Just trees. Suppose the driver had been wrong? How long would it take before she found out? And then how would she find her way to Hailcombe Cross?

Ada shivered in the biting wind and with grave misgivings, set off in the direction the bus driver had indicated, hoping he'd been right and wishing she'd worn two cardigans.

After a while, the bitter cold and the long walk had begun to hurt her knees and she wondered if she'd been hasty. Suppose no one was home? How long would she have to wait in the cold?

She'd deliberately decided against writing to Mrs Shipley because it would have taken too long to receive a reply – assuming Mrs Shipley replied at all. Mother might die at any time and then Ada would be called back to London. She needed answers now.

At last, Ada came across signs of life. The woods had long since given way to fields, but the hedgerows were tall and it wasn't until she'd turned a corner, she saw any sign of life. Mrs Shipley's was the second house along the lane. A two-storey, white building with two windows flanking a door downstairs and three windows upstairs.

Ada was exhausted by the time she reached the gate, but relief flooded through her when she saw Jacob's bicycle leaning against the wall. That must surely mean he was home. For the first time, she felt the weight lift slightly. Of course, he might be asleep if he'd been working all night. But she'd wait if necessary.

Ada hadn't expected this mission to be easy. In truth, she hadn't thought it through at all. She hadn't expected the village to be so remote. Suppose Jacob was asleep, and his landlady wasn't in? She'd have to find somewhere to wait.

Well, so be it. The sooner she knocked, the sooner she'd know what she'd have to deal with.

Ada raised the lion's head knocker and rapped.

A tall, well-built woman with grey curls opened the door. "Yes?" She wiped her hands on her apron as she inspected Ada.

"Mrs Shipley?"

"Yes." The woman's eyes narrowed suspiciously.

"Good morning. I was wondering if I could have a word with your lodger, Lieutenant Adam, please."

"And what do you want with the lieutenant?" Mrs Shipley's eyes narrowed further, and her gaze moved up and down the woman on her doorstep.

"Well..." Ada paused. How should she represent herself? Evelyn's mother? The words simply wouldn't form in her mouth after a lifetime of secrecy. Evelyn's sister? But that simply wasn't true and to deny Evelyn was her daughter was disloyal and insulting. A different tack, perhaps? "Lieutenant Adam is a friend. And I... I..."

"Yes?" Mrs Shipley crossed her arms over her large bosom. She was losing patience and obviously didn't believe Lieutenant Adam would have a friend such as Ada.

"Do you work with him?" Mrs Shipley asked doubtfully.

"No, I don't work with him. He was kind enough to mend my wireless set and—"

"If you want a repairman, there's one in Chelmsford in the High Road."

"Oh, no. It wasn't that. It's just that I... well, *we* were concerned, we haven't heard from him lately. I... that is, *we* were worried."

"We? You said, 'we'?" Mrs Shipley was losing patience.

Ada swallowed. She'd have to acknowledge Evelyn and call her 'daughter' one day. But today was too soon. No, that wasn't the problem – she was proud to acknowledge Evelyn. But if she did so, she was laying bare her guilt and shame to the world.

"Well, anyway," said Mrs Shipley, who had tired of her tongue-tied visitor. "Lieutenant Adam isn't here." She stepped back to shut the door.

"Please! Wait!" Ada said, she hadn't come all this way, jarring her joints walking along unmade roads to be turned away now and to let Evelyn down.

"Please." Something in her expression or tone must have touched Mrs Shipley. She paused with her hand on the door.

"I can explain," Ada said. "I *will* explain."

Mrs Shipley sniffed. "Well, you'd better come in then." Her tone said, 'And it had better be a good explanation.'

Ada winced as she climbed the step into Mrs Shipley's entrance hall. The smell of lavender, woodsmoke and marmalade filled the air.

"Mm, marmalade," Ada said, breathing in deeply. "Jac... that is, Lieutenant Adam brought us a jar of your marmalade at Christmas. It was delicious."

Mrs Shipley smiled. The first sign of friendliness she'd given. "You said 'us', so, I'm guessing you must be the sister of Lieutenant Adam's girl, Evelyn?"

It would have been easy to agree. But Ada had made up her mind to tell the truth. "Yes and no," she said.

Mrs Shipley gestured for her to follow along the hall.

Chapter Thirty-Six

Mrs Shipley led Ada into her parlour and seated her in one of the two armchairs in front of the fire, then went into the kitchen.

While she was out of the room, Ada glanced about. It was a clean but cluttered room. Framed photographs, candlesticks, small vases and china dogs adorned the mantlepiece and any other flat surface. Barely tamed chaos.

The chink of cups against saucers heralded Mrs Shipley's return, and she placed a tray on a small table. But before she sat in the other armchair, she held out her hand to Ada in a gesture that indicated she was expecting something. Ada looked up, confused.

"Your hand," Mrs Shipley said, with a peremptory gesture of her fingers. "Give me your hand."

Did she want to shake hands? Ada was confused but held it out anyway.

Mrs Shipley gripped her wrist firmly, keeping her palm uppermost.

Ada's instinct was to curl her fingers into a ball, but Mrs Shipley placed her long forefinger across Ada's and held them flat.

She peered at the lines on Ada's hand and made noises indicating she was alternately surprised and satisfied.

"Secrets," she said with a nod. "A life full of secrets." She paused and, with narrowed eyes, she scrutinised Ada. "Or perhaps just one large secret?"

Ada was shocked. Could Mrs Shipley really read her palm? "I... Yes..."

"That's the trouble with secrets. They always come out," said Mrs Shipley. "Sometimes it's best to get it over with."

"Yes." The sound that came from Ada was a croak.

Mrs Shipley sat down and began to pour tea. "Not that you need to tell me, of course. We're strangers. Although sometimes it's easier to unburden yourself to somebody you don't know."

"Yes," Ada said again, her mouth completely dry. How did this woman know? A lucky guess? After all, most people had secrets.

"Mrs Shipley—"

"Doris. My friends call me Doris. No need to be so formal. I can see in your palm you're trustworthy. Sad. And troubled. But trustworthy."

Had she really seen so much?

Well, what did it matter?

After Doris's earlier suspicion, this new friendliness was refreshing.

"Doris, I've come on my daughter's behalf, although she doesn't know I'm here, to speak to Lieutenant Adam. You see, they were getting on so well and then..." Ada paused.

The arrival of her mother would take some explaining.

"And your daughter would be the young lady over Dunton way, who lives with her sister?"

"Yes and no."

"You said that once before."

"It's rather complicated."

"Take your time," Doris said with a gentle smile. "We've got as long as you need. And I suspect this will take a while."

Ada hadn't realised how much of a relief it would be to tell someone about Walter, Evelyn and, of course, Mother. Doris was a good listener and, to Ada's surprise, confided that she too had fallen in love with a man who'd never returned from the Great War.

"Tom's friend, Pete, came to see me when he got home from the trenches. I'd already received the telegram, so I knew my Tom wouldn't be coming back. Pete told me they'd both fought at Passchendaele, and he'd been with Tom at the end. In fact, Tom had saved his life. Pete had been shot and had fallen in No Man's Land, and Tom dragged him back to the safety of the trench a second before a sniper got him. My Tom died a hero." Doris lowered her head and stared at her lap. "I thought I'd go mad with grief when I knew Tom had gone. He was the love of my life." She looked up at Ada and her eyes were brimming with tears. Ada's throat closed as she recalled the moment she'd learnt about Walter.

The two women sipped tea in silence for a few minutes, reliving the past.

"Pete visited quite often once the war was over. He'd been sent home. Lost part of his foot..." Doris sighed. "I suppose I was lonely. He kept on and on at me to marry him and in the end, I gave in." Her chin dropped to her chest, and she shook it gently. "I'd known about his foot and the shrapnel wounds. He was often in pain. But I'd had no idea how scarred he was mentally. Irrational anger. Bouts of depression..." She paused and swallowed. "Well, we married for better or worse and we muddled along until Pete died two years ago. But I should've remained faithful to Tom. I might've been lonely. But that would probably have been better in the long run..." She sighed.

"I'm so sorry, Doris. I made some foolish choices after I learnt of Walter's death. I did things I'd rather forget. Grief can push a woman in the wrong direction sometimes."

The two women tearfully regarded each other, both remembering crossroads in the past when different decisions might have led to better – or worse – outcomes.

"At least you have a daughter to remind you of Walter," Doris said sadly. "And you've got a chance to make up for your mother's behaviour." She nibbled her lower lip. "But I'm afraid you've had a wasted journey. Lieutenant Adam left early this morning. Training, I believe. Of course, he didn't tell me where. It'll be classified information. But I know he'll be away a few days – possibly longer. A shame because he was looking forward to a few days' leave. And between you and me, he hasn't been himself for a while. I don't mind telling you, Ada, I've been worried sick. I've grown remarkably fond of the lieutenant. He's like the son I never had."

Doris insisted Ada stay for lunch and then after a cosy chat in front of the fire, they toasted crumpets in the flames and Doris produced more butter than Ada had seen in a butter dish since the beginning of the war, and a jar of plum jam.

"I know," Doris said, holding up her hand to prevent any criticism. "I shouldn't touch black market goods, but I went without the basics for so long while Pete was alive, I can't help indulging now and again. And when Lieutenant Adam was here, it was such a pleasure to spoil him." She passed Ada a crumpet smothered in butter and jam.

"I don't know if you noticed, Ada, but there's something haunted about the lieutenant. I read his palm. Sadness was written in his hand, too. And regret. Of course, I didn't tell him what I'd seen. I just said he'd find happiness soon. And he might've done with your Evelyn. Do you know if she's written to him? He seemed to think she had but couldn't find the letter. Nothing's been delivered here. Did she write to him at work? He had a real spring in his step just before Christmas. I don't know what happened, but it's a crying shame, that it is."

Ada's face glowed with heat from the fire. And for the first time in many years, she was warm inside. She had an ally and someone she felt would become a friend. But that didn't help if Jacob was away. Perhaps he'd asked for a transfer. He could be anywhere.

As if reading her mind, Doris said, "Lieutenant Adam will be back. His things are still here. Don't you worry. We'll get them back together."

It had been so pleasant, unburdening herself and sharing memories of the men they'd loved years before, that Ada had lost touch of time. With dismay, she realised darkness was falling, and the drizzle and heavy clouds overhead deepened the twilight.

"I doubt you'll catch the last bus," Doris said. "Never mind, you'll just have to stay the night. I've got plenty of room."

As Ada lay in bed that night, she wondered whether she should tell Evelyn she'd visited Doris Shipley. Eventually, she decided against mentioning anything. After all, she had no news about Jacob, other than that he was in another part of the country. Doris was convinced he'd return but it wasn't beyond the realms of possibility he'd come back, pack up this things and leave. Ada hadn't learnt anything at all that might give Evelyn hope, so it was best to say nothing. Doris had promised if she discovered anything after Ada had gone home, she'd write. That was the best Ada could hope for.

Chapter Thirty-Seven

On Saturday morning, Evelyn was waiting at the open door when Gordon and Ada pulled up outside Mother's house in Gordon's van. During the previous few days, Evelyn's life had consisted of watching three faces: Mother's tormented features, the doctor's grave looks as he oversaw his patient and Father Brian's sanctimonious expression as he waited. Now Evelyn was desperate to look into a kind, caring face.

"How are you, my dear?" Ada clung tightly to Evelyn and, as she pulled away, she raised her eyebrows in a silent question.

"Mother's still with us," Evelyn said, avoiding the query about her own welfare. The few days she'd spent with her mother, waiting, waiting, had driven her to a dark place. The house with its gloomy rooms, particularly Mother's bedroom with its heavy, drawn curtains, was full of ghosts.

By day, Evelyn had sat in the stuffy room next to the bed, watching and waiting. Silently longing for a kind word. By night, she'd lain awake in the bed she'd left so many months before, remembering incidents she'd thought had been successfully banished from her mind. The blackness and bleakness were crushing her. Tears came easily and Father Brian had patted her shoulder when she'd broken down the previous day.

"Only to be expected under the circumstances, my child." He'd nodded at her, his hands clenched prayer-like over his chest.

Expected? He had no idea why she was crying. No one could have foreseen that even in this late stage in Mother's life, Evelyn yearned for acceptance and a sign that she was valued. But other than the tantalising moments when Mother had spoken her name, her eyes slid shut before she'd said anything else.

"Has she spoken to you?" Ada asked.

Evelyn shook her head, swallowing back the tears.

"Then let's try again," Ada said.

She led Evelyn and Gordon upstairs to Mother's room, and they sat as a family around the bed.

"Mother," Ada said gently but with determination. "Evelyn is here. I believe you have something you want to tell her. If that's so, then please speak now."

Mother's eyes opened. She glanced around the room; her gaze alighting on Evelyn. Her mouth opened and then closed; a sigh escaped from her parched lips. Her chest sank.

Three pairs of eyes stared at the counterpane, waiting for it to rise again.

After several minutes, Gordon stood. He swallowed. "I think she's gone. I'll fetch Father Brian."

Ada gathered Evelyn into her arms and together they sobbed.

Of course, a life snuffed out was always sad, but even at the end, Mother had robbed Evelyn of peace of mind.

Had she stubbornly refused to show a little affection? Or had she been willing to show it, but too weak?

Evelyn would never know.

And Ada? Why was she crying? Not for the woman who had alienated her and her daughter. Probably, knowing Ada, she was crying for the same reasons as Evelyn.

But whereas Ada valued Evelyn and had built up her self-confidence, Mother had once again destroyed it.

After the depressing week, Evelyn now saw herself through Mother's eyes. What had she ever done with her life? Nothing at all. She was worthless. Mother had silently passed her verdict, and there would never be any change.

It was final.

She was undoubtedly right.

Gordon had written to the brothers and sisters for whom he had addresses but no one had come to see Mother – no one had even replied. In the end, Ada and Evelyn offered to stay on in the house to go through Mother's belongings. They would sort out her affairs and arrange the funeral. Gordon was grateful to get back to his own family but said he'd help where he could.

Evelyn wrote to Jacob that evening telling him about her day. She put the letter in an envelope and added it to the pile of other letters she'd written to him and not posted. Earlier, she'd been afraid of asking Ada if there had been any letters from Jacob when she'd returned to Swallowmead. If there had been any, Ada would have given them to her immediately. Or perhaps not. Mother's death had eclipsed everything.

Later, she summoned the courage and asked. Ada's face fell. That was enough to answer Evelyn's query.

So, he hadn't written. He'd walked out and not explained. Well, that was a clear message that he no longer wanted anything to do with her. Perhaps what was most strange was that he'd once seen anything in her at all.

Very few people had attended the funeral. Ada, Gordon and Evelyn hadn't been surprised. Mother had never tried to make friends. Their sister Margaret, who lived in the north of London, came. It was the first time Evelyn remembered meeting her. The similarity to Mother was startling, particularly their eyes. But the crow's feet that had developed on Mother's face after years of expressing disapproval and resentment, and the bitter glitter that had lit her eyes were absent.

In fact, very little seemed to be present in Margaret's eyes. It was as though she was haunted. Had mother done that? Or had life been unkind to Margaret?

There was also a man who crept into the back of the church. Gordon acknowledged him but he'd slipped out again before the end of the service.

"That was Bob," Gordon said afterwards when they gathered in Mother's house for the last time. Margaret had not joined them, saying she didn't want to risk missing the last bus back home, even though Gordon had offered to take her in his van.

As soon as Mr Leonard, the rent collector, had inspected the rooms on behalf of the landlord, and given his approval, Gordon offered to drive Ada and Evelyn back to Dunton. They gratefully accepted. It had been tiring and depressing going through Mother's belongings and getting rid of most of them.

There had been a box of correspondence but few personal effects. Most of the letters were from years ago when their father had written to her. Those envelopes on the top, addressed in his handwriting, were unopened. Mother hadn't even bothered to read them.

There had been a few photographs of their father, but they appeared to have been discarded beneath the letters.

In the drawer next to Mother's bed, had been several religious books although they were in good condition, and it didn't appear they'd been read often. In the other drawers were legal papers and an assortment of items which meant nothing to her three children.

Not much left to mark her life.

"Her legacy was her children," said Gordon gloomily, staring ahead through the windscreen.

"Judging by her funeral, that was nothing to be proud of," Ada said. "But at least she was always kind to you, Gordon."

"That just always made me feel guilty. Now I'm wondering if it was simply relief that she'd have no more children once our father had disappeared."

When they arrived at Ada's cottage, Evelyn searched through the post but there were no letters from Jacob.

Once Gordon had gone, she went to her bedroom. It had been a harrowing few weeks, emotional journeys back in time, remembering. Sometimes laughter with Ada and Gordon, but mostly deep sadness. And always the spectre of Jacob just out of sight, lowering her mood further.

Well, Mother was gone.

They'd vacated the house in London and would never return.

Jacob had left her.

She must start afresh.

Chapter Thirty-Eight

Jacob rearranged the pillows and leaned back with a sigh. The bed creaked beneath his weight. He looked around the bedroom, remembering times when he and David, as young boys, had slept in this same bed. He swallowed, and the familiar feeling of loss when he thought of his brother dragged at his insides.

At least this was an improvement on the ward in Broomfield Hospital. He should have listened to the doctor who'd warned him he wasn't well enough to leave. It wasn't like he'd done anything useful at work since he'd discharged himself – he'd been in trouble with his supervisor for sloppy work and, much of the time, he simply couldn't remember what had happened. Jacob screwed up his eyes trying to banish the memory of the shame of being told his work hadn't been up to the required standard. Why couldn't he forget that and recall all the things he wanted to remember?

His superior officer had suggested he attend a training course in Portsmouth and warned him he'd better be more alert when he returned, or his role would be reconsidered.

Jacob didn't need telling twice.

He'd got as far as London, on his way to Portsmouth, when he'd blacked out. The next thing he'd known, he'd woken up in the London Hospital with Gran waiting by his bedside. Apparently, he'd collapsed on the platform in Liverpool Street Station.

Yet another hospital.

"Exhaustion," the doctor had diagnosed. And following the fall, he also had mild concussion, cuts and bruises. He was lucky not to have broken a bone, although he wouldn't be able to walk for a while. After the doctor had decided there would be no lasting damage, Jacob had asked to be discharged and had gone to Gran's to recuperate.

Once again, he'd felt a fraud, taking up a bed and preventing someone who might have been wounded in a bombing raid from being admitted. The hospital staff hadn't argued. They were too busy.

Gran, however, knew him better than the doctors, and hadn't been satisfied with merely knowing his bruises and cuts were healing. She'd recognised his mental pain.

"You've been pushing yourself too hard, Jake." She'd held up a warning hand. "And don't tell me we've got a war to win. I know that. But you've got to stop punishing yourself." She tipped her head to one side. "While you've been sleeping, you've mentioned Evelyn's name. But she hasn't called. Does she know what happened to you? Can I contact her? She must be worried frantic."

Jacob explained he'd written but not received a reply.

"Have you any idea why that might be? Before Christmas, your letters were full of her and how you were going to spend time with her. Did you two have a row?"

Jacob shook his head. "No. But something happened and I'm not sure how things stand between us now."

"Something happened?" Gran raised her eyebrows. "Is it anything you care to talk about?" She pulled up a chair and sat down.

Jacob wasn't sure he wanted to tell his grandmother, but keeping everything to himself hadn't worked. He'd mentally replayed everything he could remember and examined the events as closely as he could, but he hadn't spotted anything. Not that his memory was reliable, but perhaps Gran would see it through fresh eyes.

He'd tell her everything he could remember of that day, but not about the tablets Neville had given him. It was best she didn't find out about them. He'd have to admit he'd known he'd had a bad reaction to them but continued to take them anyway. Could he bear to see the disappointment and incredulity in her face at his lack of judgement? Could he explain how confused his thoughts had been lately? It sounded like an enormous excuse – even to his ears.

"I see," Gran said when he'd finished describing all he could remember. "So, you're saying Mrs Quinn turned up unexpectedly found you and Evelyn alone together?"

Jacob nodded. "But I was asleep. It had been so busy at work, I hadn't slept for... well, for days. All I remember is waking up to the sounds of shouting... And then Mrs Quinn screaming at me to leave."

"And what did Evelyn say?"

"Nothing. It was like she was under a spell. I'm not sure she even noticed I'd gone. I didn't want to leave but I thought if I stayed, I'd only make things worse."

"So, you walked out?"

He nodded.

"And what happened after that?"

He looked at her miserably. "After I came out of hospital, I did two shifts back-to-back. I might have done three... It was mayhem at work. I was waiting to hear from Evelyn to find out what had happened, but she never replied. I wanted to go and see her, but all leave was cancelled. I wondered if she'd gone back to London with her mother. I even wrote to Ada..." He paused and frowned. "At least I think I wrote to Ada. I know I was going to..."

Gran bit her lower lip. "Are you sure you didn't receive a reply from either Evelyn or Ada? I don't like to say this, Jake, but since your fall, you've been rather vague... In fact, are you sure you actually wrote to Evelyn at all?"

"Yes! Well, at least I think so. I can remember parts of the letters I wrote." He raised his eyes to the ceiling, willing the memories to return. "Although, I can't remember actually getting the words down on paper... But I must have done. I would have written. I would have..."

If only he could fill in the blanks in his memory.

Gran leaned forward and patted his hand. "You need to rest, love. You had a nasty blow to the head. It's no wonder you can't remember everything. But it'll come back. Shall I bring you writing paper? You can write to Evelyn and tell her where you are."

He nodded and thanked Gran, but he wasn't sure he'd write. If Evelyn had still wanted to see him, she'd have written. Perhaps she thought he'd failed her by not standing up to her mother. Or perhaps she'd been so intimidated by the woman, she didn't want to do anything further to displease her. Either explanation appeared to be unlikely, but he'd been surprised at Ada's reaction too. Her usual strength and good sense had disappeared when their mother had walked in. What power did Mrs Quinn have over both her daughters?

There was another reason he didn't think he'd write to Evelyn: he hadn't been honest with her and told her about his past. He didn't really deserve her. Maybe this was the price he had to pay for his guilt.

Jacob woke in the early hours, shaking and sweating. His thoughts swirled in his head, colours blazing and sounds blaring.

A REUNION IN PLOTLANDS

Too fast for him to process.

"Evelyn," he whispered, but it was as though someone had interfered with the dials on a wireless and turned the volume up to a scream.

The nightmares gradually subsided, leaving Jacob exhausted. But at least, the jitteriness and nerviness had gone.

Gran no longer needed to wipe his face with a cool cloth, nor try to soothe him during the night. "I think it's going to take you a little time to recover, Jake. You might be able to speed things up a little if you unburden yourself. There's a lot going on in your mind."

She'd provided him with a notebook, pen and instructions to commit his thoughts to paper.

His entire body ached, but in a few days, he'd be able to resume normal life – albeit painfully. He'd taken the last tablet before he'd set out for Portsmouth and now, he had no access to more.

Neither would he have taken them if he had. He was determined not to rely on them again. Ever.

Using them had been an act of selfishness – he knew that now – he'd thought they'd give him super-human powers and allow him to work harder and to have time to see Evelyn.

Instead, he'd been hospitalised twice, his work had been sub-standard and the last time he'd seen Evelyn, he'd fallen asleep.

And now, nothing was the same inside his head. Would it ever be again?

Glancing down at the pristine page again, he sighed.

He must write something before Gran returned, which he had no doubt would be soon.

But where to start? The blank paper mocked him with its emptiness and neat lines, waiting for him to write along them.

Should he start at the beginning? Perhaps that was best. Perhaps he should jot down whatever came into his mind. After all, no one was going to read it. Gran had said this was solely for his use. And even he didn't intend to read it afterwards., She'd said the act of writing everything down might help him to sort out the memories from the embellishments his mind had provided to fill in the gaps.

So many gaps.

His pen hovered over the page as he hesitated. He didn't want to write anything about the pills and yet they appeared to be central to everything. He vividly remembered the first time he'd gripped that cylindrical container in his fist and had tipped one of the tablets into his palm. Lots of people took them during this dreadful time of war. How else could people keep awake and do their duty? But Jacob had known they were not only keeping him alert but also making him sick.

Had he been trying to punish himself? Well, whatever the reason he'd taken them, it had been foolish and there'd been no point blaming the pills. Or Neville. It had been his choice.

Jacob stared at the empty page; still not a word or even a letter.

He had nothing written by the time Gran came back with a mug of tea and a biscuit. "Jake," she said reprovingly. "Just write anything. Make a start. A blank page is daunting but once you've started, you might find it flows. It's your book; you can cross out anything you like; it doesn't have to be neat. Just let the thoughts and memories tumble out. How about this? 'I am Jacob Leo Adam, son of Philip and Jessica Adam. Brother of David. My earliest memory is'..." She paused. "Start there and then move wherever your mind takes you."

She gave him a smile of encouragement and gently closed the door behind her as she left.

Jacob wrote those words down in his book, knowing it would

please Gran. He'd made a start. But now what? He closed his eyes and hunted through the darkness. Finally, he remembered a time when he'd been small, before David had been born, holding his parents' hands, as he dangled and swung between them. A tiny glimpse into the past. Meaningless on its own. Why had he remembered it?

Nothing of significance had happened other than that his parents had swung him, and they'd all laughed. Perhaps that was the point? The reason why the memory had endured, not because of what had happened, but because of how he'd felt. Happy and safe, although he'd been too young to recognise or to analyse the feelings. He'd have needed to have felt sad and afraid, to have appreciated how good that memory was. Most of his childhood had been happy and safe. He could write a book on all those times, but he knew that wasn't what Gran wanted.

She wanted him to remember those times when he felt neither happy nor safe.

He put the cap back on his pen and sipped the tea thoughtfully. Could he do this? It would mean reliving the excruciating embarrassment, his parents' disappointment, and his own fury at being seen in such a poor light. And, of course, there were so many images of Evelyn filling his mind. Her presence was all-consuming; it was hard to remember what had taken place and what he'd hoped for – and dreaded. What was real and what was imagined?

No. He couldn't do this – even if Gran expected it. But what was the alternative? At the moment, memories popped into his mind and floated like bubbles in the air, bursting as soon as he reached out to grab them. He couldn't organise his thoughts. Nor ensure they weren't false.

Writing everything down as best he could, would at least capture that bubble and fix it in place.

Haltingly at first until the words began to flow. He described his fault, his culpability.

By the time he'd finished an account of his time on board the ship, the taunting, his childish reaction, and subsequent realisation there'd been nothing wrong with being young and inexperienced, what remained of his tea was cold. He read what he'd written and looked at the scene through his parents' eyes, as best he could.

He groaned, knowing how disappointed they'd have been, and yet at the same time recognising they'd still loved him. He hadn't thought of that at the time. He'd just walked out.

Nevertheless, the humiliation on board the ship had made him stronger. He'd gone back on duty, and with strength and determination, he'd ignored the jeers and insults, brushing them away in a manner that he thought was probably more adult than he'd ever displayed before.

Eventually, the men had forgotten their game. By that time, they'd arrived off the coast of Italy.

Italy.

He put the cap back on the pen just as Gran knocked at his door. She smiled when she saw the writing in his book and nodded her approval.

"Why not have a rest? You mustn't overdo it."

He nodded. It had been harder than he'd thought it would be and yet a relief to get down on paper what had happened the last time he'd seen his parents. But after that, he'd gone back on duty aboard his ship and... No, he wasn't ready to dredge those thoughts out yet.

Perhaps tomorrow.

Chapter Thirty-Nine

Like lifting a rock and discovering so many wriggling, creeping, scuttling insects, the writing had unleashed a torrent of memories.

His dreams were disconnected, disjointed flashbacks floating in a sea of nothing.

Then in the early hours, he turned on his bedside light and started writing in his book, his heart beating wildly as he remembered his last moments in Italy.

Like a movie, he saw scenes of his voyage sailing from Messina in Sicily to the waters off Reggio di Calabria in the 'toe' of Italy.

The *boom, boom, boom* of the artillery.

The casualties.

The fallen.

Friends he'd never see again...

He'd been part of a detail of five men who'd gone into the village to look for suitable storage for supplies being unloaded from the ships. The Germans had retreated, and the village was deserted, so Jacob hadn't been worried.

Of course, there had still been the possibility of a lone German sniper, but his attention had mostly been on the intense heat and the swarms of flies that buzzed and tormented the men mercilessly.

To his right in a doorway, Jacob had spotted something blue; it was shining. He'd stopped and moved towards the building to investigate. The door had been open, and he'd given it a shove with his boot, but it was dark inside and one of the men had called at him to hurry.

Crouching, he'd seen the blue thing was a bead.

Nearby, more beads were scattered – a broken bracelet. Without thinking, he'd picked up the bead and had been about to retrieve the others when shouts had rung out and the scream of a Stuka dive bomber had drowned out everything.

He'd pressed himself against the side of the doorway and, with his hands over his ears, he'd prayed.

The bomb had fallen on the far side of the village. Beneath the doorway, Jacob had been protected, but the others in his detail had caught the full force of flying masonry and glass. Jacob alone had survived.

Saved by a blue bead. Not that he'd been unscathed. The bomb blast had hurled him backwards, and he'd passed out.

When he'd come round, he was being stretchered onto a ship with others who'd been wounded. They were on their way back to Sicily and from there, he'd been sent back to England and had begun to rebuild the strength in his back and legs in the Naval Hospital in Gosport.

The guilt had remained with him.

So senseless.

A blue bead had saved his life, but the others had died. If they hadn't waited for him, would they have been out of the bomb zone?

Might they have survived?

He should have died, too – he hadn't deserved to live. Why were good, useful people taken when he'd been spared?

Jacob slept late the next morning. He'd been up much of the night writing about his time in Italy. His guilt. His pain. At least once he'd fallen asleep, there had been no nightmares. In fact, no dreams at all. No explosions, no screams, just blessed embracing rest. Nothing.

He awoke to see Gran; her head poked around the door. Her face was filled with concern. He smiled at her and her features relaxed.

"All right, love?"

He nodded.

"I'd have left you to sleep, but you have a visitor. Somebody who works with you. Do you want to see her?"

It was only after Gran had gone that Jacob realised she'd said 'do you want to see *her*'. He'd assumed the visitor was Ronnie. Or perhaps a senior officer come to check on his progress.

Seconds later, Gran led Mary Reeves, the Wren who was always smiling, into the room. She was the one whom Ronnie had begged Jacob to take out for a drink. She greeted him and smiled shyly.

Gran's eyes darted back and forth between Jacob's face and Mary's. "Well, I'll bring tea," she said. She pulled out a chair and indicated the visitor should sit. Mary sat down, but when Gran had gone, she pulled the chair slightly closer to Jacob.

"I hope you don't mind me coming but I had a day's leave, so I thought I'd see how you were and bring everyone's best wishes. Ronnie said you're to stop shirking and get back to work. And he's borrowed your slide rule." She laughed. "And Neville says not to worry; everything's being looked after in your absence." She paused, her cheeks colouring.

What a strange message for Neville to have sent. In fact, it was surprising he'd noticed Jacob was missing at all. Perhaps he'd had to cover Jacob's work?

Mary frowned slightly and Jacob had the impression she was desperately trying to think of something to say to fill the silence. Or she had something in mind but wasn't sure she wanted to say it?

"Is Harry over the 'flu yet?" he asked, also aware of the silence and wondering how long she was going to stay. She didn't feel at ease. Neither did he.

"Yes... And Lily. She's had it, too."

He nodded. Lily who? He didn't know anyone called Lily.

Still, Mary appeared to be deep in thought, then taking a breath, she said, "Getting back to Neville... Just in case I wasn't clear. I think..." her face reddened further. "I think he was referring to that girl."

"Which girl?" Was she still talking about the Lily he didn't know?

Mary looked down and studied her hands. They lay on her lap, the thumbs circling each other. "The one who lives in Dunton. Isn't she the one you were seeing...? For a while."

It took a second for the words to filter through into his brain. "Wait! Are you saying Neville has been seeing Evelyn?"

Mary jumped at the intensity of his reply. "Err... Evelyn. Yes, that's her name. I believe that's what he said."

Was it possible? He tried to breathe in, but it felt as though a great weight was crushing his chest, squeezing all the air from his lungs.

"Yes," said Mary with certainty. She looked him in the eyes. "Yes, he said he's been to see her several times."

"How do you know?" His voice was a whisper.

"Because he told Ronnie, and I overheard. The other day he was even complaining because his car got a puncture down one of those unmade roads where she lives."

The sound of cups rattling outside the door preceded Gran arriving with their tea on a tray. Her face, once again, was troubled.

"Well," she said with what Jacob recognised as forced cheeriness. "I hope you're bringing much-needed good news, Miss Reeves. It wouldn't do to tire the patient."

Mary's cheeks flared once again. When Gran had gone, Mary gave him an account of what had been happening at work. "And you'll never guess what. Ronnie and Gladys have been out together twice. He's really sweet on her, but I'm not so sure how Gladys feels about him. That's a shame, isn't it? It's always sad when one person is keener on the other... I think Gladys still holds a torch for Neville. But his attentions are elsewhere..."

But Jacob wasn't listening.

So that was why Evelyn hadn't written – she'd found somebody new – Neville Harrington-Wade.

"So, I was wondering," Mary said, staring at her twiddling thumbs again, "when you're well... Maybe one time when you're not busy... We could go to the pictures together... Perhaps with Ronnie and Gladys. They wouldn't mind if we went with them. I asked Gladys and she said it would be fine." Mary looked up; her eyes wide with hope.

"It sounds like romance is blossoming all over the place, in my absence." Jacob tried to keep the bitter edge from his voice. But he deliberately didn't answer Mary's request. Evelyn may have found someone new, but he wasn't going to move on so fast. If at all...

"It would be nice if you could come. I'm sure you'd have fun now that... Well, that is, now Neville is seeing Evelyn."

Well, she was certainly persistent. And very tactless. Jacob didn't know what to say. Had she come all this way to make sure he knew about Evelyn and to ask him out? It seemed unbelievable. If not, she'd used up her precious leave on bringing him a few good wishes – and some bad news.

Thankfully, Gran reappeared and stood expectantly, holding open the door after picking up the tea tray. Mary stood and followed her out of the room. She wished Jacob well, saying, "I look forward to seeing you when you're back. Perhaps we could discuss that other matter then?"

Jacob smiled politely. He couldn't speak for the lump in his throat. Visions of Evelyn holding silk stockings from Neville's seemingly endless supply, and Neville holding Evelyn, seared into his brain. No, that wasn't fair. Evelyn wasn't one of those girls who was only interested in a chap for what he could give her.

But then what did he know? He barely knew her at all. He'd thought she was the woman for him. The one person with whom he could connect. Another example of his overactive imagination?

Well, he needed a fresh start away from Essex. Perhaps he'd ask for a transfer to Portsmouth where he'd been heading for training. The chief engineer had suggested Jacob transfer there, but he hadn't pursued it, wanting to stay in Chelmsford to be near Evelyn. Now, the further he was from her, the better.

Chapter Forty

As soon as Lydia Marks had shown Mary Reeves out, she rushed back upstairs.

"That's a long way to come to say hello. She's got her eyes on you, hasn't she, Jake?"

Her beloved grandson nodded slowly.

"And let me guess, you're not interested?"

Jacob shook his head. "It's worse than that," he said. "She also let slip that Evelyn is seeing someone at work."

"Let slip? Huh! I think that's unlikely. It's probably what she came to tell you, hoping you'd switch your attention to her. Do you think she might have made it up?"

"I doubt it. That would be typical of Harrington-Wade. He sees something he likes, and he reaches out and takes it."

"But Evelyn would have had a say in the matter." Lydia wanted to shake him. She longed to say, 'Oh, come on, Jake, where's your spirit? Fight for the girl!' but she must tread softly.

"Oh, he can be very persuasive. He's handsome. Always has lots of black-market goods that he gives out."

Lydia sighed. Jacob was too kind. Too good and too easily hurt. "And you think Evelyn would be tempted by presents?"

Jacob sighed. "No, I suppose not. But it doesn't matter, Gran. It's over. I have to accept that. I must concentrate on getting well and back to work; that'll take my mind off everything."

Lydia tugged at her lower lip. "Sometimes, Jake, taking your mind off things and ignoring them just delays their resolution. Sometimes you need to bring them out, give them an airing and deal with them."

"Ah," he said, tapping the notebook that was next to him on the bed.

"Exactly." Lydia wasn't sure it was helping him, but it couldn't do any harm, surely? He felt things too deeply. He always had, even as a little boy.

She wouldn't pry but she suspected he felt guilty about the dreadful bomb attack that had robbed them both of their family. It was ridiculous, of course. How could he be to blame for his parents not taking David to the shelter? But typical Jacob, taking on the guilt of the world.

Jacob sighed. "Well, your idea seems to be working, Gran. I've written down everything and it's helping straighten my thoughts out a bit."

"Do you need to talk anything through, Jake?"

"I think I might, Gran, if you don't mind."

Lydia pulled the chair closer to his bed. "Tell me all about it, son."

Chapter Forty-One

♥

Evelyn wiped her hands on her apron as she opened the front door. Once again, there was Neville Harrington-Wade on the doorstep.

He was certainly persistent. Some women might be flattered at the attention, but Evelyn had worked out what sort of man he was, and she simply wasn't interested.

He smiled, and bringing his hand out from behind his back, he held out some silk stockings. At the sight of them dangling over his palm, her heart felt as though it had stopped, remembering Jacob all those months ago on Mother's doorstep holding up a sock.

"Hello, lovely, Evelyn. I saw these and couldn't stop thinking about you." He stepped forward to hand them to her, but she raised hers to stop him.

"Thank you, Neville, that's very kind, but once again, I'm afraid I can't accept."

Surprise flickered across his face. It must be rare for anyone to turn down his bribes. For that was what they were, Evelyn knew.

"Are you denying a chap the pleasure of spoiling such a beautiful woman?"

Evelyn sighed. "I'm merely saying, no thank you. I'm very grateful, but I don't want your gifts. I think I made that clear on the other occasions you've called. I know you're still seeing my friend's sister, Val. And anyway..." She stopped there. It would be rude to tell a man who was gazing at you with adoring eyes, and holding a gift in his hand, that she couldn't abide his face.

It wasn't that there was anything wrong with his face. Indeed, he was a handsome man. And he could be charming. But he wasn't Jacob.

Unbidden, a voice inside piped up. If you don't forget Jacob and start going out soon, you'll be an old maid. What harm could it do to accept his gifts and go out with him?

But she was too empty and too tired to consider further complications.

When she'd first arrived in Dunton fresh from Mother's house and influence, she knew little about men. The women at the telephone exchange in London had spoken about their husbands and sweethearts, but it had all been so remote from her world, she hadn't taken much notice. But some of what they'd said must have gone in, and since she'd been in Dunton, she'd paid more attention to Phyllis and the others where she worked. She knew about this type of man now, and she recognised he wasn't interested in her. He merely wanted to satisfy himself. She probably represented a challenge.

"Come for a spin and we can talk about it. I'll take you wherever you want to go..."

She smiled sweetly. "Thank you, but no. And please don't come back." She couldn't make it plainer than that. As she shut the door, he stepped forward and put his foot in the gap.

"If you're still hankering for your romantic hero, he's gone." Neville's eyes were now icy.

"Gone? Gone where?" The words tripped over themselves in her haste to find out.

Neville smiled, stepping away from the door, certain he'd got her interest, and she wouldn't slam the door on him. He chuckled and raised his eyebrows in a knowing look. "So, you *are* still interested in him? How much do you want to know where he's gone?"

Had he just said that to gain her interest? Or had Jacob really gone? And if so, where?

Does it matter?

The answer was no, it didn't matter. If he'd gone and not told her, then he obviously had no interest in her at all.

"So, how about drinks tonight? I could pick you up and we could discuss it then… I might be able to find out a little more."

Although she was desperate to know, Evelyn couldn't bear the thought of spending any more time in this man's company than she had already. She shook her head. "That's very kind but, I've already told you, no, thank you."

His nostrils flared. He'd obviously run out of patience. "Well, if you must know, he's gone to Portsmouth. Transfer. He won't be back."

"Thank you," said Evelyn. She shut the door. And turning, she leaned against it, tears trickling down her cheeks. Outside, she heard Neville's footsteps recede as he walked down the path. The gate swung and slammed shut.

Minutes later, the engine started, and the car screeched off.

Chapter Forty-Two

The conversation with Gran had been thought-provoking. Of course, she'd known he'd visited his family prior to the bomb blast that had killed them. It had been his birthday and she'd known he'd had leave. But to his shame, he'd never told her what had happened during his visit nor why his parents had been so disappointed with him. It was yet another reason for his guilt. But it had been time to tell all. He'd go to Portsmouth and start anew amongst people who didn't know him. But first, he had to own up to his grandmother.

To his amazement, she hadn't blamed him. "Each person has an allotted time on earth, Jake. I firmly believe that. You had nothing to do with your family's tragic end. Your mother hated going into the air raid shelter. I know she often ignored the warnings and stayed in the house. A stray bomb could have fallen on any of those occasions. It just happened to fall on that evening. And as for what you call your 'utter and unforgivable foolishness', well, I don't suppose there's a person alive who hasn't been young and foolish at some time. You are a fine young man. Your parents would have been so very proud of you."

She'd wiped away a tear and continued. "And as for the matter in Italy, again, the time was up for the men you were with. You were destined to live. And to do anything other than to make the most of your life now would be a travesty."

She'd patted his hand. "War is a terrible thing, Jake. But even so, some men thrive. Other, more sensitive men – those who think deeply about things – don't fare so well. All those senseless deaths were out of your hands. It's time you let it all go. I hope you believe me."

The more Jacob thought about Gran's words, the more the enormous weight that had been bearing down on him lightened. And her idea of writing everything down and clearing his head appeared to be working. Not that making a few notes and having one conversation would erase the wretched thoughts from his brain, but it was a start. And best of all, he didn't feel so isolated or alone.

He picked up his pen.

Evelyn. He must put his thoughts about her to rest. He'd start with all the good things about her and hopefully, the more he wrote, the more he'd remember.

The words flowed. He pinned his memories down on paper, recording the time and place. The first occasion he'd looked into her eyes on that Sunday when he'd called at her house in Barnes Street, Stepney. Holding her in his arms at the dance before Christmas. Then, walking her home that star-spangled evening along the frosty avenues of Plotlands and their first kiss.

That dreadful occasion in Ada's cottage when her mother had screamed at him to leave.

His thoughts turned once again to the time he'd told Evelyn about his stupidity onboard his ship. She'd appeared sympathetic at first, although less so when he'd explained how he'd argued with his parents and then walked out, leaving them to their deaths. Then, he'd described to her what had happened in Italy and had registered the disappointment on her face. She'd opened the fabric wrapping around the blue bead and... And what? Oh, why couldn't he remember?

Write it down. It'll come to you.

He held his pen over the notebook but there were no words. The images in his mind shifted. The conversation had surely taken place in Ada's house. But where and when? He couldn't remember a time when they'd been alone for long enough for him to have explained.

No, of course he hadn't told her in Ada's house; the conversation had taken place when Evelyn had accompanied him to the main road while he wheeled his bicycle.

Hadn't it?

But no, there hadn't been enough time to explain everything during that short walk.

So, when had he told her?

Indeed, *had* he told her?

Increasingly, it appeared he hadn't. That conversation simply hadn't taken place at all. He'd imagined telling her, but it appeared he'd never spoken those words.

She didn't know about his parents or what had happened to him in Italy. She hadn't looked at him in disgust. It had simply been his imagination.

Jacob wasn't sure whether to feel dismay he hadn't owned up to her, or relief Evelyn hadn't expressed her repugnance of him.

Or was his mind playing tricks on him again? Had the conversation taken place but had been so painful his memory had selectively deleted it?

After all, if he hadn't told her and she hadn't been disappointed with him, why hadn't she replied to his letters?

Had he inadvertently offended her? He searched his memory for what he'd written, but nothing came. Surely, he should be able to remember what he'd said. Then, a dreadful thought. He drew in a deep breath and held it, listening to the sound of the blood pumping through his ears. Perhaps he hadn't written to her at all? Was that possible? The air rushed out of him in a groan.

But he definitely remembered sitting at his bench after a shift writing her a letter. Yes! He could even see his words in his mind's eye.

And did you post it?

Well, of course he'd posted it.

Hadn't he?

But try as he might, he couldn't remember dropping it in the post box.

Was it possible he'd been so tired and confused while taking those tablets, he hadn't actually written to her at all?

That would be unforgivable.

If only he could walk, he'd get on a train right now. He'd go to Laindon, find Evelyn and ask. It might be too late for them to get together now Neville had claimed her, but at least he could explain and apologise. And anyway, he wanted to know how she was.

Then it came to him. The blue bead in its fabric wrapping had been in the drawer of his bedside table. His memories of him giving it to Evelyn changed each time he inspected them. The more he thought about it, the more he doubted he'd given it to her at all.

Well, there was one way to find out. If it wasn't in his drawer, he'd given it to Evelyn, and those memories of him telling her about his brush with death in Italy and her disgust were true. And that would explain why she hadn't contacted him again.

However, if the bead was in his drawer, then he couldn't trust his recent memories and the conversation hadn't taken place at all. And if it hadn't, then it was possible that his memories of having written to her were false, too.

If she hadn't heard from him, she might believe he didn't care enough to find out how she was. Not that it mattered to their relationship. That was over. But he wanted to understand what had happened and to apologise.

He focused on the bead. It flashed blue in his mind's eye. The concentric circles on one side staring at him like an eye.

He hastily wrote a letter to Mrs Shipley explaining what had happened to him and where he was. It was possible no one had told her he hadn't arrived safely in Portsmouth. He'd paid his rent in advance until his return from training, but now, he didn't know how long it would be before he'd be back.

He also requested she look in his bedside table drawer for the piece of fabric she had once given him and described how something small was wrapped inside it and tied up with a blue ribbon. Please could she confirm that little package was there as swiftly as possible?

Chapter Forty-Three

Lydia put Jacob's letter to his landlady along with a letter that she'd written in her basket. She'd go to the post office first, before she joined the queue at the shops. One of the good things about having so many people staying with her in the house was that the tasks could be shared.

Sidney, a quiet bachelor who'd recently almost died when his home had been bombed, was in the garden checking over the winter cabbages and sowing a few broad beans.

Marjorie, an elderly widow who'd been with Lydia for several months, was looking after the baby of one of the other guests. The baby's mother, Eileen, was a young woman, recently widowed – her husband had lost his life fighting in North Africa. Eileen was queuing at the butchers for some meat for the household. She'd certainly be there a while and was grateful for the chance to gossip with the other women without having to comfort a fractious baby. Everyone helped out.

Eileen usually did most of the shopping, but on that day, there was one item Lydia wanted to buy herself. First, she posted Jacob's letter. He'd been quite agitated about it, and when Lydia had looked at the address, she'd been puzzled. She'd expected it to be addressed to Evelyn. Instead, it was to Mrs D. Shipley, his landlady in Hailcombe Cross.

If only that wretched Wren hadn't come and bothered Jacob with her tales.

Still, Lydia had done as Jacob had asked and now, on to her important task. She joined the queue outside Graham's Bakery, and with her hand in her basket protectively over her letter, she waited. Finally, she reached the head of the queue and smiled at the pleasant young man who usually served.

"Good morning, madam, what can I get you?" he asked cheerily.

She asked for a loaf and as she handed over a sixpence and three pennies, she held out the letter. "Thank you, Mr Quinn, and I would appreciate it if you could give this to your sister Evelyn, please."

The man looked first at Lydia, then down at the letter in surprise.

"I would appreciate a reply as swiftly as possible, please," she said.

"Do you know my sister, madam?" He regarded her suspiciously, through narrow eyes.

"I do not. My name is Lydia Marks… Jacob Adam's grandmother."

"Ah," he said, crisply. "The man who left my sister without any word of explanation."

It was now Lydia's turn to be confused. She shook her head. "No, no! I think you'll find it was the other way round."

"Get a move on, will yer! I've still got to queue at the butchers," the woman behind Lydia said loudly.

"I'll be taking lunch in…" Mr Quinn checked his watch. "In twenty minutes. Perhaps we could have a cuppa in the café opposite. There are obviously matters we need to discuss?"

Chapter Forty-Four

Gordon led Mrs Marks to a table in the corner of the bustling café, and once they had been served, they eyed each other warily over the tops of their steaming mugs.

Gordon spoke first. "The obvious question is, why didn't your grandson write to Evelyn, Mrs Marks?"

She gnawed her lower lip. "I understand he believed he had written to her."

Gordon frowned for an instant before she continued. "You have to understand, Mr Quinn, Jacob has been working extremely hard since he last saw your sister. In fact, he recently collapsed with exhaustion."

Gordon could see there was more to it than that, but for the moment, at least she'd provided a reason.

"But that doesn't explain why your sister didn't write to Jacob," Mrs Marks said, regaining some of her resolve. "The least she could have done is to let him know it's over."

"Our mother recently died," Gordon said. "We've all been dealing with that, and I'm afraid Evelyn has borne the brunt of it."

Mrs Mark's face fell. "I am so sorry to hear that, Mr Quinn. Then it is completely understandable. Please accept my condolences." Her earlier self-assurance had been shaken.

"Thank you." Gordon hesitated. Usually, he wouldn't discuss family matters with a stranger, but if Evelyn and Jacob got back together, the truth would come out. Better that it emerged now.

"But perhaps I need to explain, Mrs Marks... There's more to it than that. I won't pretend anyone in our family has been grief stricken. Our mother was a... complicated person and she made our lives difficult. Evelyn's most of all. If Evelyn didn't write, it was probably because she was ashamed."

Mrs Marks looked up sharply. "Ashamed of what, may I ask? Ashamed of her mother dying?"

Gordon swallowed. He explained about Mother's visit and her revelation. "I know Evelyn was afraid Jacob was shocked. She was waiting for him to write and hopefully let her know how he felt about her unfortunate beginnings."

Mrs Mark's brows drew together, and she pinched her lower lip between forefinger and thumb as she considered. "I'd be very surprised if that had changed Jacob's opinion of Evelyn," she said slowly and thoughtfully. "Of course, I may be wrong, but that doesn't sound like Jacob at all."

"I understand your grandson had a wonderful childhood and that upholding family values is very important to him. Evelyn wondered if perhaps her... er... circumstances went against those ideals."

"Ah," said Mrs Marks, "I'm afraid there's more to it than simply a celebration of family life." She tapped her lower lip thoughtfully. "I appreciate your candour, Mr Quinn, and I feel I can trust you, so I'm going to explain a little about what happened."

Gordon listened as she told him about the guilt Jacob had carried. "My grandson is a kind and honourable man. He feels things deeply and has shouldered more guilt than necessary. I knew he'd been wounded in Italy, but only just discovered exactly what happened. He survived. The others in his party died. Poor Jacob felt that keenly too and blamed himself."

"I see." Gordon put down his mug. "That is very sad. We have two people carrying more than their fair share of worry and guilt."

"Yes, indeed. Perhaps two people who could have healed each other?"

Mrs Marks shook her head sadly. "Although I fear it's too late. I understand your sister has moved on and is now seeing somebody else."

Gordon spluttered on his tea. "Not as far as I know. I received a letter from Ada this morning and there was no mention of another man."

They peered at each other over the tops of their mugs.

Mrs Marks pinched her lower lip again. "Interesting. Jacob had a visitor from work. A young Wren who told him someone had driven over to Dunton on various occasions to see her."

"Driven? Ah, that would be the chap with the double-barrelled name and the Rolls Royce. The man Evelyn keeps sending away. Well, I can assure you, if that's the man you mean. She's not seeing him."

"Really? That is interesting." Mrs Marks laced her fingers together. "It seems to me we have two people who belong together. And we have all the information we need to get those two people together."

Gordon considered her words and then nodded. "Yet, I'm not sure if others should meddle. My mother did her best to interfere in my relationship and before that, in Ada's. She was acting in her own interest with terrible consequences for Ada. Thankfully, my marriage is strong, but it's still taken its toll. If we step in, we wouldn't be doing it for our benefit, but it would be interference, nonetheless. Let's give it further thought and see what develops."

Chapter Forty-Five

Mrs Shipley must have acted immediately. The small package arrived two days after Gran had posted Jacob's letter. Along with a message, wishing him well, was a small fabric-wrapped, ribbon-tied parcel.

Jacob pulled off the ribbon and opened the package to find the dazzling blue bead. He blinked, expecting the sight of it to whisk his mind back to that far off day in Italy, but it merely sat on the fabric on his palm. He rolled it until the concentric circles stared up at him.

It had saved his life, but it had been unconnected to his comrades' deaths. If Gran was correct – and he wanted to believe her – their time had been up on that awful day, but he'd been allowed longer to live.

The bead now represented hope. Its unblinking stare looked right through him.

He hadn't explained to Evelyn, and she hadn't rejected him. Well, at least now he knew that. Sadly, it was too late. He'd lost her.

Then all the more reason not to waste any more time. As soon as he got back to work, he'd request a transfer. The war wouldn't last forever.

He'd build a new life. Peacetime world needed the developments he'd been working on, detecting planes and ships using electromagnetic waves. Direction finding at microwave frequencies had given them the advantage of better identification of enemy craft and better directional accuracy. What sort of uses could those technologies be used for in the future? Well, he would find work looking into those possibilities.

Chapter Forty-Six

Lydia had given the matter much thought during the days following her meeting in the café. Mr Quinn had probably been right about not interfering. She certainly didn't want to risk causing more trouble. And yet... didn't her Jacob deserve to know there had been a good reason why Evelyn might not have written?

The poor girl had been forced to come to terms with her illegitimacy after so many years. That would have been enough of a shock without shortly after suffering the death of the woman she'd believed was her mother. However troubled the relationship had been, a death in the family was always difficult.

The more Lydia thought about it, the more she was certain. Jake deserved to know Mrs Quinn had died, and she expected he'd be keen to send his condolences.

Something puzzled her, though. Jacob hadn't mentioned the shocking news Mrs Quinn had delivered to Evelyn. Had he not mentioned it out of respect for Evelyn's feelings? That was possible. Or maybe he hadn't thought it important enough to mention. Still, it was strange. Was it possible he didn't know about her illegitimacy?

But he would definitely write to express his condolences, and who could tell what might come after that?

She hardly dared to admit she was hoping a letter from Jacob might bring the two together. No, she wouldn't allow that thought room in her head.

Nevertheless, wouldn't it be lovely if it happened?

Gordon's advice to Mrs Quinn had been that they ought not interfere. She'd agreed, but the last time she'd come into the bakery, she'd told him Jacob now planned to transfer to another part of Britain.

Surely Evelyn would want to know. Would telling her be considered interfering? Gordon decided to talk it over with Ada the next time he took Sarah and Tommy to see her. Sarah had been pleading with him to move out to Essex now she was expecting again, and they'd made a few trips to Plotlands to look at the area.

The idea of moving to the country was appealing, although he didn't like the idea of letting Mr Graham down at the bakery. But surely baking bread in one place was as good as another? People had to eat, wherever they were.

He'd need to find a job first... But it wouldn't hurt to take Sarah and Tommy on a visit at the weekend and explore the possibility of moving. Ada and Evelyn would love to see them. And if he should accidentally drop the information that Jacob would be moving away soon to Ada and possibly a few other things that Mrs Marks had told him... Well, Ada would know what to do.

Chapter Forty-Seven

Evelyn had been thrilled when Gordon, Sarah and Tommy had visited and suggested they might soon be neighbours. Sarah had fallen in love with Dunton. Tommy had never seen so much open space and he was so excited, running back and forth in Ada's garden; he didn't even cry when he tripped over a tree root and grazed both knees. In no time, he'd even made a friend in the cottage next door and was soon running about in the neighbour's garden.

Gordon was undecided, but usually, Sarah got her way, so it was probably only a matter of time before they moved to Dunton.

Evelyn could see Ada was pleased, although preoccupied – perhaps even worried. She'd been jittery all day after receiving a letter that morning. Evelyn hadn't recognised the writing on the envelope and Ada hadn't spoken about it.

But Evelyn had forgotten once Gordon and his family had arrived. She'd chatted to Sarah about the child she was expecting and had even walked along the avenue, looking at the two empty cottages. Meanwhile, Gordon and Ada had kept an eye on Tommy in the garden and had appeared to be deep in conversation when Sarah and Evelyn had returned from their walk.

"Aren't you keen on Gordon moving to Dunton, Ada?" Evelyn asked when he'd left. "You looked so serious when you were talking in the garden."

"Oh yes! Of course, I'm keen on them moving here. How lovely it would be to have them living nearby." Ada's face lit up and it was obvious that wasn't what was troubling her. "But I... I think Gordon's worried about finding work and I know Sarah is anxious about leaving her friends behind."

"Sarah? She didn't say that to me. In fact, she couldn't wait to come."

"Yes, but..." Ada paused, as if groping for something to say. "Friends are so important..." she finished, then she looked away.

Strange. Ada obviously had something on her mind. Sarah was a friendly girl who would have no trouble making friends.

"In fact," Ada said quickly, "I have a new friend."

Evelyn recognised Ada had changed the subject. Well, if something was bothering her about Gordon's move, she'd tell Evelyn eventually. It was best to simply follow the conversation.

"A new friend?" Evelyn asked. Could she mean Mr Farrell? Ada had spoken of him fondly on several occasions lately.

"In fact, I'd very much like you to come with me to my friend's. Perhaps tomorrow?"

"I... er, well, yes."

Ada had hurried into the kitchen and Evelyn didn't pursue the matter.

It was obviously sensitive.

But how marvellous it would be if Ada and Mr Farrell became friends. More than friends, even. Ada deserved to find happiness.

Perhaps Ada's strange mood was more to do with her new friend than Gordon's move. Well, Evelyn would find out more the following day.

The next morning, when they arrived at the bus stop, Evelyn was surprised. "We're going by bus?"

Ada nodded.

"But I thought Mr Farrell lived in Laindon."

"He does. But we're not going to Mr Farrell's house." Ada avoided Evelyn's gaze and turned to peer down the road for the bus.

"So, where are we going?" Perhaps Mr Farrell was meeting them out somewhere.

"Oh, nowhere you've been before." Ada waved her hand vaguely as if pointing the way.

Why was Ada so defensive?

It was most unlike her. She wasn't just being defensive, she was on the verge of irritation, and Evelyn wondered if it was too late to walk home and leave her to it.

But perhaps she was being unfair. Ada rarely asked her to do anything, and this obviously meant a lot to her.

Was she worried Evelyn would resent her happiness because Jacob had left her? Surely, she wouldn't believe that.

Well, Evelyn would simply have to show Ada she was thrilled she had a friend or if it turned out Mr Farrell was more than a friend, then she was delighted about that, too. To resent Ada's happiness after all she'd been through, would be unforgivable.

Evelyn was still examining her thoughts when the bus appeared around the bend. She'd simply stop asking questions and do exactly as Ada wanted. She wouldn't risk upsetting her and when they arrived at wherever they were meeting Mr Farrell, Evelyn would be extremely polite.

As they found seats, Evelyn had a thought. Perhaps they weren't going to meet Mr Farrell. Was it possible Ada had a different friend? Was that why she was behaving so oddly? She'd seemed rather on edge after reading that letter earlier. Well, Evelyn would simply have to wait and see.

Soon the bus was travelling along roads Evelyn didn't recognise and the fields and woods gave no clue to their destination. Eventually, the bus driver pulled up at a crossroads in what appeared to be the middle of nowhere and, to Evelyn's surprise, Ada indicated they should alight.

"This way," Ada said, setting off along a lane flanked on either side by woods.

After a while, Evelyn wondered if Ada was lost. They'd walked a long way without any sign of a village, and she was about to ask where they were when she glanced at Ada. Her jaw was clamped resolutely, and Evelyn guessed she was in pain after such a long walk. The words died on her lips. There didn't appear to be any doubt in Ada's expression, so they must be on the right road and if it was worth it to Ada, then wherever they were and whatever they were about to do, was worth it to Evelyn.

Finally, they reached the edge of a village and through clenched teeth, Ada said, "We're here." She opened the gate leading to a large white house and hurried up the path.

Ada knocked at the door and a tall, well-built woman with curly, grey hair opened up a few seconds later. Her face lit up and she smiled delightedly when she saw Ada.

"You got the letter, then?" she asked.

"Yes, thank you." Ada said. The gratitude in her voice was obvious.

Was this Ada's friend? Evelyn was slightly disappointed. She'd been so sure they'd be going to see Mr Farrell. But perhaps this woman was related to him. A sister, perhaps?

"Doris, this is my daughter, Evelyn. Evelyn, this is Doris," Ada said with no other explanation.

Doris wiped her hands on her apron and shook Evelyn's hand. "Oh, my dear, how pleased I am to meet you." Her enthusiasm appeared to grow. "Yes, indeed, so pleased to see you. I've heard so much about you. Come in, come in."

She ushered them into her living room and, after taking their coats and hats, she ensured they were seated in front of her fire. A roaring fire, Evelyn saw. There was obviously no shortage of coal in this house.

Once she was sure they were comfortable, Doris held out her hands towards Evelyn who looked at her in confusion. "Indulge an old lady, would you, my dear? May I read your palms?"

Evelyn held out her hands. This was altogether the strangest day she'd ever passed. She glanced at Ada, but instead of the disapproval and consternation she'd expected to see, there was eagerness and respect.

Doris narrowed her eyes and peered at Evelyn's palms, nodding and making mewing noises of satisfaction. Finally, she raised a finger as if to ask Evelyn to wait and turned and left the room. Footsteps rang out on the wooden staircase going upstairs and seconds later, down again.

"Let's have tea," Doris said as she entered the parlour. "Ada, dear, I'm just in the middle of baking; perhaps you'd help me get the tea?"

Evelyn rose to help. Ada would appreciate a rest in front of the fire. "Shall I hel—"

"No!" both women said sharply. The force of their words almost knocked Evelyn back into her chair.

Surprisingly, Ada almost leapt to her feet without wincing and hurried after Doris into the kitchen. "I'll help Doris, Evelyn. You warm yourself in front of the fire."

Evelyn sighed and looked around at the ornaments and trinkets that covered every surface. Her eyes alighted on an ornate frame that surrounded a sepia image of a soldier from the last dreadful war. Perhaps that was why Ada and Doris had become friends, they were of a similar age and would have experienced the same horrors of their men at war. Perhaps Doris had lost someone, too.

The sound of a man clearing his throat behind her brought her back to the present. Perhaps it was the man in the photograph? Doris's husband? Her brother? Mr Farrell?

Evelyn looked up, expecting a man who was old enough to have served in the Great War. The blood drained from her face, and a strangled sound came from her mouth.

The man at the door was Jacob.

His face was as shocked as hers.

Chapter Forty-Eight

Jacob stepped back slightly, his eyes wide in surprise and embarrassment. "M... Mrs Shipley asked me to come down, I..."

So, he hadn't known she was there. She blinked rapidly and stared at him in silence. So many thoughts jostled for prominence. She couldn't make sense of anything.

Jacob appeared to recover first, and she saw the shock turn to pleasure. Was she imagining it because that was what she wanted to see?

He smiled, that lopsided smile that made her stomach somersault, and a strangled cry came from her throat again.

Jacob walked towards her. "I'm so pleased to see you."

She stood up quickly, her head so light, she wondered if she was going to faint. "Are you? Pleased, I mean." Her voice was a whispered croak.

"Oh yes, I am," he said, so fervently she couldn't doubt he meant it.

Then Jacob stopped. The pleasure in his face died, leaving a blank

– perhaps even a haunted look. "But, of course, I understand you have someone else in your life now." His voice was formal. Polite. The hands he'd extended towards her dropped to his sides.

"No," she said, stepping forward to reduce the space between them. "There's no one. I have no one in my life. There's no one at all!" The words came out in a rush, and he jumped at her vehemence.

She groaned inwardly, silently chiding herself for her lack of dignity. Jacob was behaving formally. She must do the same.

"Harrington-Wade?" His eyes drilled into her. "I understand you've been seeing him."

"Harrington-Wade?" She was aghast. How could he think she'd been seeing that dreadful man? "Neville Harrington-Wade is a nuisance. He's arrived uninvited at Ada's cottage on several occasions, and each time I've asked him to leave. He just doesn't listen." She smiled mischievously. "Although the last time he came, I told him in rather unladylike language that I never wanted to see his face again. I suspect after that he might have got the message. But who knows? That man seems incapable of taking no for an answer."

"He can be very persuasive," Jacob said, his brows knitted and his eyes slightly narrowed.

Didn't he believe her? It was more of a question than a statement. Was he testing her?

She held her head high and looked directly into his eyes. "He can be very persuasive if you're open to persuasion. But I'm not. If you're referring to his seemingly limitless supply of silk stockings and chocolate, I turned them away. The man is repulsive. I didn't like him the first time I met him and each time I see him, I dislike him more."

Hope now lit Jacob's eyes and he stepped forward an inch. "I wasn't sure... It's just that... well... one of the Wrens I work with told me you were seeing him."

Evelyn drew back slightly and crossed her arms over her chest. "Ah," she said, "that would be Mary... Now, what did Neville say her name was? Something beginning with 'R'. Yes, Reeves. Mary Reeves, your new lady friend." Well, two could play at that game. How dare he question her about Neville Harrington-Wade when he'd moved on with another woman?

"My new...?" Jacob stepped back in surprise. "I don't have a new lady friend, Evelyn... I...I've only ever wanted you."

She stared at him. He truly was shocked, and his voice was filled with sincerity.

"But Neville said..." Evelyn paused.

Forget what Neville Harrington-Wade had said. Jacob had just told her he only wanted her. Could that be true?

"In that case, I think there's a lot we need to discuss," she said.

"There is, Evelyn, but we can speed things up considerably if you like. Just one question will do it."

She nodded.

"Do you still have feelings for me? Do you still want me?" He winced as if waiting for her to reject him.

"That's two questions," she said with a smile. "But the answers are yes, yes and yes!"

Jacob tipped his head back and closed his eyes. She saw his Adam's Apple dip as if swallowing a lump in this throat. When he opened his eyes again, the anxious lines around them had gone. The brown depths were filled with longing.

He closed the gap between them and held out his arms to her. She stepped into them, and he held her tight, his cheek against hers. A tiny sound came from his mouth and caressed her skin. It was a sigh of relief.

Evelyn squeezed her eyes tightly shut and clasped her hands together behind Jacob's back. She breathed in deeply, filling her nostrils with the scent of him. How right this felt to be in his arms.

A voice whispered inside. This was too good to be true. It had happened so fast; surely it would be over just as rapidly? Evelyn held Jacob tighter, trying to blot out the voice of doubt. If she clung to him in silence, then what could go wrong?

Please, she thought, don't say anything. Don't spoil this moment by letting words come between us.

Chapter Forty-Nine

Jacob inhaled slowly, his breath ragged with relief, with joy, with fear.

She still had feelings for him.

This was so fragile – one wrong word and it might force them apart again. But now he knew she wasn't interested in Harrington-Wade, and indeed, had never been. And she knew he didn't have anyone either.

They both wanted each other.

Surely, they could work anything else out? He caressed the back of her head, allowing his fingertips to slide into her hair, relishing the sensuality of it.

Determination rushed through him. He loved this woman, and he would not allow anything to come between them if she still wanted him.

The kitchen door opened a crack, creaking as softly as a whisper. Jacob glanced up, and guessed Mrs Shipley was peering out at them. As reluctant as he was to let go of Evelyn, they couldn't stay there forever. It was the landlady's parlour, and they couldn't remain like that trapping her in the kitchen. How had Evelyn come to be there, anyway?

She'd appeared to be as surprised at seeing him as he'd been when Mrs Shipley had told him an old friend had called to see him and he'd found Evelyn sitting by the fire. There were so many questions, and before he could make any more decisions about his future, he must find out the answers.

Jacob cupped Evelyn's face in his hands, and her eyes opened. He saw her alarm, and recognised that she, too, feared something might come between them again. Smiling, he kissed her lips, and then with noses touching, he said, "We have so much to discuss. Shall we go for a walk?"

She looked up at him fearfully and nodded.

"We will work everything out," he said firmly, and relief lit her eyes.

Chapter Fifty

"What's happening?" whispered Ada, craning her neck to see through the small gap between the door and jamb.

"Lieutenant Adam's helping your daughter into her coat."

"What! Is she going? Is he sending her away?"

"Shh! No!" Doris batted her hand behind her to quieten Ada. "Ah! How romantic. No, he's not sending her away, he's going with her. Here, you look."

Doris moved out of the way and Ada put her eye to the gap. Jacob still stood behind Evelyn, having helped her into her coat. He'd wrapped his arms around her. Ada could see both their faces; Evelyn's half-turned, looking up towards Jacob's face, and his cheek resting against hers. They were radiant with joy.

Tears pricked her eyes, and she swallowed the lump in her throat. Such a perfect moment didn't need a witness. She gently closed the door, but she was glad nevertheless to have seen them. There was no doubt in her heart they belonged together.

"Evelyn and I are going out for a walk, Mrs Shipley. We won't be long," Jacob called from the front door.

"Rightio," shouted Doris, trying to sound normal. "Take your time. No need to rush. See you later."

Once the front door had clicked, Ada and Doris giggled like schoolgirls and hugged each other tightly.

Ada steepled her hands and held them to her mouth as if in prayer. "I do so hope they sort everything out."

"Oh, they will," said Doris with certainty. "I saw it in Evelyn's palm. Such a troubled life to start, but it will all become smoother. And as for Lieutenant Adam's hand. I saw a long smooth life with a few problems in the middle. He's passed those now. Yes, they're perfect for each other. Of course, I'm not saying there won't be a few problems to iron out along the way. Aren't there always? But they stand a better chance than most." She handed Ada a tea towel. "You've just wiped flour on your face. Right, let's get those scones in the oven so they're ready when our lovebirds get home. A long, cold walk will be just the thing to give them an appetite."

Chapter Fifty-One

Ada waited at the door of Swallowmead, hand shielding her eyes against the low spring sunshine. On the other side of Second Avenue, the door of a cottage opened, and Sarah turned and called a goodbye over her shoulder. Closing the door behind her, she placed her hands protectively over her large belly and walked down the path. She waved to Ada when she saw her.

Behind her in the kitchen, Doris called out, "Is Sarah here yet?"

"She's just coming."

Ada heard the oven door open and sniffed at the tempting aroma of freshly baked scones that was beginning to fill the cottage. She sighed with contentment. For so long, she'd held her guilty secret close and pushed people away.

That dreadful day when Mother had appeared and told Evelyn the truth would be indelibly marked on Ada's memory. At first, the shock. Then the mind-numbing shame. And above all, the fear she'd lose Evelyn's respect and love. Perhaps even lose Evelyn herself.

Yet, that day had been so important in her life. Mother had done Ada a great service, although that obviously hadn't been her intention.

Of course, it hadn't appeared like that at the time. Evelyn and Jacob's fragile, new friendship had floundered, and Ada had despaired.

But thankfully, Jacob and Evelyn had found each other again – with a little help from Jacob's grandmother, Gordon and Doris.

Not only found each other. Evelyn would marry Jacob at the end of the month and, although Ada had never dared dream of such a thing, she would be at the ceremony as the mother of the bride. Tingles of pride ran up and down her as she anticipated the day. She'd been worried people would shun her, but her new friend, Doris, had given her the confidence to claim that right – mother of the bride. She whispered the words now, while watching Sarah wave as she crossed the grassy avenue.

Remarkably, no one had yet drawn attention to her new position as mother of the bride. The one person she'd dreaded finding out had been Ted Farrell. Not that he'd ever portrayed himself as being righteous – quite the opposite. But she'd realised his good opinion of her mattered a great deal and Ada, in revealing her secret, might have lost it.

She'd gone to work early one morning and met him on the way to school to tell him. Best that he knew before everyone else. It would have made working with him difficult, but they were adults. They'd have had to deal with it somehow. However, he had been remarkably accepting, too.

"We've both lost someone we loved," he'd said when she'd told him about Walter. "War's a dreadful thing, Ada. It robbed me of time with my beloved wife and robbed you of the man you would otherwise have married."

There had been no blame, simply recognition of shared tragedy. And as a result, they'd become close friends. In fact, he would be giving Evelyn away at her wedding.

Sarah had reached the garden gate and smiled as she pushed it open. "Am I late?" she asked.

"No, I was just watching out to make sure you got here safely." Ada smiled at how ridiculous that sounded. After all, Gordon, Sarah and Tommy had moved into a cottage across the road. Sarah could hardly have got lost. But who cared? Why shouldn't Ada look out for them all?

"Tea's up," Doris called from behind her. "Come and get the scones while they're hot. I think I'm finally getting the hang of your oven, Ada. These are all quite evenly browned."

Ada stood back for Sarah to enter. For a second, she had a pang of regret that Evelyn wouldn't be there to share tea with them that morning, but she was at work.

At least Doris was with her. She was staying at Swallowmead for a few days, and at the end of the month she would come and stay again when Lieutenant and Mrs Jacob Adam would have the white house in Hailcombe Cross to themselves for their first few days of their married lives.

Sarah breathed in deeply as she entered Ada's cottage, her eyes closed in appreciation. "Mmm, that smells so good."

The aroma of freshly baked scones filled Swallowmead.

"And you've got honey?" she asked, her voice rising in amazement as she saw what was on the table. "I can't remember the last time I had honey. I'm wondering why we didn't make the move into the country sooner."

She eased herself into a chair and, as Doris poured the tea, the conversation flowed smoothly between the three women. Ada let it envelop her like the comforting smell of Doris's baking.

Three women enjoying each other's company, laughing, sharing and just... being.

Ada had never known anything like it. She'd lived on her own for so long. Keeping herself remote; afraid people would discover her secret and judge her. Afraid of tainting Evelyn's life.

It had been Doris who'd made her realise she hadn't been alone in wishing her past had been different. How many others had made decisions that had appeared sensible at the time until hindsight had shown otherwise?

Doris's life would have been completely different if Tom had returned from the war. What if she'd turned down Pete's proposal? Years of loneliness? Or years of peace? Pete hadn't been the man of her dreams, but his careful management of their money had left her very comfortably off. She certainly wouldn't have owned the large, white house in Hailcombe Cross. But without Pete, might she have met someone else? There was no point dwelling on the past and wondering 'what if?'.

Looking back over Ada's life, what would she have done differently? She had loved Walter – body and soul. But suppose she'd done as society expected and hadn't snatched moments of love with him, then Evelyn wouldn't have been born.

She couldn't bear to think of that possibility. But was that fair? She now had supportive friends who accepted her. If the illegitimacy had impacted negatively on Evelyn, Ada would have been more remorseful.

But Ada saw her daughter's face when she looked at Jacob, and she knew Evelyn was glad to be alive – whatever the circumstances.

And Jacob always returned her adoring gaze. What would he have done without Evelyn? Of course, tongues would wag in town, and there would always be mean-spirited people who'd snub Ada, but now she had the strength to stare them in the eyes and ignore their narrow-minded judgements.

And surprisingly, Ted Farrell had been one of the most supportive.

Having been almost speechless at the honour when Evelyn had asked him to carry out the duties of the father of the bride, he'd remarked how proud Ada must be of Evelyn and how he envied her seeing her daughter's wedding day.

"Perhaps outside of school, you might call me by my given name?" he'd asked. "Mr Farrell sounds so formal."

Ted had even bought a new suit. "There hasn't been any reason to worry about new clothes," he'd said. "So, I had enough coupons."

During the weeks leading up to the wedding, Ted and Ada had become closer. She wasn't looking for romance. Neither was Ted, she was sure. But they enjoyed each other's company and recently, had begun to make each other laugh, too. The sound basis for a good friendship. And if it should develop further...

"Ouch!" Sarah said, wincing in surprise. She placed her hands on her bump. "I think I've been eating too much and too fast. Indigestion. But these scones are so delicious."

Doris shot Ada an alarmed look. They stared at each other for several seconds, sending silent messages.

"And when are you due, my dear?" Doris asked in a conversational voice as she studiously rearranged the scones on the plate.

"Oh, not for several weeks yet," said Sarah, taking another bite of scone and honey.

"Excellent, excellent. And did you say earlier that Gordon's going into town this morning?"

"Mr Cresswell's showing him around his bakery. And then tomorrow, Gordon's got an appointment with the bank manager. I can't believe he might buy into his own bakery. It's a dream come true... Ouch. My word, the baby's lively today."

"And will Gordon be back soon?" Ada asked casually.

At last, Sarah detected the undercurrent of anxiety. Her voice was a whisper, "You don't think the baby's coming, do you? Only it's early and it wasn't like this with Tommy. I didn't get pains anywhere near as strong as this. Ow!"

"Well, who can say?" said Ada nonchalantly. "But how about we get you back to your cottage and we call the midwife? Just a precaution, of course. Nothing to worry about…"

Doris held Sarah's arm as they walked sedately back to her home, and Ada set off in the opposite direction for the post office to telephone the midwife.

Oh, how marvellous, another child on the way! What a blessing. And Ada would be able to watch this little one grow up. Her heart skipped a beat with delight, and she hurried faster.

It suddenly occurred to her that she was moving rather speedily, and that although her knees were hurting, they weren't troubling her as much as usual. In fact, she felt lighter and more sprightly. There was too much distraction to worry about painful joints. It was just the shock of realising Sarah was probably going into labour. Once things had quietened down, her knees would be agony. Nevertheless, her life recently had been so pleasurable, she hadn't had time to dwell on the discomfort. And surely that was also a blessing.

Gordon arrived back at his new home full of optimism. Mr Cresswell, who owned a successful bakery in the High Road, wanted to retire in a year or two, and he liked the idea of having a junior partner to take the pressure off him. Eventually, if things worked out, he intended to sell his entire business to Gordon and move to Sussex to be near his brother. This was such a wonderful opportunity; Gordon could scarcely believe it. As he opened the door to his new home, his mind was full of figures; profits, outgoings and possibly, even expansion.

If only the dreadful war would finish, he thought as he took off his jacket. He was pulled back to the present with a jolt, as he heard what sounded like a new-born child wailing. Ada came out of his bedroom, followed by her friend.

"Oh, my dear," Ada said, her voice catching. "You have a beautiful daughter. Mother and baby are doing well."

Gordon ran into his bedroom to find the midwife packing her bag. Sarah held a tiny infant in her arms and next to her, Tommy looked on with wide, surprised eyes.

"Well," said Doris as she and Ada walked back to Swallowmead, "when you suggested I stay with you for a while, I didn't foresee anything quite so exciting happening. Hailcombe Cross is a fine place, but nothing ever happens there. My life certainly changed the day you knocked on my door, Ada."

"And so did mine. For the first time, I confided in someone about Evelyn. I'll always be grateful you listened and didn't judge me. That made such a difference to me and now, at last, I can acknowledge I'm a mother."

"And shortly, you'll be the mother-in-law to a very fine man, don't forget. I've grown so fond of him; it almost feels like he's my son. The one I would have loved."

Ada made more tea, and they finished the scones in silence, both lost in their own thoughts. Once, Ada's family had been large and had fallen apart as her brothers and sisters fled. Now, she had people around her – some related, some not – but they were the ones who mattered.

Chapter Fifty-Two

Once outside Baxter's Teashop, Evelyn held onto Jacob's hand and smiled at him. How happy he looked. How carefree. As if all his worries had been swept away. Not that they had, of course. It would take time before he let go of all his guilt. Evelyn knew that was so, because despite his assurances that she was worthy of love, from time to time, Mother's voice whispered in her head, and she doubted herself. Guilt and doubts weren't so easily banished. But together, they would help each other through the dark times.

Together.

They truly were together now. Man and wife.

Sarah stepped forward and, with her tiny daughter in one arm, she tossed a handful of rice over Evelyn's head.

"Yes, I know, I know. A dreadful waste of food, but a wedding's not a wedding without rice." Sarah grinned.

Evelyn shook her head scattering the grains and looked back at the group of people who were cheering. Best man, Gordon, with Sarah and their two children, Jacob's grandmother and next to her, holding the arm of a painfully thin man, was Phyllis.

Her fiancé, Tim, had arrived home the previous week. No word had been heard from him for months while one group of French

Resistance members hid him, then passed him to the next. Finally, at the French border, he'd been led on foot over the mountains into Spain. It had taken many more months to get home from there, but eventually, he'd arrived on the coast of England and had made his way home to Phyllis, emaciated and fever ridden. But alive.

Phyllis and Tim would be the next couple to be married. Their wedding would be arranged more speedily than Evelyn's – and for good reason. They'd already lost too much time.

Another couple stood next to them. Jacob's friend Ronnie Howell gave the thumbs up sign to the newly-weds and he turned to smile at the girl on his arm. She was one of the Wrens Ronnie had never noticed because of his infatuation with Gladys, but she appeared to have won his heart. Perhaps they would be the next couple to marry.

Ada stood nearby, her arm through Mr Farrell's. On her other side, was Doris.

It was a modest wedding party, but they were the most precious people in Lieutenant and Mrs Adam's life.

The few days leading up to the wedding had been so hectic, Evelyn hadn't had time to think. As soon as Jacob had proposed – insisting on painfully getting down on one knee – they hadn't wanted to wait. What would they have been waiting for? They'd decided to spend their lives together. Why not start immediately?

The time had come to say goodbye to the guests, but it suddenly occurred to Evelyn she didn't know how they were going to get to Doris's house in Hailcombe Cross where they would spend their forty-eight-hour honeymoon. Presumably they'd catch the bus.

Well, it wasn't as though she was wearing a bridal dress – she wouldn't stand out too much. Ada had somehow produced enough coupons for a bridal gown, but Evelyn had asked, instead, if she could borrow the lilac crepe dress with matching embroidered bolero jacket

A REUNION IN PLOTLANDS 249

that Ada had worn to the Christmas dance.

At the time, Evelyn hadn't known why Ada had wistfully replied she'd never worn the outfit. It was only later she realised it had been what Ada had intended to wear on her own wedding day.

Phyllis had helped with the alterations and Evelyn had walked down the aisle on Mr Farrell's arm wearing the dress and jacket her mother would have worn to marry her beloved Walter. It was a tenuous link to her father, who'd never met her, nor known about her existence.

But at least in a dress and jacket, she wouldn't look like a runaway bride on the bus. The luggage had already been delivered to Doris's house, so it wasn't as though as they'd have to struggle with that.

Jacob brushed some rice grains out of her hair and smiled a knowing smile.

"Do we need to leave now?" she asked.

Jacob nodded, and his smile grew wider and then something clouded his face.

"Oh," he said, and she saw his Adam's Apple bob. She knew him well enough to know he was nervous.

"Your dress... I hadn't thought." He nibbled his lower lip.

"What's the matter with my dress?"

"Nothing. Oh dear, I hope this is all right..." He peered over her shoulder, and as Evelyn turned around, she saw Gordon wheeling a tandem bicycle towards them decorated with ribbons.

"Your carriage awaits, madam," Gordon said with a sweeping gesture of his hand towards the rear saddle.

"I hope this is all right," Jacob said, his eyes wide with dread.

"It's perfect, Jacob." He'd visited her so many times on a bicycle, now she would get to see the journey he'd taken after he'd left her.

They could take their time, perhaps stop in several places before they arrived in Hailcombe Cross. Time to consider the next part of the day. The part that Evelyn had tried not to think about.

She threw her bouquet over her shoulder in Phyllis's direction and was delighted when she turned around to see her friend had caught it. Then Gordon held the tandem bicycle steady, and she mounted. Jacob climbed on and, as they began to pedal down the High Road, their wedding party cheered again.

Evelyn turned briefly and her eyes sought Ada.

"Thank you," she mouthed.

Ada held both hands to her mouth and blew Evelyn a kiss.

Chapter Fifty-Three

Evelyn was tempted to reach out and touch Jacob's back, to place her hands on him and feel the muscles ripple beneath his shirt. However, she dared not take her hands off the handlebars. He was in control of the steering, so there was no danger the tandem bicycle would veer off the road, but she knew it would distract him.

She gripped the handlebars with determination and, in an attempt to take her mind off Jacob's muscles, she admired her new bracelet with its single blue bead.

On the day Ada had taken her to Doris Shipley's, she'd gone for a walk with Jacob, and he'd told her how he believed it had saved his life. He'd brought it home and kept it until he'd met her and then he'd wanted her to have it as a good luck charm. She'd been touched and her reaction had moved him.

"I wasn't sure you'd want something so... well, so insignificant," he'd said.

"But it's not insignificant at all!" She'd been aghast at his comment. And that had prompted him to tell her about how guilty he'd felt at having survived while the others had died. It had been a revelation. Never before had she thought how people might feel if they'd been saved while others had been lost.

"You weren't responsible, Jacob." She'd taken his hands and looked into his sad, brown eyes.

"But I didn't deserve to live," he said simply. And then, he'd told her about what he'd called his 'stupidity'.

"Oh, darling Jacob! You weren't at fault at all. Just finding your way. You know Mother was furious with me for including my address in those socks. Well, suppose I'd done exactly as she wanted all the time? I'd never have dared to include it, and then I'd never have met you. Mother would have said I'd been stupid because I'd done something she wouldn't have agreed with."

"Gran says everyone has a certain length of time on earth..." He'd tailed off and looked at her with a question in his eyes.

"I don't think anything you did or didn't do would have made any difference."

He'd rested his forehead against hers in silence for several minutes. "I think I've woven grief and guilt together until I couldn't separate them. But if I'd seen blame in your face, I wouldn't have been able to bear it."

She'd assured him he hadn't been responsible. As someone who'd felt guilty from an early age without knowing why, she was sympathetic.

"We'll convince each other neither of us is to blame," she'd said.

Later, Jacob and Evelyn had taken the vibrant blue bead into a jeweller to have it attached to a chain. The jeweller had inspected the bead with interest. "One o' them foreign things what keeps away the evil eye," he'd said, pointing at the concentric circles. "I saw lots o' them during my time in the army. The last war, that is... Gallipoli..." He'd fallen silent then and they hadn't pressed him. Another soldier with overwhelming memories.

But he'd done an excellent job setting the bead on a dainty silver chain and Evelyn knew she'd treasure it forever. How appropriate to discover it was supposed to keep away bad luck. It had saved Jacob and now, it was part of their new life together.

They'd shared their feelings, but as part of that confession, Jacob had told her about his first experience with women. She had to admit, she'd been shocked and hurt, but she'd seen his shame in letting down his family and not standing up to his fellow officers had been punishment enough. He'd carried too much guilt for too long and it wouldn't be fair to start out a life together, unless both started afresh.

But her nervousness had increased when it suddenly occurred to her that Jacob would be able to compare her awkwardness and incompetence to the women he'd known.

He hadn't been able to meet her gaze when he'd explained he'd been so drunk, he remembered very little and admitted he had no idea what he should do.

On the days leading up to the wedding, there had been too much to think about to let the honeymoon worry her. She'd put it to the back of her mind and assumed they'd deal with the situation later. After all, the kisses they'd shared had been unexpectedly delicious. She'd not suspected such a cascade of sensations would ripple throughout her body when their lips touched. What might it feel like when they were alone?

Ada's embarrassed explanation of what men and women did when they were together had been interesting, but baffling. Perhaps it was best if she and Jacob got that awkward part out of the way first and then carried on with the pleasurable part – the kissing. She planned to ask him later.

The tandem had taken some getting used to, but they'd cycled slowly and stopped for breaks.

"I'm not sure this was such a good idea," Jacob had said each time they'd stopped, his eyes searching hers for signs of dissatisfaction, but she'd been touched by the thought he'd put into their farewell, and anyway, the slow journey was delaying the inevitable awkwardness.

By the time they finally arrived at Doris's house, Evelyn's leg muscles were aching at the unaccustomed activity.

"I'm so sorry, Evie. I should have thought. I remember what it's like to have aching muscles after doing something you're not used to. I must admit, my legs ache, too. It was harder than I thought it would be. What a stupid, stupid idea."

Evelyn's heart sank. This wasn't how she'd wanted to start married life, with Jacob angry at himself.

Jacob breathed in sharply and his eyes opened wide. "But I may just have the perfect cure."

He smiled, that lopsided grin that made her heart flutter.

Fetching towels from the bathroom, he laid them on the bed, then went downstairs and came back with a small bowl.

"The doctor told me to massage my muscles with a little oil if they ached. I didn't bother for myself, but since I caused your pain, the least I can do is to put it right."

She'd stripped down to her underwear, feeling rather embarrassed and with trepidation, lay down on the towels on the bed. It was only because of his pleasure at believing he could cure her aches, she agreed to go through with it. Whatever 'it' might be.

However, it turned out that Jacob had magic hands. His touch on her calves had been light and enjoyable – exciting even. Gradually, his hands had slid up her legs to her thighs and she forgot all about muscle aches and her earlier embarrassment. Wherever Jacob touched her, he left a trail of exquisite pleasure – and she wanted more. Each silky soft stroke of his fingers as they glided over her skin, exploring more of her body had her gasping for pleasure, until she lay naked in his arms.

A REUNION IN PLOTLANDS

"My turn," she said and made a place for him on the bed, then straddling him, copied the way he'd caressed her.

Later, they soaped each other down in the bathroom to remove the oil, and that had proved equally exciting.

A little oil had gone a long way they discovered, and the following day, they'd shared the washing and cleaning. She'd never suspected wash day could be quite so entertaining. By the time they'd finished washing the bed sheets and the floor, they'd been drenched and covered in soapsuds. They'd peeled the clothes off each other and held each other close.

Evelyn wondered what she'd been worried about on their way to Hailcombe Cross. Their honeymoon night and the following morning had been perfection. Slippery, but perfect.

Chapter Fifty-Four

♥

It was the second and final day of their honeymoon. In the morning, Doris would come back to her house and Jacob would start work. They would alternate between the white house in Hailcombe Cross when Jacob was working, and Ada's cottage when he had time off. In the meantime, they were saving hard.

One day when the war was over, they'd buy a cottage in Plotlands near Ada and Gordon. Jacob wanted to buy a car so he could continue working at Marconi should he still have a job there. Although he was toying with the idea of cycling each day.

Well, that was far in the future.

They'd make up their minds when the time came.

The afternoon was cool with a half-hearted sun in the blue sky, but having already cycled several miles on the tandem, they were hot, and the fresh breeze was welcome. In the basket on the front there was everything they'd need for a picnic, and soon, they'd find somewhere suitable along the river whose course they were following.

Evelyn was tempted to suggest they stop now but decided against it.

The tandem wasn't just a means of transport, it was Jacob's bid for fitness. Of course, after such dreadful injuries as he'd sustained in Italy, he'd never be completely free of pain nor walk without a limp, but the exercise helped.

And her massage, of course.

Evelyn blushed, her body filling with a rush of warmth as she remembered the previous night and earlier that morning. How wonderful it was to have discovered so quickly how to please each other. She smiled at the memory of her wedding-night nerves and once again fought back the temptation to reach out and touch Jacob's back. The shirt fabric strained across his muscles as his legs pumped up and down.

Jacob called over his shoulder, asking if she was all right. She shouted back that she was fine.

Oh yes, she was more than fine!

On their left, through enormous weeping willows, the river glinted, and, on their right, fields swept to a rise. She wondered how far they were from Chelmsford. She was thirsty.

"Shall we stop here?" Jacob called over his shoulder.

They spread the blanket beneath a weeping willow next to the river and, after their picnic, sat close together watching a narrowboat moored on the far bank. Other than the wind rustling the leaves in the trees, the birds skimming the water and the gurgling and occasional splash of the river as it flowed past, it was quiet.

"We could be the only two people on the planet," Jacob said.

They were silent for a few moments, both aware the war was still being waged, and the peace they were appreciating was just a temporary respite from their usual world of air raids and reports of battles and destruction.

Jacob put his arm around Evelyn's shoulders and pulled her closer. "I sometimes try to imagine I can see all those radio waves surging through the air. The messages carried on them. The music. The calls for help. The transfer of information from one distant place to another," Jacob said. "People sending messages out into the air, hoping someone will hear."

Evelyn had only ever considered the sounds coming out of a wireless, but now, she tried to imagine the waves carrying the sounds. "I wonder how many calls for help are never heard? I wonder if that poem I put in those socks was a bit like that? A call for... well, not help, exactly, but a call for something?"

"And if I hadn't found it, I'd never have met you. I'd still be calling out for help. All those hopes and dreams thrown out into the universe and still floating unheard."

"That's a very sad thought." She looked at him anxiously.

He stroked her hair. "Yes, but I'm actually thinking how lucky I am to have found you. In my job, I've seen the power of the electromagnetic wave and its potential, but there's something to be said for the power of socks!"

Grey clouds slid across the sun, instantly cooling the air. Evelyn and Jacob gathered up their things and repacked them in the bicycle basket.

"The last one home is a loser," Jacob said.

Evelyn laughed. On the tandem, they'd arrive home together. Surely a wonderful omen for their lives.

Fat drops of rain began to fall. "Come on, Evie, let's get home as fast as we can. And don't worry about being sore. I have a cure for that."

They picked up speed down a slight incline. Evelyn pedalled faster as they climbed the other side. She wanted to get back to the white house as quickly as possible. Not because she wanted to avoid a drenching – it was too late for that – she was already wet. But because she was anticipating their arrival home. They would slowly remove each other's soaking clothes and kiss away the raindrops.

Evelyn reached forward and stroked Jacob's back. He shivered, and she knew it wasn't from the cold or the rain.

END

Dawn would be thrilled if you would consider leaving a review for this book on Amazon and Goodreads, thank you.

If you'd like to know more about her books, you can find out more from her newsletter on her website: Blog: https://dawnknox.com. Please sign up for her newsletter to receive a welcome gift, containing an exclusive prequel to The Duchess of Sydney, short humorous stories and two photo-stories from the Great War.

About the Author

Dawn spent much of her childhood making up stories filled with romance, drama and excitement. She loved fairy tales, although if she cast herself as a character, she'd more likely have played the part of the Court Jester than the Princess. She didn't recognise it at the time, but she was searching for the emotional depth in the stories she read. It wasn't enough to be told the Prince loved the Princess, she wanted to know how he felt and to see him declare his love. She wanted to see the wedding. And so, she'd furnish her stories with those details.

Nowadays, she hopes to write books that will engage readers' passions. From poignant stories set during the First World War to the zany antics of the inhabitants of the fictitious town of Basilwade; and from historical romances, to the fantasy adventures of a group of anthropomorphic animals led by a chicken with delusions of grandeur, she explores the richness and depth of human emotion.

A book by Dawn will offer laughter or tears – or anything in between, but if she touches your soul, she'll consider her job well done.

Following Dawn:

Blog: https://dawnknox.com https://dawnknox.com

Amazon Author Central: Dawn Knox https://mybook.to/DawnKnox https://mybook.to/DawnKnox

Facebook: https://www.facebook.com/DawnKnoxWriter https://www.facebook.com/DawnKnoxWriter

X: https://twitter.com/SunriseCalls https://twitter.com/SunriseCalls

Instragram: https://www.instagram.com/sunrisecalls/ https://www.instagram.com/sunrisecalls/

YouTube: https://tinyurl.com/mtcpdyms https://tinyurl.com/mtcpdyms

Also by Dawn Knox

A Cottage in Plotlands
The Heart of Plotlands Saga – Book One
London's East End to the Essex countryside - will a Plotlands cottage bring Joanna happiness or heartache?
1930 – Eighteen-year-old Joanna Marshall arrives in Dunton Plotlands friendless and alone. When her dream to live independently is cruelly shattered, her neighbours step in. Plotlanders look after their own. But they can't help Joanna when she falls in love with Ben Richardson – a man who is her social superior… and her boss. Can Joanna and Ben find a place where rigid social rules will allow them to love?
Order from Amazon: https://mybook.to/ACottageInPlotlands
Paperback: ISBN: 9798378843756 eBook: ASIN: B0C4Y9VZY9
Also A Folly in Plotlands, **A Canary Girl in Plotlands, A Reunion in Plotlands** and **A Rose in Plotlands**

The Duchess of Sydney
The Lady Amelia Saga – Book One

Betrayed by her family and convicted of a crime she did not commit, Georgiana is sent halfway around the world to the penal colony of Sydney, New South Wales. Aboard the transport ship, the Lady Amelia, Lieutenant Francis Brooks, the ship's agent becomes her protector, taking her as his "sea-wife" – not because he has any interest in her but because he has been tasked with the duty.

Despite their mutual distrust, the attraction between them grows. But life has not played fair with Georgiana. She is bound by family secrets and lies. Will she ever be free again – free to be herself and free to love?

Order from Amazon: https://mybook.to/TheDuchessOfSydney
Paperback: ISBN: 9798814373588 eBook: ASIN: B09Z8LN4G9
Audiobook: ASIN: B0C86LG3Y4

Also, **The Finding of Eden, The Other Place, The Dolphin's Kiss, The Pearl of Aphrodite** and **The Wooden Tokens**

Printed in Great Britain
by Amazon